STRANGE BIRDS

A FIELD GUIDE TO RUFFLING FEATHERS

by Celia C. Pérez
Author of *The First Rule of Punk*

PUFFIN BOOKS

Readers love *Strange Birds*!

"*Strange Birds* respects its readers' intelligence and sophistication. Pérez's charming story explores what is means to belong to a community while being willing to stage small but significant revolutions, all the while reveling in the joy of childhood."
—Erika L. Sánchez, *New York Times* bestselling author of the National Book Award Finalist *I Am Not Your Perfect Mexican Daughter* for *The New York Times Book Review*

"An inspiring story about the power of truth, and of true friends."
—Rebecca Stead, *New York Times* bestselling author of the Newbery Medal winner *When You Reach Me*

"Thought-provoking, timely, and laugh-out-loud funny."
—Aisha Saeed, *New York Times* bestselling author of *Amal Unbound*

★ "Writing with wry restraint that's reminiscent of Kate DiCamillo . . . a beautiful tale." —*Kirkus Reviews* (starred review)

★ "[An] engaging, well-plotted second novel from Pérez."
—*Publishers Weekly* (starred review)

★ "A perfect title for school and public libraries."
—*School Library Journal* (starred review)

★ "Perfect for preteens becoming aware that friendships can be complicated, and that the world is more so."
—*The Horn Book* (starred review)

Washington Post Best Children's Books of 2019 • An ALSC Notable Children's Book • *Kirkus* Best Children's Books of 2019 • Chicago Public Library's Best of the Best Books of 2019 • CSMCL's Best Multicultural Children's Books of 2019 • A 2020 Rise: A Feminist Book Project List selection • A 2019 Middle Grade Fiction Nerdies selection

Three cheers for *The First Rule of Punk*!

"Malú rocks!"

—**Victoria Jamieson**, author and illustrator of the
New York Times bestselling and Newbery Honor Book *Roller Girl*

★ "Charming." —*Kirkus Reviews* (starred review)

★ "Vivacious." —*School Library Journal* (starred review)

★ "Exuberant." —*Publishers Weekly* (starred review)

A 2018 Pura Belpré Author Honor Book • A 2018 ALSC Notable Children's Book • A 2018 Tomás Rivera Mexican American Children's Book Award Winner • A 2017 ABA Indies Introduce Title • A Kids' Indie Next List Pick • An E. B. White Read-Aloud Middle Reader Award finalist • A 2018 *Boston Globe–Horn Book* Fiction and Poetry Honor Book • An Amelia Bloomer List Book • CCBC Choices 2018 • 2017 Nerdy Book Award Winner • A 2018 Judy Lopez Memorial Award for Children's Literature Honor Book • *Publishers Weekly* Flying Start • 2018 Américas Award Honorable Mention Title • NPR Best Books of 2017 • *Kirkus Reviews* Best Fiction of 2017 • School Library Journal Best Books of 2017 • A *Horn Book* Fanfare Selection • Center for the Study of Multicultural Children's Literature Best Books of 2017 • NYPL Best Books for Kids 2017 • Chicago Public Library's Best of the Best Books 2017 • Evanston Public Library 101 Great Books for Kids 2017 • A Seattle Public Library Top 10 Children's Chapter Book of 2017 • A UPenn Graduate School of Education Best Book of 2017 • 2018-2019 Dorothy Canfield Fisher Children's Book Award Nominee • 2018–2019 Sunshine State Young Readers Award Nominee • A 2018 Great Lakes, Great Reads Award Winner • 2017 Nerdy Book Award Winner

For best friends

For the birds

For you

PUFFIN BOOKS
An imprint of Penguin Random House LLC, New York

First published in the United States of America by Kokila,
an imprint of Penguin Random House LLC, 2019
Published by Puffin Books, imprint of Penguin Random House LLC, 2020

Visit us online at penguinrandomhouse.com.

THE LIBRARY OF CONGRESS HAS CATALOGED THE KOKILA EDITION AS FOLLOWS:
Names: Pérez, Celia C.
Title: Strange birds : a field guide to ruffling feathers / Celia C. Pérez.
Description: New York : Kokila, [2019] | Summary: After Ofelia, Aster, Cat, and Lane fail to
persuade a local girls club to change an outdated tradition, they form an alternative group that
shakes up their sleepy Florida town. Includes tips for beginning birders, characteristics of crystals,
a cookie recipe, tips for aspiring journalists, directions for creating badges, and facts about the
killing of birds for fashion. | Includes bibliographic references.
Identifiers: LCCN 2019013146 | ISBN 9780425290439 (hardback)
Subjects: | CYAC: Clubs—Fiction. | Social action—Fiction. | Friendship—Fiction. |
Family life—Florida—Fiction. | Florida—Fiction. | BISAC: JUVENILE FICTION / People &
Places / United States / Hispanic & Latino. | JUVENILE FICTION / Nature & the Natural World /
Environment. | JUVENILE FICTION / Social Issues / Friendship.
Classification: LCC PZ7.1.P44747 Str 2019 | DDC [Fic]— dc23
LC record available at https://lccn.loc.gov/2019013146

Printed in the United States of America

Puffin Books ISBN 978-0-425290453

1 3 5 7 9 10 8 6 4 2

Design by Jasmin Rubero
Text set in Diverda Serif Com

I never had any friends later on like the ones I had when I was twelve.

Stephen King
The Body

CHAPTER 1

The pencil Ofelia tapped against her reporter's notebook was part of a set, a last-day-of-school gift from her favorite teacher, Ms. Niggli. She'd given them to all the newspaper staffers who were moving on to middle school. Ofelia knew they were nice pencils. Not generic twelve-for-two-dollars pencils. Each one was topped with a black eraser, and on its natural wood color was a quote by a man named Woody Guthrie: "All you can write is what you see."

She had asked Ms. Niggli what the quote meant, and Ms. Niggli had answered in the way teachers do. "What do *you* think it means?"

Ofelia hoped it didn't mean that all you could write was, literally, what you saw. Woody Guthrie had obviously never lived in Sabal Palms, Florida.

What she saw outside the window of her mother's car on that first Monday morning of summer break was the same thing she saw every Monday morning. There was Doña Amalia from next door wheeling her overflowing blue recycling bin across her driveway. The wheels crunched over gravel as she struggled to drag it. Once at the curb, she opened the lid and pulled out the topmost object. Then she aimed it at Chucho.

Chucho was a rooster that had shown up one day after a tropical storm battered their town. He moved into the tree in front of Doña Amalia's house and never left. Someone on their street—no one remembers who—named him "Chucho," and it stuck.

Chucho had the prettiest burnt-orange feathers, but his handsomeness didn't outweigh his bad habits. The rooster pooped on cars when Doña Amalia had company parked out front. And if that wasn't bad enough, he crowed all day, like his internal alarm clock was out of whack, drawing the wrath not just of Ofelia's neighbor, but of the entire street.

As a rinsed-out can of Goya black beans flew through the air, it occurred to Ofelia that the only thing that really changed from week to week was the item Doña Amalia threw at the bird with all the strength her seventy-something-year-old arm could muster. The can missed its mark but startled the rooster who flew from his perch, squawking angrily as he strutted down the street.

Ofelia watched her mom make her way toward the car, purse hanging on her right shoulder, keys in hand.

"Dale, Doña Amalia!" Mrs. Castillo called out. "If you hit that bird, I'll make arroz con gallo for us."

Ha-ha, Ofelia thought. She pulled off her glasses and wiped them on her T-shirt. She didn't need them to see that the two women were now laughing like it was the first time her mom had made that joke.

She held up the pencil to her nose and inhaled the cedar scent. It smelled like an amazing story. It smelled like the truth. *That*, she realized, was all she could write. And *that* was what would win the Qwerty Sholes Journalism Contest.

Five lucky seventh-graders from around the country were picked each year to attend a summer journalism camp in New York City. Winning the contest not only meant being recognized for her writing. It meant going away without her parents and proving to them, once and for all, that she could be responsible and independent. But as she watched Doña Amalia push down the contents of her recycling bin, close the lid, and head back up her driveway, she saw her Qwerty Sholes dreams circling the drain.

Ofelia sighed and looked at the blank page.

"Let me remind you that you are not to write anything in your little notebook," Mrs. Castillo said, settling into the driver's seat and glancing in Ofelia's direction. "Nothing you see, nothing you hear."

"What kinds of things might I see or hear that I *shouldn't* write about?" She wiggled her eyebrows at her mom.

"Ni una palabra, Ofelia," Mrs. Castillo warned again. "None of your Nancy Drew business."

"Nancy Drew is a sleuth," Ofelia said. "She looks for clues to solve mysteries. I'm a journalist. I look for stories to write."

"Hmm," Mrs. Castillo said. "Both sound nosy to me."

Ofelia thought about what her mother said. She knew that she wanted to be a journalist when she learned about the muckrakers in social studies class. In the late-nineteenth and early-twentieth centuries, journalists like Ida B. Wells, Nellie Bly, and Ida Tarbell exposed corruption. They noticed injustices and then, through their stories, forced the world to notice them too.

Ms. Niggli said no one really used the term *muckraker* anymore, that today they call them investigative journalists. Still, Ofelia relished the idea of raking the muck off and exposing things. Like raking the tomato sauce off the "meat-balls" in the school cafeteria and exposing them for the textured vegetable protein balls they really were. Or like the topic of her very first story in the second grade—an exposé on the three wise men—after she caught her parents, not los Reyes Magos, leaving gifts for her on January 6. It made her wonder what else the adults in her life were hiding.

Maybe she could be Nancy Drew *and* Ida B. Wells all in one. She certainly didn't want to be a Lois Lane type of journalist who didn't even realize that Clark Kent was Superman wearing glasses.

"But what am I supposed to do there all summer, Ma?" Ofelia asked, struggling to keep from whining.

In books and movies, summer break meant spending your days outside looking for adventures. Her friend Andrea was flying alone to visit her cousins in California, and then she was going to sleepaway camp. Ofelia, on the other hand, got to go to work with her mom.

She squirmed with embarrassment and wondered how many twelve-year-olds had parents as overprotective as hers. She knew kids who were unsupervised after school and during the summer and went to the movies with friends, not with their parents.

"When I was a little girl in Cuba, we would make a whole game out of an empty box," Mrs. Castillo said, proudly. "You can help me if you need something to do. I'm going to be very busy with the preparations for the Floras Centennial."

"Just point me to the nearest box, please," Ofelia said with fake enthusiasm.

"Bueno, read, be bored," Mrs. Castillo said. "It's not the worst thing in the world."

Ofelia stuck the pencil in her mouth and bit down so hard the thin glossy coat over the word *can* cracked between her teeth. It was as if even the pencil had known she was doomed.

Being bored, being stuck in an old, dusty house all summer, those *were* the absolute worst things in the world. Ofelia pressed the steely gray lead of her pencil against the page and wrote:

Dead Body Found at DiSanti Mansion.
Boredom Sought for Questioning.
By Ofelia Castillo

CHAPTER 2

In Lane's memory, the tree house had been a lot higher up in the branches of the old banyan. It was a scary climb when she was little, even with one of her older brothers leading the way and the other following behind. They allowed her up only when their parents insisted, so she never let on that she was scared, no matter how much the ladder wobbled beneath her feet.

She squinted up at the makeshift flagpole and blew a strand of hair out of her sweaty face. Her brothers' flag, an old pillowcase with a large *D* for DiSanti sloppily written on it in red marker, still hung from the pole.

Lane noticed a peacock nearby, watching. The way the bird looked at her intently, its head tilted, one eye turned in her direction, made her feel like it knew something about her that even she didn't know. She didn't like the feeling.

"Whatcha looking at, weirdo?" she asked the bird, before

wrapping her fingers around the sides of the ladder. She was twelve now. The climb wasn't as high or as scary. She didn't need her brothers.

At the top, Lane pulled off her backpack and tossed it into the tree house. She looked around at the familiar space. A hammock made of thick, interwoven ropes was strung across one end, a crocheted afghan lay in a ball inside it. She pulled out the afghan. It had once been a bright green and blue, but the colors had faded after years of lying in direct sunlight that came in through the opening in the roof. Lane held her breath and shook it out, watching dust motes swirl and scatter. She hung the afghan over a windowsill to air out.

She could see that the bird was still standing where she'd left it. She dug out a granola bar from her backpack, broke off a few pieces, and tossed them down to the bird. Her grandmother's property was overrun with peacocks, and she had warned Lane not to feed them. Lane watched the bird scurry away, but not so far that it didn't quickly return to investigate what had been dropped.

Lane turned back to her work in the tree house. Besides the hammock, the only other furniture in it was a wall of cubbies, some long and rectangular, others small and square.

Most of the cubbies were empty, but a few still held items her brothers had left behind: a game of checkers and a deck of cards, a box of matches and a flashlight, a deflated football, and a few books whose pages were stuck together, their covers warped from rain. Everything was covered in a layer of grit. She collected her brothers' old things into one cubby. Even if the items were no longer useful, she couldn't throw them away. They were relics of a time when her family was still a family.

Lane had her own room in her grandmother's house, but in the tree house she stashed the things that would help her survive the summer. In one cubby, she unpacked her paints, brushes, and sketch pad, along with her X-Acto knife, an item that would probably alarm her grandmother if she found it inside. In another cubby, she placed a small canvas pouch with her collection of crystals. She had found a box of tiny, battery-operated string lights in the attic, which she now hung around the doorway.

When she was younger, she'd loved the tree house because it reminded her of her favorite picture book about a boy whose family didn't like him building things inside their house. One day he runs away and builds his own house where he can do as he likes. Soon he's joined by other kids whose families don't like their pets and their hobbies, their dirt and their noise. The boy builds them all houses, and the children create their own little village.

Lane felt like the boy in the book as she pulled in the flagpole and removed her brothers' old pillowcase flag. Except that in the story, the families all realize how much they miss the children. And the kids realize they miss their families too. They reunite and go home together and live happily ever after. Just like people always do in books, Lane thought.

She was glad to have the tree house to herself, a place of her own, away from her family. A place where no one was looking for her. Not her parents, not her brothers, and not her grandmother.

CHAPTER 3

Aster cradled the six yellow boxes of microfilm in her arms as she walked to the reference librarian's desk. They felt like baby chicks threatening to hop out and fall to the floor.

"Here you go, Ms. Falco," she said.

"Anything else for today?" Ms. Falco asked, relieving Aster of her load.

"Mm, he needs the *Miami Herald* from February first to February fifteenth, 1909," Aster said, squinting at her grandfather's tiny handwriting on a sheet of legal pad paper. "And I think that's it, but you know my grandpa."

Ms. Falco nodded before disappearing among the beige microfilm cabinets behind her desk and returned a minute later with a single yellow box.

Aster walked it back to where her grandfather sat. He spent so much time at the Sabal Palms Public Library that he had his own microfilm machine. It didn't really belong to him, but it might as well have his name on it since he was probably one of the last people, besides Ms. Falco, who even knew how to use it.

It wasn't that her grandpa didn't appreciate new technologies. He wasn't about to churn butter or even make it by shaking cream in a jar like Aster had shown him. And he loved his frozen microwave dinners. He used the old microfilm machine because there were some things new technologies still couldn't do.

For example, if he wanted to find out what the citrus industry was like in South Florida the year he was born— a year that Aster knew only because she found his missing birth certificate while helping him look for his also-missing Social Security card—he had to go to the library. Sure, he might be able to find some bits and pieces of information online, but for the real meat of it, what her grandpa called "primary sources," sometimes the internet wouldn't cut it. Plus, he liked to argue, technology took some of the mystery and wonder out of the world.

"Grandpa, we have to go soon," Aster said, looking at the clock on the wall.

"Mm-hmm," he responded.

She watched the reflection of the microfilm on his glasses

as he rewound it. The end of the film reel swooshed between the plates of glass and released, spinning and flapping on its spool, until her grandfather turned the knob to stop it.

"All done with this one," he said. He removed the reel from the machine and handed it to Aster. "How much time do we have?"

"The matinee starts at two," she said. "A half hour at most."

"Plenty of time," her grandfather said and unboxed the reel she had brought him.

Once a month, Aster and her grandfather went to the Sabal Palms Cinema where they only screened old movies. Aster liked that there were no computers or cell phones or people wearing shorts and sneakers in the movies. Instead, the actors wore fancy hats and coats and always had their hair done. When she didn't find a movie very interesting and she had run out of popcorn and Milk Duds, the red velvet seats were just comfortable enough for napping.

"How does coq au vin sound for dinner?" Aster asked, flipping through the library's reference copy of the cookbook with the white cover and little orange fleur-de-lis and turquoise stars.

Her grandfather glanced at her over the top of his glasses.

13

"It's chicken, Grandpa," she explained. "In red wine. It has onions and bacon and mushrooms. Sounds good, right?"

Her grandfather nodded, but she could tell he was concentrating on his microfilm reel.

"What is this word?" she asked, pointing to the list of ingredients. "Do we have any at home?"

Her grandfather glanced at the book.

"Cognac. The 'g' is silent and the 'nac' sounds like the Three Stooges' laughing—nyuk-nyuk-nyuk," her grandfather said.

"I'm going to make a copy of the recipe," Aster said, shaking her head at her grandfather's joke.

She carried the book to the photocopier, dropped two dimes in the coin slot, and watched the sheets of paper slide out of the machine. When she turned, she almost bumped into one of her neighbors.

"Hey, Asteroid," Ken from two houses over said. He carried his football shoulder pads in one arm and a stack of books in the other. "How's it going?"

"I'm good," Aster said. "But you look like you need help."

"Nah, I got it," Ken assured her. "But thanks. Tell the professor I say hi."

"I will," Aster said.

The professor was what everyone in the neighborhood called her grandfather. Not Mr. Douglas or Benjamin or Ben. Benjamin Douglas was the first Black professor hired to teach at Sabal Palms University, and their community was proud that he was their own.

Sometimes Aster called him Professor Grandpa because he was both her grandfather and her homeschool teacher. Soon he would just be Grandpa, though, since she would be starting seventh grade at Hurston Middle School that fall. The thought of going to school made her stomach ache, like the time she ate a bad oyster sandwich at the county fair.

The plan had always been for her to eventually go to a public school. Her mom thought she needed to have a "real" school experience with other kids and other adults. And now that her grandpa was busy working on his book, a history of the Douglas family, who were some of the earliest Bahamian settlers in Sabal Palms, it seemed like the perfect time.

"Coq au vin? Nice," Ms. Falco said, interrupting her thoughts. "You have one lucky grandfather."

"Tell that to him. I'm trying to expand his taste in food, Ms. Falco," Aster said. "Grandpa could eat box macaroni and cheese every day no problem."

"I'm sure he appreciates your delicious cooking," Ms. Falco said.

"Oh, he does," Aster said. "But he thinks eating is just one more distraction from doing other things, like *working*."

"Well, some people just don't have a passion for good food like us," Ms. Falco said and winked.

"I think eating is like . . . " Aster thought for a second. "It's like looking at art in a museum. Except better."

"Art you can eat," Ms. Falco said. "Want me to take that?" She held out her hands.

Aster inhaled the smell of the cream-colored pages one more time before giving Ms. Falco the book. Her desire for dinners that weren't microwaved in plastic trays and that didn't taste like cardboard had led her to the library's cookbook section, where she learned about cuisines from all over the world. But her favorite was the book dedicated to "La Belle France."

She loved everything about it: the list of measurement conversions; the line illustrations of cutting techniques; the way the recipe names were all in French, and she had to look them up online to hear how they were pronounced.

She folded the photocopies and filed them inside the vintage wooden DiSanti Citrus recipe box she carried with her. It had been a promotional item that once contained recipes using DiSanti citrus products. She had found it at the flea market, emptied of its original contents. Now it kept her own ideas, as well as those she copied from cookbooks and magazines at the library.

"It's time to go, Grandpa," she announced, adjusting her backpack. "*A Raisin in the Sun* awaits."

"Yes, can't be late for Sidney," her grandfather said, putting the last microfilm reel back in its box. Aster grabbed the boxes and placed them in the return tray on Ms. Falco's desk while her grandfather stuffed his folder of papers into his satchel.

"Did you know Sidney Poitier was the first Black man to win an Oscar for best actor?" her grandpa asked.

"I do now," Aster said, grinning. "Ready to go, Professor?"

Her grandfather nodded and they headed for the exit.

"Goodbye, Mr. Douglas, Aster," the librarian called to them.

"Goodbye, Ms. Falco," Aster said with a wave before walking out into the humid afternoon with her grandfather.

CHAPTER 4

The Floras House reminded Cat of a quinceañera cake on display in the window of a Cuban bakery. It was a two-story wooden house painted orchid purple with pink window shutters, a white porch, and a white balcony that wrapped around the second level. On the front lawn stood a sign that read THE FLORAS OF SABAL PALMS, EST. 1918.

Cat remembered how she had anxiously looked forward to her seventh birthday when she would finally be old enough to join the Floras, just like her mom and her sisters. But on that Thursday afternoon, five years later, she felt like she was on her way to the gallows. She wished to be anywhere but in the meeting room where girls greeted one another, talked about summer plans, drank iced tea, and nibbled on lemon-thyme shortbread cookies while they waited for Mrs. McAllister to call the meeting to order.

Alice Vargas walked in and looked around the room,

giving Cat a quick little nod before making her way over to where Emma Hannigan stood. Alice and Cat had been inseparable for years. Cat would often ride to school with Alice and her dad. Alice made Cat her first pair of binoculars for birding out of two halves of a paper-towel tube. They'd even joined the Floras together. But everything changed when Alice transferred to a different school at the start of sixth grade.

To Cat, it felt like it had happened as fast as the beating of a ruby-throated hummingbird's wings. One day they were best friends, and then they weren't. Days would go by before Alice would respond to Cat's text messages. She stopped coming over on weekends. Eventually, they were seeing each other only at Floras meetings, where Cat would save a seat for Alice, only for Alice to pretend not to see and sit next to Emma, a classmate at her new school.

Cat held her binoculars to her eyes and looked out a window that faced the backyard. The Floras property stretched past the purple house and ended at a drop. Beyond that was the bay. There had been plans to build a fence at one point. Cat remembered that someone's dog had gotten off its leash and bolted across the yard, falling right over the edge of the property. Poor pup, she thought. The dog was rescued, but no fence had been put up yet. A rusted chain was still the only barrier between the end of the property and the tangle of mangrove roots below. A short wooden pier, its planks rotted with age, jutted out from the yard like a tongue lapping water. The pier had been used back in the days when the only way to get to South Florida was by boat, but now a KEEP OUT sign was posted at its entrance.

Cat spied a couple of brown pelicans bobbing in the water. She imagined a little boat at the pier waiting to rescue her.

"Good afternoon, Floras," Mrs. McAllister said, walking into the room. "Find a seat, please."

Cat let her binoculars drop, adjusting the strap that had become tangled in the lavender Floras bandanna around her neck, and settled into the nearest chair. The head of the Floras reminded Cat of a male Osceola Turkey. She had skinny legs and a huge bosom that seemed to lead her when she walked. She also had a wattle, and her hair color changed every few months, which Cat imagined to be similar to the way the heads of wild turkeys can change color depending on their moods. Today, Mrs. McAllister's hair was a glowing bluish white.

When the woman finished writing the agenda on the

rolling chalkboard, she opened the glass door of one of the display cabinets that lined the wall behind her and pulled out a shiny gold hatbox that she set on a table. She motioned for the girls to stand and recite the Floras oath.

"As a Flora, I promise to obey and follow the laws of the troop to my fullest ability." Cat mouthed the words. Unlike when she was younger, she didn't get a thrill from taking the oath anymore.

The oath was followed by the eight laws. There were seven twelve-year-olds so each girl was tasked with calling out one, which the group then repeated. Mrs. McAllister called out the final law. Cat didn't mind this part because she had been assigned the best of the eight.

"A Flora is a friend to all living things," she said. She waited for the group to repeat.

When they had taken their seats, Mrs. McAllister asked each girl to give an update on her brownie sales. Cat hated selling brownies. She wasn't a very good salesperson, but she had an especially hard time because she didn't even like chocolate. How was she supposed to sell something she didn't like?

"Catarina?" Mrs. McAllister called her name.

"One hundred dollars," Cat said, recalling the amount in

the envelope she had left on her dresser. "I'll bring it in next week."

"Please do," Mrs. McAllister said, jotting down the number next to Cat's name in her log. "Every penny counts."

This year's brownie funds were going toward the big centennial celebration, so Mrs. McAllister was being extra pushy about sales.

"If there are no other updates, we'll close this agenda item," Mrs. McAllister said. "And don't forget to let your parents know that we'll be setting up a table at the Bahamas Day Festival in a few weeks. We have lots of brownies to sell, girls!"

Mrs. McAllister began passing out sheets of paper. When she received her copy, Cat looked at the ballot.

"We need to decide on a summer volunteer project," Mrs. McAllister said. "We'll only be working on the project with the most votes so please choose carefully."

Cat read the three projects listed:

❐ Sabal Palms Soup Kitchen
❐ Friends of the Library Book Sale
❐ Beach cleanup with the Olas Club

The item that wasn't on the list was her idea. She had proposed a project that included different community organizations and businesses collaborating to commemorate the centennial of the Migratory Bird Treaty Act.

At their brainstorming session, Cat had suggested working with the Aves Society to plan activities such as growing native plants like seaside goldenrod and scarlet bush for local birds and working with owners of high-rise buildings to place decorations on windows that would help prevent bird collisions. None of that was on the ballot.

Cat raised her hand.

"Yes, Catarina," Mrs. McAllister said.

"My bird project proposal isn't on the list," Cat said.

"As you know, our summer project should be one that is easy to execute and that will make an impact in a short period of time," Mrs. McAllister said. "The project you suggested would require a lot of outreach and planning with different groups."

"Yes," Cat said. "But couldn't it at least have gone on the ballot? I thought there were no bad ideas."

"I didn't say it was a bad idea, did I?" Mrs. McAllister smiled. "But there are better times for some ideas."

With three older sisters, Cat had learned to recognize

that there were different kinds of smiles. While some were warm and genuine, others were not. Mrs. McAllister's smile at the moment was not of the warm and genuine variety.

"It would take more time to implement than we have this summer. Why don't we table it for another meeting and discuss it as a long-term project?" Mrs. McAllister offered. "For now, you girls should vote from these three options."

Cat saw Emma lean into Alice and whisper. They giggled. The old Alice would have backed her up. Cat sighed and drew an X next to the beach cleanup.

Mrs. McAllister collected the ballots, counted the votes, and wrote Friends of the Library on the board. Great, Cat thought. They had volunteered for the book sale before, and it meant sorting through dusty books in a windowless storage room of the Sabal Palms Public Library, helping them prepare for their annual sale.

"The next item on today's agenda is the Miss Floras contest," Mrs. McAllister said. Cat noticed that the woman's smile was now a genuine one, one that was so big it threatened to spill off the sides of her face.

She could feel the buzz of excitement ripple through the room as the girls anticipated the unboxing of the hat. All twelve-year-old Floras were automatically entered in the competition unless they opted out. No one ever opted out. Being Miss Floras was the ultimate goal for any girl who had gone through years of meetings and brownie sales. And like Cat, most Floras tended to come from families where there had been other Floras, so participation in the contest was expected.

Every summer a Miss Floras was selected by a committee made up of one member of the Sabal Palms Garden Club, one member of the Sabal Palms Botanical Society, one member of the board of directors of the Floras, and a former Miss Floras. The girl was picked based on volunteer work, salesmanship, etiquette, knowledge of local flora, and adherence to the Floras oath and laws.

Year after year, she had been like the other girls in the room, excited to see the hat that Miss Floras wore. But this year, she felt sick as Mrs. McAllister pulled it out of its box.

Cat had no intention of wearing the hat. Ever. Not after having done a research project on the history of the Migratory Bird Treaty Act, which held people and businesses accountable for harming birds, both intentionally and unintentionally.

"Bird murder," Cat mumbled under her breath.

"Did you say something, Catarina?" Mrs. McAllister

asked, holding the hat in the palm of her hands like it was a delicate flower she was afraid of crushing.

"Bird murder," Cat said louder. "Did you know that birds were killed to make that hat?"

A few girls, including Emma and Alice, giggled and rolled their eyes. Everyone was used to Cat's bird obsession. So much so, that some of the girls had given her a nickname.

"That's an unproven accusation," Mrs. McAllister said. But Cat couldn't help notice that the woman looked a little nervous.

"A hundred years ago, around the time that hat was made, people thought it was okay to kill birds and wear them, Mrs. McAllister," Cat said. "That's a fact."

"Oh my gawd," Emma said. "Seriously, Nerdy Birdy?"

Cat couldn't tell if she was questioning the seriousness of Cat or of her statement. Either way, she had the group's attention so she went on.

"Seriously," Cat said, standing up. "And we really should think about not using it anymore."

Mrs. McAllister let out a laugh that Cat knew was *not* genuine.

"Not use it? What is going on with you, Catarina?" Mrs.

McAllister asked incredulously. "Where is all this coming from?"

"Don't any of you care that innocent birds were murdered?" Cat asked, looking at the other girls, ignoring Mrs. McAllister.

"I care," a Flora named Olive said. She raised one of her long black braids into the air along with her hand. "Why would they do that, Mrs. McAllister?"

A few of the younger girls began to whisper.

"That's enough, everyone," Mrs. McAllister said, returning the feathered hat to its box. "Catarina, why don't you and I talk after the meeting?"

Cat didn't want to talk. Especially not to Mrs. McAllister.

"Isn't it funny that she loves birds and her name is . . . Cat?" Emma said. A few girls laughed.

"It's just some feathers, Cat," Alice whispered. "Chill out."

Hearing Alice call them "just some feathers" and telling her to chill out made something inside Cat snap like a dead limb on a tree. She grabbed her bag off the floor and before she could think, she ran.

"Where are you going?" Olive called after her.

"Catarina, come back here!" Mrs. McAllister yelled.

But Cat kept running. Through the parlor, out the front door, across the porch, and down the steps. Away from Mrs. McAllister. Away from the Floras. And away from the awful feathered hat.

CHAPTER 5

"I don't think there really is a Mrs. DiSanti," Ofelia declared at dinner.

"It *is* a little strange that she doesn't show her face, no?" Mr. Castillo agreed. He pointed to his palomilla steak with his knife. Ofelia knew this was his invitation for her to deposit any grilled onions she wasn't going to eat onto his plate.

"Viejo, don't encourage her," Mrs. Castillo said. "La señora is a very private person. We're lucky she's even allowing me to bring you to work. Now, let me eat my dinner in peace, por favor."

Ofelia's mom looked tired. She was Mrs. DiSanti's assistant, which, Ofelia gathered, meant she did anything and everything the woman needed. In her first week at the DiSanti house Ofelia had helped her mother stuff hundreds of envelopes with Floras Centennial invitations. She also read three library books, saved two lizards that had fallen into the swimming pool, and took a nap on the fanciest and most uncomfortable couch. But she had yet to see Mrs. DiSanti. The only proof she had that the woman existed was that her mom was always stressed out. Mrs. DiSanti was like a ghost. And who knew ghosts were so demanding?

Whenever she ate lunch in the kitchen, Ofelia would watch as Mira, Mrs. DiSanti's cook, prepared a tray for the woman. Mrs. DiSanti always ate upstairs, and she always had the same thing for lunch: a boiled egg with a sprinkling of paprika served in one of those old-fashioned egg cups like in *Bread and Jam for Frances*, a salad of arugula, avocado, and radishes, no dressing, and a cup of tea with a slice of lemon. Food for phantoms, Ofelia thought.

"Why is she so private?" Ofelia scraped the onions off her steak and onto her father's plate. "Is she hiding something? Adults are always hiding stuff."

"That's none of your business," Mrs. Castillo said. "Your business is to be quiet and stay out of the way."

"Fine," Ofelia said. "I'll stay out of the way. Did you read over the Qwerty Sholes application?" she asked.

She saw her parents glance at each other and anticipated what was coming.

"Did you hear the part about enjoying my dinner en paz?" Mrs. Castillo asked.

"But there's a deadline," Ofelia insisted. "I need you to sign it."

"We read the application, but I don't know if we are ready to sign anything," Mr. Castillo said, shaking his head. "A summer in New York City?"

"Not a summer. Just four weeks." She looked expectantly at her dad. "The winners get to work with Qwerty Sholes journalists and editors and photographers to create a real magazine." She was almost out of her chair thinking about it.

"New York City is not a place for a young girl to be alone," her mother said.

"You've never even been to New York," Ofelia said. "How would you know?"

"Don't get bocona with me," Mrs. Castillo said with a frown. "I'm old enough to know that a place like New York City is dangerous."

"I wouldn't be alone," Ofelia assured her. "It's like a sleepaway camp. There would be adult chaperones keeping an eye on us." Ofelia made sure to emphasize the word *chaperones*.

"We don't know anything about these adults," Mr. Castillo said. "How do we know they aren't—"

"Pa, please," Ofelia interrupted. "Qwerty Sholes is one of the biggest publishers in the country. Do you know how many contest winners have gone on to win Pulitzer Prizes in journalism? Don't you want me, your only daughter, to be a Pulitzer Prize winner?"

"But you've never even stayed home alone for more than an hour," Mr. Castillo said jokingly. "How are you going to survive four weeks in New York without your viejos?"

"I *could* stay home alone if you would just let me," Ofelia said, not amused by her father's joke.

Ofelia hated that her parents suffered from OCS—Only Child Syndrome. They hovered and questioned and acted like danger lurked around every corner. They treated her like a baby, their only baby, that needed constant protecting. She'd loved all the attention when she was a little kid, but she wasn't a little kid anymore.

She found herself wishing her parents would have another child just to take some of their focus off her. But that would never happen because her dad was right about them being her viejos. Her parents were old. Maybe not grandparent old, but definitely older than any of her classmates' parents. She was what they called their milagrito, a little miracle that came along when they had given up on the hope of ever having children.

"This is something Pa and I have to talk about," her mother said with finality.

Ofelia knew they would discuss it to death and figure out all the ways in which it was a terrible idea. She didn't understand her parents at all. They had left Cuba, an island in the Caribbean that looked like the gnarled finger of a witch, when they were just a little older than Ofelia. They should want her to be as brave and independent. Instead, they seemed to work hard to make her afraid of the world.

Maybe, Ofelia thought, she just needed to prove to her parents that she wasn't afraid, and that the world was more than its scary parts. Maybe bravery was like a muscle. She had to exercise it for it to develop. It couldn't be any harder than attempting a pull-up in PE.

"We'll think about it," Mr. Castillo said. He stood up and began clearing the table.

"Sure," Ofelia said. But she knew *we'll think about it* usually meant no.

"Have you seen la nieta?" Mrs. Castillo asked, carrying

plates to the sink. "She came in last week. Se llama Purslane."

"Maybe a summer friend, right?" Mr. Castillo said, hopefully.

"I don't know," Ofelia said. "Maybe."

She had seen the girl a few times since she arrived, skulking around her grandmother's property, dressed all in black like the girl from that old television show about the family of monsters. She didn't seem very friendly. Ofelia was pretty sure the girl might have hissed at her once.

In her room that night, Ofelia thought about what her mother had said at dinner. Not the part about New York City being a dangerous place for young girls. The part about Mrs. DiSanti. She wondered if her mother had any idea that the worst thing you could say to a journalist, especially a muckraker, was that someone is private or that something is off-limits. She would be quiet all right. So quiet she would blend into the background, all eyes and ears.

She opened her reporter's notebook and dug out her pencil from her backpack. Ofelia wrote:

What Secrets Hide in the DiSanti
Mansion?
By Ofelia Castillo

* The whole place is cold and quiet, like a museum no one ever visits.
* There are so many statues of little fat babies with curly hair and creepy eyeball-less stares.
* The mopey granddaughter hangs out in the tree house and hisses at people.
* Peacocks are always sneaking up on a person; bunch of strange birds.
* The big, old trees in the yard look like giants <u>pretending</u> to be trees.
* There's no sign of the mysterious Mrs. DiSanti.

Maybe, Ofelia thought, sticking her pencil through the wire of the notebook spiral, Mrs. DiSanti's house held the story she needed.

CHAPTER 6

Lane rubbed her thumb and forefinger against the smooth sides of the crystal that hung from a piece of black yarn around her neck. She and her grandmother sat in silence as Mira cleared the table of the dinner dishes. If Lane believed in Santa Claus, she could imagine Mira as Mrs. Claus. She had a sweet face with a hint of wrinkles and the bluest eyes. The gray apron she always wore matched her hair. But what Lane liked most about Mira was that she was always so kind and attentive.

"Enjoy," she said to Lane, as she placed a bowl of pistachio gelato in front of her before disappearing into the kitchen.

Lane scooped a bite. The solitary clink of the spoon against her bowl seemed to echo in the large dining room.

"Purslane," Mrs. DiSanti started, "I don't know if your father spoke to you about this, but I would like you to think about joining the Floras while you're here."

Lane let the gelato numb her tongue. Her father had made the pitch. He also knew her well enough to realize there was no way she was joining the Floras.

"The Floras were founded by Charlotte DiSanti, and all DiSanti women have been members," her grandmother went on. "Floras are well-rounded and go on to make great contributions to their communities. Besides being tradition, it's a good place for a young girl to learn about social etiquette and gain leadership skills, to volunteer and study the natural environment. I think you would enjoy it."

"That sounds really great, Grandmother." Lane was sure the woman was quoting the Floras' website word for word. "But I'm going to be busy this summer. Dad probably forgot to mention it. He doesn't remember anything I tell him."

"What will be keeping you so busy?" Mrs. DiSanti asked.

"Well, I have to read fifteen books before the school year starts," Lane said. "*Fifteen.* Schools in the United States don't seem to believe in summer vacation like they do in England." She let out a little laugh.

Her grandmother stared at her for an uncomfortably long minute as if trying to get to the truth by reading her face. Just like the peacock in the yard.

"Fifteen books are not a lot," Mrs. DiSanti said.

"I'm a very slow reader," Lane countered.

Her grandmother continued to give her the peacock stare, her dark eyes shining.

"The Floras sound like a good organization, but . . ." Lane hesitated. If she were with her parents she would just let her indignation roll out like a tidal wave, but the last thing she wanted was for her grandmother to insist on it. She had to play it carefully. "I'm not sure they're my thing."

"And what is your thing?" Mrs. DiSanti asked.

"I like to make art," Lane said. She didn't expect her grandmother to know her. She had only seen her twice in the last four years since her family moved to London for her father's job.

"Well, that's wonderful," Mrs. DiSanti said, clasping her hands on top of the white tablecloth. "The Floras offer opportunities to learn about the arts. Some of our board members are involved with the Atlantic Ballet and the Sabal Palms Museum of Fine Art."

"No," Lane said, slowly shaking her head. "Not like *gallery* art."

"What other kind of art is there?" Mrs. DiSanti asked, furrowing her brow.

Lane thought about the art she saw around London in

Brick Lane and Shoreditch and Brixton. Homemade stickers on light poles, beautiful paper cutouts wheatpasted onto brick walls, and stencils spray-painted on the corners of buildings, in alleys, on the sidewalk. It was art that you only noticed if you were really paying attention. Her grandmother didn't understand that there was art that lived outside of museums.

She shrugged in response and scraped the last streaks of gelato from her bowl.

"I hope you'll at least think about it," Mrs. DiSanti said. "It will make the summer go quicker to be around other girls your age."

Lane wasn't sure if she wanted the summer to go quickly or slowly. She was currently stuck between two unknowns: being with her grandmother, a woman she barely knew; and being in New York, starting a new life with her mother. Neither unknown appealed to her.

"Yes, Grandmother," Lane said. "May I be excused?"

Mrs. DiSanti looked at her a little longer, as if trying to figure out where Lane had come from.

"You're excused," the woman said finally.

That night, while Lane was in bed wondering what her parents and her brothers were doing, there was a faint knock on her bedroom door. She quickly turned over onto her stomach and closed her eyes. She listened as the door creaked open.

"Purslane?" Mrs. DiSanti whispered. "Are you still awake?"

She sensed her grandmother walk toward her bed and heard the slight thump of something on her bedside table. Lane tried to breathe like a sleeping person, steady, slow, peacefully, while she waited for her grandmother to leave. The smell of vanilla and orange tickled her nose. *Do not sneeze*, she thought, willing her nose to ignore the scent. Peeking through her eyelashes, Lane watched the woman, who seemed to float through the room in her long, white nightgown, finally flick off the light.

Lane waited and listened to her grandmother's footsteps move quietly down the hallway to her own room. When she heard the door close, she went back to breathing normally and turned on the flashlight she kept under her pillow for late-night reading.

She ran her hand across the top of the bedside table and grabbed the book her grandmother had placed on it. Gold-embossed flowers framed the frayed purple clothbound cover. In the middle, in fancy cursive gold letters, was written *The Floras: A Handbook for Sabal Palms Girls*.

Lane saw her grandmother's name written inside the book: Elizabeth Felice DiSanti. Lane knew the story about how her grandmother had kept her maiden name when she married, which was almost unheard of in the olden days. But she was the heir to the DiSanti fortune, and if your name was DiSanti in Florida, people understood not changing it.

Lane opened the book. She read the history of the Floras, followed by the Floras oath and the eight laws. *A Flora is courteous. A Flora is cheerful. A Flora is helpful. A Flora is loyal.* Loyal to who, Lane wondered. She read about the Floras uniform and their symbols and signs. She read tips on proper dress and behavior for Floras. Floras did things like tuck in their shirts and comb their hair. Lane ran her hand through her bob and tugged at a knot until she managed to loosen it. The Floras would be appalled.

Floras were grounded, the book declared. To illustrate the point, there was a drawing of a Flora looking up at a boy climbing a tree, a smile on her face. Lane certainly didn't want to be grounded if it meant not climbing up to the tree house. She wanted to draw a scowl on the girl. Were Floras allowed to be angry at the injustices of life? Because if they weren't, there was definitely no place for her. She felt angry a lot of the time, especially since leaving London.

The book gave instructions on how to identify local trees and plants, how to tell the age of a tree from its rings, how to press flowers, and how to use Morse code, which didn't sound so terrible to Lane. There were also recipes for tea made from local plants and for the original Floras brownies. She read about Miss Floras, who Lane imagined was the queen of the Floras.

Her eyes, heavy with sleepiness, rested on an illustration. *A group of Floras is called a cluster*, she read. Lane liked the names given to groups of specific things. She imagined a bloom of jellyfish unfolding underwater like flowers. And her favorite, a skulk of foxes, creeping up on their prey. Until recently she had been part of a family of DiSantis. But that group had broken apart, and now it was just her. A single jellyfish, a single fox, a single DiSanti.

Her grandmother had said being around other girls her age would make the summer pass more quickly. Lane yawned and turned off the flashlight. As she slipped into sleep she thought that maybe her grandmother was onto something.

CHAPTER 7

Lane pressed a finger against the paint on each invitation to make sure they were all dry and ready to roll. She had sketched out the image that would represent her Scout troop. Then she drew the symbol onto a piece of cardboard from a box she found in the recycling bin and carefully cut out the shape with her X-Acto knife. She tore a paper grocery bag into sheets and painted the stencil image onto these. Finally, she handwrote the details and set the sheets aside to dry.

Lane was happy with how they had turned out. Once she was sure they would not smudge, she rolled up each invitation and tied them with pieces of bakery string from the spool Mira kept on the kitchen counter.

Her first mission was to find the girl's backpack *without* the girl. She had seen Mrs. Castillo's daughter around the property, usually with her nose in a book or writing in that little notebook she carried, chewing on her pencil like it was a carrot stick.

Lane placed the invitations in her bag, climbed down from the tree house, and walked to the kitchen. She could see Mrs. Castillo's back as she worked at her computer in the office just off to the side. The girl's red backpack was on the floor near her desk.

Lane walked up to the doorway and cleared her throat. Mrs. Castillo swiveled in her chair.

"Oh, hi, Purslane," she said, tucking a strand of hair behind her ear. "How are you? Did you need something?"

"My grandmother wants to see you," Lane said, trying not to look like the nervous fibber she was. "She's in her library."

Mrs. Castillo studied Lane's face, then looked at the phone on her desk.

"Hmm, she didn't call," the woman said, frowning. "Are you sure?"

Lane hadn't thought about the phone.

"Yes," she said quickly. "Something about a document to scan and send out. I think."

"Okay, I'll go check on her," Mrs. Castillo said, standing up. "Thank you."

Before she left the office, Mrs. Castillo turned back to Lane.

"Ofelia is around here somewhere," she said. "She can be a little shy."

Lane nodded and watched Mrs. Castillo walk away. She was absolutely not just going to go up to a stranger and say hello. That might have worked when she was five, but not anymore. It was too awkward. Putting an anonymous invitation in the girl's backpack seemed a lot safer. She wouldn't know who it was from, so if she decided not to show up, Lane didn't have to feel like it was a personal rejection. Lane knelt by the girl's backpack and stuck the invitation inside.

She had two more invitations to leave somewhere, ideally where kids hung out. It also had to be a place *she* liked. The way she figured, kids who spent time in places *she* liked were more likely to be kids she could potentially hang out with. She went to her room and collected a couple of library books to return.

As she biked to the public library, Lane wondered how people made friends. It seemed like a thing that happened unconsciously. One day you realized you had friends that weren't friends before. But when you were *searching* for friends, it was too . . . scary. At the moment, her only friend was one particular peacock she'd named Eunice who had taken to perching in the banyan when Lane was around. She

45

knew it was the same bird because it had a little bald spot on the right side of its head. Animals were easy, Lane thought. You just had to give them food and they'd keep coming around.

Somehow, she had managed to make friends in London. But things were simple when you were eight and the new kid from "across the pond." Little kids don't judge one another so quickly or automatically think someone is weird if they aren't exactly like everyone else.

Now that she and her mom were back in New York, she had to start all over again. Her mom didn't seem to have a problem with that. She had old friends from before they moved. She had transferred her business in London, a yoga studio, to someone else, and had already picked out a new local studio space to rent in New York. But it was different for Lane. She wasn't the same person who had left four years ago. She couldn't just pick up where she left off.

Lane walked into the library. Just inside the entrance of the children's room hung a board with community and library announcements. As she looked at it, she knew she couldn't just tack up her invitations like she was looking for a missing cat. This required a little more thought. Hers wasn't a "friends wanted" flyer with a list of likes (street art, the color black, old *Twilight Zone* episodes, crystals) and dislikes (people who talked too much, vegetables, air-conditioning, moving). That seemed too desperate. The flyer was supposed to catch the attention of someone who was curious, someone interested in mystery. Someone like her.

She noticed the yellow kids' book-club bags hanging next to the librarian's desk. Ms. Falco was helping a patron at a computer, so Lane walked over and grabbed two of the bags. Inside were copies of that month's book club selection. She pulled these out, placing them on the librarian's desk, and dropped an invitation in each bag. Then she found two copies of her favorite book in the stacks and put one in each bag for good measure. Maybe the kids who found them would see the book as a message too. Wanted: someone to run away with to the museum.

Lane knew she couldn't just leave the bags on a table, or Ms. Falco might pick them up and place them back on the rack. So, she headed to the girls' restroom. She dried the counter with a paper towel and placed one bag there. She hung the other on a hook behind a stall door. Then she closed her eyes and rubbed the crystal around her neck, making a wish, before leaving.

CHAPTER 8

Cat locked her bike at the rack outside the library and watched as Floras walked up the porch steps and went inside the purple house. She should have been going in too, but she had known as she rode up the street that she couldn't.

"Hi, Cat." It was Olive, waving to her from the sidewalk in front of the Floras House. "Are you coming?"

Cat shook her head. "Can you tell Mrs. McAllister that I'm not feeling well?"

It was the truth. The thought of returning to the Floras House, of facing Mrs. McAllister and the other girls, made her feel dizzy.

She watched as Olive looked left, right, and left again, before crossing to her side of the street.

"Are you okay?" the younger girl asked, a look of concern on her face.

"Yeah, I'll be better soon," Cat said, eager to be rid of the girl.

"I'll let her know," Olive said. "You can count on me."

She shot Cat a big, partially toothed smile.

"Thanks, Olive."

"I hope you feel better soon," Olive said, waving before crossing toward the house.

Cat watched and waited for Mrs. McAllister to close the front door of the Floras House before making her way to the nearby nature preserve.

She had recently discovered that going for a walk with her birding binoculars was magic for untangling mind knots. And her mind was like a constrictor knot that afternoon. She swatted mosquitoes and wiped her face with her Floras neckerchief. It was shady under the trees, but still so hot. She thought about how nice and cool it was in the Floras House. Where her mother thought she was at that moment, preparing to become the next Miss Floras.

Mrs. McAllister had called her mom after she ran out of the previous week's meeting, but Cat managed to intercept the message and delete it from her mom's phone. Now her feelings were in the middle of a tug-of-war that rivaled the one between the fifth and sixth graders on field day. She still felt terrible. Not about deleting Mrs. McAllister's message, but about doing something to betray her mom's trust. She knew it was wrong, but she felt like she had no choice. If her mom found out, she would have forced her to apologize. And she didn't think that wild turkey, Mrs. McAllister, deserved an apology. She also didn't want to be anywhere near Alice and Emma or the hat.

Her mother would kill her if she knew she wasn't with the Floras. Not literally, of course. Virginia Garcia would just be heartbroken with disappointment. Cat was, after all, the Last Great Garcia Hope.

Mrs. Garcia had been a Miss Floras when she was twelve. Or, as she made clear to Cat and her sisters, the first *Cuban American* Miss Floras. And there had been no other since her.

"It's all political," Cat's sister Clara had said one night at dinner when Mrs. Garcia had been going on about Cat entering that year. "It's not about you. It's about who you know, who your family is, and how much they can donate to the groups that judge the whole thing."

"Well, apparently not," Mrs. Garcia had retorted. "Otherwise *you* might have been Miss Floras."

"It's not the end of the world if you aren't Miss Floras," Clara assured her, ignoring Mrs. Garcia. "Look at us." She motioned around the table at Cat's sisters.

That exchange led to a blowup between her mom and her sister that ended with Clara storming out of the room. Which, when Cat thought about it, wasn't an uncommon occurrence. Storming out in anger was a special talent of the Garcia sisters.

Being in the Miss Floras contest was something Cat had thought of as part of the natural progression of her time as a Flora. Her mother talked about it like it was something important, and so, she had always thought of it that way too.

Her mom credited her own successes in life in part to her involvement with the Floras. It was a big deal to her.

Cat had seen photos of her mother at twelve, beaming proudly into the camera with the feathered hat resting on her long dark hair. Mrs. Garcia dreamed of a Miss Floras legacy with her four daughters. But so far, she was zero for three. Neither Cari, Carmen, nor Clara had been Miss Floras. And Mrs. Garcia saw this as a reason why none of them had achieved her idea of success.

Cari worked in a salon where she painted cool designs on people's nails, and at night she worked on her own paintings. Carmen was a clerk at the post office. Clara worked at the supermarket and took improv comedy classes. Cat liked when Cari painted tiny birds on her nails and when Carmen told her about how far a package that came through the post office had traveled. And even though she didn't think Clara was very funny, she would never have told her so because Cat believed in everyone having their own dream.

Her sisters seemed happy. Wasn't that important? Maybe her sister was right. Maybe it wasn't the end of the world, even though her mother acted as if it was.

Cat's dream was to be an ornithologist. Her mom didn't have a problem with that because it meant going to college and "using her brain." She and Cat's father had even given her a pair of starter binoculars for her birthday. But there was no discussion when it came to the Floras and the Miss Floras contest. Cat might not have cared about just doing it for her mother's sake. As the youngest daughter, she was used to doing what she was told by everyone. But seeing the feathered hat again—especially after learning about how bird populations were harmed—made her realize she didn't want to be a part of something that went against what she believed in and cared for.

The sound of a whistle snapped Cat out of her thoughts.

She put her binoculars to her eyes and searched for the source of the sharp single note followed by a melodic trill. She spotted a bird wearing a black mask perched on a branch. It looked a little like a blue jay but it was gray with black-and-white wings. She made a mental note to stop in the library before going home to see if she could find it in *The Sibley Guide to Birds*.

She searched the trees overhead for who else might be hiding out with her. Leaves rustled, and she waited for the bird to appear in her line of vision, but it flew away too fast for Cat to see anything but a flash of red.

Cat thought about all the years she had spent with the Floras as she followed the path back out of the nature preserve. She had loved being part of a group of girls, but it was like her friendship with Alice. Something had changed. Not in the Floras, but in her. And she knew things wouldn't be the same. It made her sad. But disappointing her mom made her both sad and terrified.

At the end of the path, Cat stopped at the welcome sign to take a sip from her water bottle. As she hooked the bottle back onto her bag, she noticed the donation box. The welcome sign informed visitors that while it was free to enter the nature preserve, a donation of any amount was appreciated. Cat unzipped her backpack. The only money she had was the brownie money she was supposed to turn in at the meeting that afternoon. She pulled out the white envelope and peeked inside. She ran her thumb along the edges of the bills. She had sold twenty boxes of brownies at five dollars apiece.

Cat freed the stack of bills from the envelope, and before she could stop herself, she had folded it in half and shoved it into the slot in the wooden box. Her stomach twisted with nerves. An explosion of twittering that sounded like laughter rang out in the trees above her as she hurried out of the nature preserve.

At the library, Cat was greeted by a welcome gust of cold air. She made her way to the children's room where Ms. Falco was working. She grabbed *The Sibley Guide to Birds* from its spot on a shelf, as well as her favorite book about John James Audubon's paintings.

There were a lot of gray birds in the *Sibley Guide*, but after searching and being distracted by other birds, Cat hadn't found the one she was looking for.

"Have you seen the Audubon app?" Ms. Falco asked. She was pushing the pop-up library cart that lived outside the building a few times a week.

"There's an Audubon app?" Cat asked eagerly. "Show me."

Ms. Falco opened the app on her own phone. It included a field guide with bird songs and calls. Users could also see what kinds of birds had been spotted in their area.

"This is great," Cat said. "I'm going to add it to my phone. Maybe I'll find the bird I saw at the nature preserve. Thanks, Ms. Falco."

"You're welcome," the librarian said. "When I heard about it, I immediately thought of you."

Ms. Falco continued on her way out, and Cat flipped through the Audubon book. She found her favorite painting of the regal snowy egret, *Egretta thula*, plate 242, standing in what looked like a marsh. She imagined Audubon seeing the beautiful bird for the first time.

Cat checked her phone. The Floras meeting would be ending soon. She'd planned to pick up her bike and head out before the girls were dismissed so she wouldn't risk the chance of running into anyone.

She placed the books back in their places, collected her bag, and made a bathroom stop before leaving the library. At the sink counter, someone had left a yellow bag, the kind the library used to hold multiple copies of the book-club selection. She washed and dried her hands, then grabbed the bag to drop it off on Ms. Falco's desk on her way out.

She had participated in the kids' book club with Alice last summer, before everything changed. Cat peered in the bag, wondering what they were reading this season. Inside was a paperback. On the cover of the book, a girl and boy carrying satchels and instrument cases looked up the stairs of the Metropolitan Museum of Art. At the bottom of the bag lay something that looked like a scroll.

Cat pulled out the paper thinking it might be a book-club-participation certificate someone left behind, but it was made of thick brown paper and tied with a string. She untied the scroll and opened it.

Inaugural Meeting of the Ostentation of Others and Outsiders
A (Secret) Scout Troop

15 Horned Lark Lane (in the tree house!)
Thursday, June 28, at 2:00 p.m.
Open the mailbox for further instructions.
KIDS ONLY.

CHAPTER 9

Most of the desserts in *Mastering the Art of French Cooking* weren't easily portable. Especially in the Florida heat. Aster couldn't put something made with a bunch of egg whites in her bike basket and expect it to not be a runny mess by the time she got to 15 Horned Lark Lane. The closest thing in the book to cookies was a recipe for ladyfingers, so she decided to make those.

"Grandpa!" Aster called from the kitchen. "Where are you? I need you to try something."

Aster lived with her grandfather in the same house he had grown up in. It was a small, green shotgun house on the east side of Sabal Palms. Her grandpa had explained that the shotgun style had been brought over to the area by their Bahamian ancestors. It was called a shotgun house because the rooms were built in a row and if a gun were fired into the entrance of the house the bullet would travel straight through and out the back door. Aster wondered why the explanation had to be so morbid. Especially since the houses were built that way because the design worked well in hot climates. You could open the front and back doors and air could travel and circulate through the house like a natural air-conditioning system.

Aster found her grandfather in the backyard.

"Would you like a ladyfinger?" she said, walking across the grass to where her grandfather was bent over picking up avocados that had fallen from their tree.

"Whose finger?" he asked suspiciously.

"No one's finger," Aster said. "They're ladyfingers with apricot preserves."

"I'm sorry, but I only eat gentlemen's fingers with blueberry jam." Her grandfather chuckled. "I thought you knew that."

"Good one, Grandpa," Aster said, smiling at his joke.

"Gimme that," her grandfather said, taking Aster's offering.

She had made thirty ladyfingers, spread fifteen with apricot preserves, and placed the other fifteen on top of each one to make sandwich cookies. She packed them in a plastic container for safe transport.

"How does it taste?" she asked.

Her grandfather had eaten it in two bites.

"Mmm," he answered.

"Does that mean they're good?"

"Do you know where these come from?" he asked, ignoring her question.

Aster looked at the avocado in his hand.

"From that tree?"

"David Fairchild shipped hundreds of them to Washington, DC, from Chile in 1899," he said.

Aster knew her grandpa was in his research rabbit hole.

"David Fairchild," he repeated. He held up the avocado before placing it in a paper bag with the others. "We have these everywhere because one person made the decision to collect them and send them from one country to another. Amazing, isn't it?"

"Yeah, amazing," Aster said. "Is it okay if I go out?"

"Mmmm," her grandfather answered, feeling an avocado for firmness.

Aster took that as a yes.

"Okay, bye, Grandpa," she said, backing away toward the screen door. "I sure hope no one kidnaps me and tries to make ladyfingers out of *my* fingers."

"Be home before dark," her grandfather called back. "With all your fingers!"

Aster grinned as she walked back through the house. She collected her things, secured the plastic container and her backpack in her basket, then wheeled her bicycle through the front yard.

She had barely begun pedaling when she almost hit Harold Hendricks, who tore out of the house across the street, followed closely by his sister Helen. Aster clutched her brakes. The four Hendricks children, ages five to eleven, were collectively known on her block as Hurricane Hendricks. Even the neighborhood dogs ran for cover when one or more of them was outdoors. Mrs. Hendricks came out of the house, calling warnings and instructions like a drill sergeant as she left.

"Keep an eye on them if you can, okay?" Mrs. Hendricks asked Aster.

"I'm on my way out," Aster said, tapping her handlebars. "But I'll check on them when I'm back."

One of the things Aster loved about her street was that everyone kept an eye out for one another. Her grandpa said they were lucky to be a part of a community where people still knew and cared for their neighbors.

"Once developers come in and start putting up fancy condo buildings, it's over," he said.

Aster couldn't imagine all the little wooden houses on her street gone. Each house was painted a different color—cotton-candy blue, butter yellow, sunset orange, carnation pink—and as she rode down Whistling Duck Avenue, Aster thought her street looked like it was lined with petits fours.

As she biked away from her neighborhood, Aster thought about the invitation. She had been intrigued by the piece of paper she found inside a library book-club tote. It was tucked in with a copy of one of her favorite books. Who *didn't* love a story about kids who ran away to a museum?

But as she crossed Gray Kingbird Avenue, also known as the Wall, she considered turning back and going home. She had to remind herself why she had accepted the mysterious invitation. The paper read *kids only*. Going to a public school in the fall meant having to do a lot of new things, including making friends her age.

She passed between the columns made of coral that led to Horned Lark Lane. Once on that road, it was an easy ride. It was a secluded area full of huge fancy homes. If her street was a box of petit fours, Horned Lark Lane was lined with gingerbread houses covered in gumdrops and icing.

The only traffic came from the few people who lived on the street, delivery trucks, and the occasional peacock blocking the road.

She pedaled up to the address on the invitation and stared at the imposing gate. Orange blossoms welded out of iron crept across the top of the entrance. It's not too late to leave, she told herself. But she wasn't turning back. Even before arriving at the house, she had known exactly where she was going. The address, 15 Horned Lark Lane, was the DiSanti property.

As one of the founding families of Sabal Palms, the DiSantis were what Aster called history-book old. Everyone in Florida, even a homeschooled kid like her, learned about them right along with the Spanish conquistadors, Henry Flagler, and Julia Tuttle. If you went to public schools, you probably got little cartons of DiSanti Citrus orange juice with your cafeteria breakfast. The Douglas family was history-book old too, but they weren't millionaires credited with growing some of the earliest orange groves in the area.

Aster climbed off her bike and wheeled it toward the entrance. She looked at the invitation again. *Open the mail-*

box for further instructions. Security cameras sat on top of the gate at either end, their lenses staring at her like one-eyed owls.

She felt more nervous than she had on the bike ride over. She hoped Mrs. DiSanti wouldn't call the police on her. After all, she was farther on the other side of the Wall than she typically ventured.

Aster opened the mailbox next to the gate and stuck her hand in. Inside, she found another scroll. She opened it and read a series of instructions.

Dial 6291 into the intercom.

Ask for Eunice Peacock.

Eunice Peacock? Aster shook her head, took a deep breath, and punched the numbers into the intercom's key pad. It rang three times before someone answered.

"Who are you here to see?" a voice asked.

"Umm, Eunice Peacock?" Aster responded, leaning closer to the intercom.

"You seem unsure," the voice said.

Aster looked at the instructions again.

"I'm here to see Eunice Peacock," she repeated, this time without hesitation.

"Do you come by foot or by wheel?"

"I'm on my bike," Aster said. She rang her bike bell once as if to provide proof.

"Leave it outside the gate," the voice instructed.

"I can't leave my bike out here," Aster said. "It might get stolen."

She guessed bikes rarely got stolen on Horned Lark Lane, especially not dinged-up, secondhand bikes passed down by a neighbor. But it was her bike, and she wasn't leaving it outside.

Aster waited for a response as the intercom crackled.

"Fine," the voice said. "Bring it in, but leave it just inside the gate. Whatever you do, don't roll it over the grass or my grandmother will have our heads. Oh, and the lion holds the map."

The gate slowly opened, and Aster pushed her bike inside. She flipped down the kickstand and lifted the container of ladyfinger sandwiches out of her basket.

She had seen photos of the house, and she knew some facts about it from helping Grandpa with his research. She knew that it took almost three years to build and that like the other mansions in the area built in the early 1900s, it was supposed to look like something from the Mediterranean area of Europe. It was a massive structure of limestone and coral and tiles imported from Cuba. But nothing she read in a book prepared her for the sight of the house and its surrounding gardens.

Her grandfather never used the word *palatial*, but that was exactly what it was. The whole place looked like a picture from a book about the Renaissance. She felt like she'd walked into a different time and place, somewhere far from Sabal Palms.

"The lion holds the map," the voice from the intercom repeated impatiently.

"Oh yeah," Aster said, looking around. "The lion."

There were several lions, stone faces carved into a wall along a path that led away from the gate. The lions' mouths were open in roars and had little holes in them from which they spouted water into a stone pool full of koi fish. A few of the lions seemed to be out of commission. One held a rolled piece of paper in its mouth like it was on a smoke break. Aster pulled out the paper and opened it to find the map.

She followed the path past the lions and a reflecting pool, past the groundskeepers' cottage, to the banyan tree marked with an X on the map. A ladder hung down from above. Her eyes followed it to the top, where it ended at a tree house that looked like a bird's nest, pieced together with wood of different origins and sizes. She grabbed the rope that hung next to the ladder and swung it back and forth, causing wind chimes to announce her arrival.

Aster could see movement in the tree house. Out of the corner of her eye, she saw something suddenly run toward her.

"What the—" Aster shrieked, almost dropping her container.

A peacock had charged and now stood watching her from a couple of feet away. It eyed her suspiciously. Or maybe expectantly. She wasn't sure. And at the moment she didn't want to find out. Aster hooked one arm tightly around her container of ladyfingers and with the other grabbed the ladder and began her climb.

CHAPTER 10

"Welcome," Lane said, clearing her throat. She was out of breath from sprinting to and from the kitchen, where she had buzzed in the girls. They were all now sitting on the floor of the tree house, staring at her. Lane rubbed her crystal, feeling its cool surface in her fingers, before continuing. "Welcome to the first meeting of the Ostentation of Others and Outsiders."

She looked at the faces of the three girls. There was Ofelia, Mrs. Castillo's daughter, squinting at her through a pair of green-framed glasses, her hair pulled up in a bun, notebook in hand. The girl next to her was tall, taller than Lane, and wore a blue oversize button-down shirt, sleeves rolled up to her elbows, with jeans that hit above her ankles like she'd outgrown the pants and no one had bothered to buy her a new pair. Lane noticed she had set a leftovers container on the floor next to her. Lane felt the girl's dark eyes focused on her. The third girl wore her light brown hair in a braid down her back, a pair of forest-green binoculars hung around her neck. She kept fiddling with the strap and looking at her phone as if she had somewhere to be.

Lane cleared her throat again and put her hands on her hips. She had heard that the superhero pose was supposed to help you feel confident and in control. It was worth a try.

"Each of you either found or was given an invitation to be a part of this secret Scout troop."

The three girls looked at one another, then back at Lane.

"I'm Lane DiSanti," she said. "And that's Eunice the peacock." She pointed to where the bird had perched in the doorway.

"*That's* Eunice?" the girl with the too-big shirt asked, twisting a curl from her ponytail.

"Actually," the girl with the binoculars said, "Eunice is a *peahen*. The word *peacock* applies to males. You can tell the females and males apart because of their feathers. See how Eunice has a brown-and-tan body? Peahens aren't as colorful as the males because the male is the one that has to impress the female for mating purposes."

The girls looked at Eunice. Eunice turned her pointy

face away from the group, as if she knew they were talking about her and didn't appreciate it, before flying down from her roost.

"A peahen, huh," Lane said. "Duly noted."

"I'm Cat Garcia," the bird girl said. "I didn't mean to sound like a know-it-all, but I love birds."

"Why do people call them peacocks if they aren't all peacocks?" Lane wondered out loud.

"I'm not sure." Cat shrugged. "Probably just lack of information. Sometimes people can't be bothered with those details. It's easier to just label everything that looks similar the same, I guess."

"Hmm," Lane said thoughtfully. She liked the bird girl already.

"I brought snacks," the girl with the oversize shirt announced out of the blue. She pushed the leftovers container into the center of the group.

"They're ladyfingers with apricot preserves. I didn't make the preserves although I could have but the apricot selection at the store wasn't great, and I didn't get a chance to go to the farmers market so I just bought a jar of preserves. It's not the same as homemade but it's still good.

Unless you prefer gentlemen's fingers with blueberry jam in which case you might not care for these anyway." She scrambled to her knees and opened the container.

"But these are definitely ladyfingers," the girl rambled on, taking a cookie. "Because there's no such thing as gentlemen's fingers. That was just my grandpa's joke."

There was an awkward silence. Lane felt exhausted listening to her. The girl stuffed the cookie into her mouth and chewed.

"You brought ladyfingers," Lane said, "with apricot preserves?"

"I wasn't sure what would be appropriate for this get-together," the girl explained. "But now that I know the meeting is in a tree, I'm glad I didn't plan to make a cherry tart flambé."

"What's a flambé?" Ofelia asked. Lane watched Mrs. Castillo's daughter write something in her notebook.

"It's when you set a dessert on fire," Lane answered.

"Why would you set a dessert on fire?" Cat asked, looking perplexed.

It *did* sound tragic, Lane thought.

"It's a little more than just setting a dessert on fire," the ladyfingers girl said. "It's when you caramelize sugar on top of a dessert. You warm a liquor and then you pour it over the dessert. *Then* you set it on fire. It's fun. I mean, I've only seen it done on cooking videos, of course. My grandpa won't let me do it in the house. He says, 'Girl, this house survived the great hurricane of 1915, and it won't be burned down by a cherry tart!'" The girl laughed at her own impersonation of her grandfather.

Cat giggled.

"How do you put out the fire before it just burns the whole thing and keeps spreading?" Ofelia asked. Lane watched as the girl drew big flames around the word *flambé* in her notebook.

"With a fire extinguisher," Lane cracked.

The ladyfingers girl shook her head.

"No," she said. "The alcohol in the liquor will burn off, and the flame will go out on its own. I tried telling my grandpa, but he still wasn't having it."

"Good to know," Lane said. "And who are *you*? Julia Child?"

"Oh, my name's not Julia Child. It's Aster," the girl said, wiping off apricot jam that had dripped onto her jeans with her thumb. "Aster Douglas, but just call me Aster."

Lane couldn't help laughing at how serious she seemed.

"Thanks for the treat, Aster," Cat said, taking a ladyfingers sandwich.

Lane motioned to Ofelia to introduce herself.

"I'm Ofelia," the girl said. "My mom works for Mrs. DiSanti. Your grandmother."

"Yeah, I know the lady," Lane said.

"So, what is it that makes this troop secret?" Aster asked. She held up the invitation. "Are we not allowed to tell anyone about it? If not, why?"

"Very good questions," Ofelia said.

"Well," Lane said with a frown, wondering if Aster had ever read books about secret clubs and societies. "We keep our business to ourselves. We do our own thing. No adults. We'll have our own handbook, make our own rules." She held up a blank journal with a black cover.

"Like the Floras," Cat said. She looked at her phone again.

"Kind of," Lane agreed. "But different too."

"We aren't going to slice our palms open and seal our sisterhood with bloody handshakes, are we?" Ofelia asked.

"No," Lane said. "But that's not a terrible idea."

She gave Ofelia what her father called her flatline smile.

"Have you ever heard of blood-borne pathogens?" Aster asked, with a raised eyebrow.

"I was kidding," Lane said, studying the girl. "Ha-ha?"

"I think we should definitely make treats a part of our meetings," Cat said, holding up her ladyfingers sandwich. "These are really good."

"Thank you," Aster said.

"The Floras have a sign-in book," Cat told the group. "You sign it when you join and then again when you leave the Floras for good."

"How do you know that?" Lane asked.

"I just do," Cat said, shrugging. "Doesn't everyone know that?"

Lane observed the bird girl with curiosity.

"I like that," Ofelia said, writing in her notebook.

Lane opened the blank book and uncapped a black marker. At the top of the first page, she wrote MEMBERSHIP. Below the heading, she drew four lines.

"What's an ostentation?" Ofelia asked Lane.

"It's a group of peacocks," Lane said. "I mean . . . " She looked at Cat for help.

"Peafowl," Cat said. "That's a good name. They symbolize power and wisdom and beauty."

"Are *we* supposed to be the others and outsiders?" Aster asked.

The four girls looked at one another. No one said anything.

Lane stood, picking up a little stack of notepaper and pencils from a cubby. She was starting to fear she hadn't planned enough for them to do. Even the strange girl had thought to bring something to eat.

"Let's each write one question on our paper," Lane said. "We answer our own question first and then the others have to answer it too."

"What kind of question?" Ofelia asked. "Does it have to be personal?"

"With all due respect," Aster said, looking at each girl, "I just met you, and I am not telling you my personal business."

"No," Lane said, ignoring Aster. "It can be a question about anything. Just so we know something about each other, okay?"

She passed out the notepaper and pencils and waited for the other girls to start writing before letting out her breath and turning to her own paper. The girls sat in silence for a few minutes until all had written a question.

"Who wants to go first?" Lane asked.

"Me," Cat said eagerly. "My question is, what is your favorite bird? My favorite is the snowy egret. Do you know it? It's so beautiful." Lane saw the moony look in the girl's eyes. She wasn't kidding when she said she *really* loved birds.

"I have to go with the peacocks," Lane said. "I mean *peafowl*. Mostly because my grandmother hates them. But also, because I think Eunice is great. She's smart, and she keeps me company. Even though she didn't want to hang out with us today."

"Why does your grandmother hate them?" Cat asked.

"Because they're loud and they crap all over the place," Lane said gleefully. "Did you know that their poop can damage the paint job on cars?"

"They sound like Chucho," Ofelia said. "Can my favorite bird be a specific bird?"

"Sure," Cat said.

"Okay then, Chucho is my favorite bird," Ofelia said.

"What's a Chucho?" Aster asked, a puzzled look on her face.

"The rooster that lives on my street," Ofelia explained. "He also poops on cars. No wonder my neighbor hates him."

"You have a *rooster* living on your street?" Lane asked.

"What?" Ofelia said. "You have peacocks living on yours."

"True," Lane acknowledged.

"What about you, Aster?" Cat asked. "What's your favorite bird?"

"Poulet rôti," Aster said.

"And that means . . . ?" Lane asked.

"Roast chicken," Aster responded, as if it were the most obvious thing. "It's the best with rainbow carrots."

"I don't think that's what she meant when she asked for your favorite bird," Ofelia said.

"Yeah," Lane agreed. "Way to be gross."

"I'm sorry," Aster said, glancing at Cat.

"It's okay," Cat said. "I'm not offended. Even though I don't eat birds myself."

"I'm not sure I have a favorite bird," Aster said, thinking. "Well, truthfully, I've never really thought about birds. Except when I cook them."

"You did it again," Lane said incredulously.

"Can we just move on?" Cat asked. "Next question?"

"What is your favorite school subject?" Ofelia asked. "Mine is journalism class. I want to be a journalist when I grow up. Assuming my parents ever allow me to grow up."

Cat laughed as if she knew exactly what Ofelia meant.

"Science," Cat answered. "I like learning anything about animals. Especially birds, of course."

"Of course," Lane said. "I guess if I had to pick a favorite subject it would be art. I like to draw and paint and make things. What about you, Julia Child?"

"I don't know if this is an actual school subject because I'm homeschooled," Aster said. "But I like cooking."

"You don't go to school?" Ofelia asked, wide-eyed.

"I do," Aster said. "I just don't go to the same building every day."

"Isn't that against the law or something?" Lane asked. This girl was the strangest bird she'd ever met, with her ladyfingers and no school.

"Of course not," Aster said. "I have school. At home, in the public library, in nature preserves, in museums."

"The world is your school," Cat said, opening her arms wide.

"Exactly," Aster said, looking approvingly at Cat.

"I wish *I* didn't have to go to school," Lane said. "Sorry, Mom, Dad. I'm just going to go teach myself stuff out in the world."

"That sounds great," Ofelia said.

"It's been good. My grandpa is my teacher," Aster said. "But I'm going to a public school this year. It'll probably be really different, right?"

"You don't know the half of it," Lane said, shaking her head. "It's your turn to ask a question."

"What is your favorite meal of the day?" Aster asked. "I am partial to dessert. If you think about it, dessert is kind of like all the subjects rolled into one. It's part science and art. And it's part history and math and geography and storytelling too."

"Did you just make something as delicious as dessert sound like school?" Lane asked, making a face.

"I think she made something like school sound as delicious as dessert," Ofelia corrected.

"Two left." Aster picked up the lid and held out the container. "Anyone want them?"

"You aren't leaving, are you?" Lane asked. The girl was a little odd, but she didn't want the meeting to end already. "We have one more question."

Cat and Ofelia grabbed the last two ladyfingers.

"Ask away," Aster said, waving the lid before snapping it on.

"What's your favorite color? Mine is—"

"Wait, don't tell us," Aster said, closing her eyes as if trying to conjure the answer. "It's black."

Lane looked down at her black T-shirt, black shorts, and

black high-top sneakers. Her grandmother had asked if she owned anything that wasn't black and offered to take her shopping. She quickly declined.

"Wrong," Lane said. "It's green. Fern green to be exact." It was her second favorite, but Aster didn't need to know that.

"Good," Aster said. "Because black isn't a color. It's the absence of color."

"I knew that," Lane said.

"I like the color orange," Aster said. "Like the fruit." Lane felt like the girl was directing some hidden message the way she looked at her.

"Ofelia?" Lane asked, trying to take the attention off herself.

"Red," Ofelia said. "Just plain old crayon-box red."

Lane could see Ofelia writing something in her little notebook. Was she taking notes on the meeting? Was she going to share them with her mom? Or, more important, would they get to her grandmother? She didn't want her grandmother anywhere near her business.

"I like purple," Cat said. As soon as the words left her lips, she checked her phone once more and jumped up. "I have to go."

Lane stood, too, and looked at the group.

"Wait. Let's meet again, okay?" she said. "Same time. Next week? How about at the Frosty Dream?"

"I'll try to make it," Cat said, before hurrying off.

Aster picked up her container and, without saying a word, made her way down the ladder.

"Goodbye," Lane called, peering down from the entrance. "It was nice meeting you!"

There was no response from Aster.

"I guess I should go check in with my mom before she thinks I've been kidnapped," Ofelia said, closing her notebook.

"You can come back and hang out here if you want." Lane tried not to seem too eager. "Whenever."

"Thanks," Ofelia said, looking around. "I like the tree house."

"Yeah. I'm surprised it's still here," Lane said. "My grandmother hates to see children have fun."

"Sounds like she and my mom have a lot in common," Ofelia said, with a smirk.

Lane watched the last girl climb down over the side of the entrance. She dropped into the hammock. As she swung from side to side, she wondered if any of them would show up at the Frosty Dream. The blank journal she had brought to the meeting, imagining it could be their very own handbook just like the Floras', lay on the floor. Lane slipped out of the hammock and picked it up. She opened to the membership page and saw that no one had signed their names.

CHAPTER II

When Aster hopped down from the ladder, she meant to head back out the way she came in, grab her bike, and never return. Cat and Ofelia seemed nice, but just thinking about Lane made her squirm. The girl was what her grandpa called a sour lemon. But her feet seemed to have a mind of their own, because instead of leaving, she found herself venturing deeper into the DiSanti property.

The verdure of the space was dizzying. It felt like entering into a vortex of green. There were palms that looked like Hawaiian dancers in hula skirts and a beautiful live oak that reminded her of her grandpa. Even though it was old, it looked big and strong, its long, dark branches extending like an open embrace. It seemed unfair to Aster that one person could own all of this.

Aster walked down a path where grapevines twisted and draped from stone archways. She wondered where else there might be hidden security cameras. Something dripped from the archway she was about to step through. She stopped and looked up in time to see a peacock, definitely not a peahen, sitting above like a feathered spy.

Water flowed from a stone urn held up by a statue of a naked man that looked like Michelangelo's *David*. Aster looked away quickly.

In the middle of it all sat the massive house like a fortress. If not for the fact that she had just met Lane, and that Ofelia had said her mother worked for Mrs. DiSanti, Aster would not have imagined that anyone actually lived in the house.

When Aster thought of the DiSantis, she thought of two things: first was the famous Winter Sun pie. Winter Sun pie was to Sabal Palms, what key lime pie was to Key West.

Of course, folks from Sabal Palms thought their signature dessert was the better of the two, and Aster had to agree. To her it was the perfect combination of a lemon meringue pie and a key lime pie, but with its own special flavor. It had a graham cracker crust like a key lime pie and a snowdrift of meringue on top like a lemon meringue pie. Sandwiched in the middle was what made it a whole other thing: a layer of smooth Winter Sun orange filling.

Just as key lime pies were traditionally only made with key limes, the Winter Sun had been made with only Winter Sun oranges until the big hurricane struck in 1915 and destroyed the existing trees. Ever since, people made the pie with a combination of navel oranges and vanilla to give it the orange Creamsicle flavor the Winter Sun oranges were known for.

Aster's mouth watered thinking about Winter Sun pie. And then she remembered the second thing she thought of when she thought of the DiSantis: her grandpa.

With the research her grandfather was doing for his book, he was hoping to find some kind of evidence that the Winter Sun orange originated in the area with the Douglas family and not the DiSantis. Aster sometimes wondered why her grandfather was so determined to prove something that didn't seem to really matter anymore. Still, she knew it meant a lot to him, and she wanted to help him somehow.

Aster had almost walked the perimeter of the property when she stopped and dug through her backpack for a blank recipe card. She wanted to write down what she saw—the statues and trees and plants—before she forgot. Maybe some of it would be useful to her grandfather.

As she made her way back to the entrance around the

east side of the property, she noticed a shorter path that veered to the southernmost end of the yard. Aster wondered what was there, but the sound of a lawn mower starting up somewhere nearby made her hurry back to her bike near the entrance.

She looked at the iron gate and realized there was no way to get out without someone opening it from wherever the magic button lived. Aster remembered riding past a side entrance and carried her bike, careful not to trample any plants or roll over grass, in that direction. When she found the door, she turned the knob and was relieved to find that it opened without a problem.

Aster took one last look at all the green that stretched behind her. She wondered what her grandpa would say if she told him where she'd been. She rolled her bike out of the property and listened to the door click shut. Aster tried the handle, but she was locked out. She hopped on her bike and pedaled home.

CHAPTER 12

"Lucy, I'm home!" Ofelia's father hollered in his best Ricky Ricardo impersonation. "Who's hungry?"

Mr. Castillo came into the kitchen in a cloud of delicious smells. He kissed Ofelia on top of her head and placed on the table a bag of takeout from La Reina de las Fritas.

Her parents said takeout was "para los ricos." But once a month her dad would come home with Chinese food or burgers. Never Cuban because why get takeout if they were just going to eat the same things they could have cooked themselves for less? La Reina was the exception. It was, technically, Cuban food, but they always got the fritas.

"Me muero de hambre," Mrs. Castillo said, tearing into the bag. "This has been the longest week of my life. I barely even have time to eat at work."

"Drown your tiredness in a shake, vieja," Mr. Castillo said, handing her a cardboard cup holder.

"I went up to the tree house today," Ofelia announced, unwrapping her burger. A mountain of shoestring fries spilled out onto her plate.

"The tree house?" Mrs. Castillo said. "People have been known to fall from those things and break their necks."

"Seriously, Ma?" she asked, giving her mother a questioning look.

"Why would I lie about that?" Mrs. Castillo said. "¿Trigo o mango?" She held up two cups for Ofelia to pick a shake.

"Mango," Ofelia said, wondering why anyone would ever choose puffed wheat.

"I don't know about people falling out of trees," her father said, "but aren't you a little old to be climbing a tree like a monkey?"

Ofelia frowned and shook her head.

"What were you doing up there?" Mrs. Castillo asked. "I told you not to go getting into places you don't belong."

"Lane invited me," Ofelia said, chewing.

"¿La nieta?" her father asked.

"Yes," Ofelia said. "What do you know about her, Ma?"

"Me? Nada," Mrs. Castillo said. "I go to work and stay out of their business."

"What business?" Ofelia asked. She wondered if it would

be rude to open her reporter's notebook at the table and jot down notes.

"She's always very polite," Mrs. Castillo said. "I see her floating around the house like a little dark rain cloud when she isn't outside. The other day she came to my office and told me Mrs. DiSanti needed to see me. I walked all the way up to her library, and the woman wasn't even in there. So strange. Como la abuela."

"Eccentric, vieja," Mr. Castillo said and chuckled. "Rich people aren't strange, they're *eccentric*."

"She seems okay," Ofelia said. "Pa, she's always dressed in black. Like, *all* the time, right, Ma?"

"Sí, she looks like a widow," Mrs. Castillo said. "And she's going to sweat away into a puddle. Maybe all that black works in London, but not here."

"She's from *London*?" Ofelia asked. "That's amazing. She's an artist too. That explains a lot."

"Artists dress in black?" Mr. Castillo said.

Ofelia watched her dad bite into his frita and shuddered. He always got it with a fried egg and the yolk dripped onto his plate. It was so gross.

"Of course, Pa," Ofelia said. "It's edgy."

"¿Y qué tú sabes de edgy?" Mrs. Castillo said, winking.

"Absolutely nothing." Ofelia let out a sigh. If it were up to her parents she would remain as edgy as a kickball.

"Did you have a good time with her?" Mr. Castillo asked.

"I guess," Ofelia said. "Lane is starting a club. With two other girls." She didn't tell them it was supposed to be a secret troop or their nosy radar would have exploded.

"What is this club?" Mrs. Castillo asked. "Like una pandilla?"

"Yes, Ma, a gang," Ofelia said, rolling her eyes.

"Just remember that Lane can afford to buy her way out of trouble, but not you."

"So we shouldn't knock over banks?" Ofelia said.

"That's not funny." Mrs. Castillo shot her a glare. "That girl is a little fragile anyway. Be careful."

"Fragile?" Ofelia asked. "How? What's wrong? Did something happen? Is she sick? Did someone die? Is that why she dresses in black?"

The girl she had met earlier wasn't someone Ofelia would have described as fragile. Sure, she was so skinny she looked like she could use a couple of fritas from La Reina, but she wasn't like the fine china sitting in the antique vitrine in Mrs. DiSanti's dining room. She looked tough. Or maybe, Ofelia thought, it was something else pretending to be toughness.

"Her parents are getting divorced. Ay, it's a mess. The mother in New York, the father and brothers in London. Can you imagine?" Mrs. Castillo shook her head.

"Divorced?" Ofelia repeated.

"That's too bad," Mr. Castillo said.

"Mrs. DiSanti mentioned that her father may be moving back to Miami next year. That might be good for Lane, to be near her abuela," Ofelia's mother continued. "Okay, ya, I have said enough about things that don't concern us. Don't try to distract me with twenty questions, niña. I want you to be careful in that tree. And with that girl. *And* with those birds too. They carry disease."

"Not Eunice," Ofelia whispered, feeling bad for Lane.

"Who's Eunice?" Mr. Castillo asked.

"No one." Ofelia took a sip of her shake.

She tuned out her parents' conversation about work and weather and corrupt politicians and thought about Lane. She tried to imagine her own parents getting divorced. It felt scary. Scarier than the thought of falling out of a tree. And were there really so many people falling out of tree houses and breaking their necks? That sounded like one of the lies her parents told her to prevent her from doing anything.

In their defense, Sabal Palms was literally crawling with danger. Just last week, an eight-foot alligator had been seen lumbering down a residential street. And there was water everywhere—the ocean, lagoons, bays, retention ponds, a river. For a girl who could just barely swim, it was one big death trap. She felt a momentary relief that she had parents that kept her from wandering the streets where alligators also roamed freely.

However, as a reporter it was her job to sniff out the truth. And this story about people falling out of trees to their untimely deaths? It smelled like mom bologna.

When her dad began to clear the table, Ofelia opened her notebook and looked over her notes from the meeting.

Lane: too eager but also aloof, pretending; needs something

Aster: awkward; like an adult trying to figure out how to be a kid?

Cat: antsy; seems troubled; hiding something

Eunice: peahen (not a peacock); observer; good keeper of secrets

Under the flame she'd drawn, she wrote a new headline:

Orange Juice Heiress Creates Secret
Scouts: An Undercover Exposé
By Ofelia Castillo

CHAPTER 13

When Aster wanted her grandpa to drop everything, she knew there was one thing that always got his attention: her chips-and-chips cookies. The recipe she used wasn't anything special. In fact, it came from the back of the chocolate chips bag. But what her grandpa really loved was how she sprinkled potato chip crumbs on top of the cookies before putting them into the oven. Hence, chips and chips. The potato chips gave them a salty crunchiness to balance the sweet gooeyness of the semisweet chocolate chips.

Today, she had two things she needed to talk to him about. And as expected, when the cookies hit the seven-minute mark and started to smell, she heard the *slap-slap-slap* of his rubber flip-flops making their way toward the kitchen.

"Did you call me?" her grandpa asked, poking his head in the doorway.

"Nope," Aster said. "But since you're here, would you like one of my cookies?"

"There's no 'my' in this house, young lady," Grandpa said, grinning expectantly and taking a seat at the table. "How long?"

"When are we going back-to-school shopping, Grandpa?" Aster asked, holding up the timer to show four minutes.

"Back-to-school shopping?" her grandfather said. "For what?"

"I *need* school supplies," Aster said.

"Says who?" Grandpa scratched his head and looked at the oven door pointedly. Aster could tell he was starting to suspect he'd been lured into the kitchen under false pretenses.

"Says the school." Aster pointed to the Hurston Middle School supply list on the refrigerator. "Says everyone." She shook the store ad insert that had come in that day's newspaper. It was only the end of June, and already the stores were rushing into the next school year. "I need pencils, paper, one-subject wide-ruled notebooks. *Seven* of them."

"Don't we have paper and pencils all over the place?" her grandpa asked. "Things don't have to be new, you know? That's just our consumer culture brainwashing you

94

into thinking you have to buy brand-new things because it's a new school year. What? That pencil you used yesterday is suddenly no longer good? Hmph. Not getting my money." Her grandfather clasped his hands on the table and waited. "Did you put the potato chips on top?"

Aster was beginning to regret baking cookies. She imagined herself showing up to school still wearing her dad's old shirts and carrying a manual typewriter. Instead of a cell phone, she'd bring in the yellow landline from her room.

"Yes, I did," Aster said.

Her grandfather got up and opened the refrigerator.

"Milk?" he asked, holding up the carton.

"Please," Aster said, turning to the cabinet where the glasses were kept.

"Now, don't let them burn," her grandpa warned.

Aster placed two glasses on the table, then opened the oven door to inspect the first batch just as the timer rang.

Besides the topic of school supplies, she'd originally called this unofficial cookie meeting to tell her grandfather about going to the DiSanti house. But now she had a feeling that telling him right away wasn't the thing to do. She wasn't sure if she'd go to the next meeting, and she wasn't sure how being there would help her grandfather with his research.

She decided that she needed more information before she could figure out her plan.

Her grandfather rubbed his hands in anticipation as she placed the cookie sheet and spatula on the table.

"They have to cool," she warned. "Or they'll fall apart. Not to mention burn your mouth."

"Nah," Grandpa said, as he scraped a still-hot cookie off the sheet onto his plate.

"Hey, Grandpa," Aster said, sitting down. "Tell me about the oranges again."

"You mean the Czars of Citrus?" her grandfather asked. "The Monarchs of Mandarins?" He peered at her over his glasses and wiggled his eyebrows.

"Yeah, *those* oranges," she said and laughed.

"Well," her grandpa said, "the story people tell is that Anthony DiSanti was visiting family in Italy in 1902 when he came across a tree that bore an odd-looking fruit."

"Odd how?" Aster asked. She'd heard the story many times, but wanted to make sure there weren't any details she wasn't already aware of.

"It was the size and shape of an orange, but it looked like a snowball," her grandfather said. "Its skin was cream colored and inside was the brightest orange flesh—the sun inside a wintry white outside."

"That sounds good," Aster said.

She shook her head as she watched her grandfather blow out to keep the bite of cookie in his mouth from burning.

"Sure does. Especially if what you're used to eating is pretty limited," her grandfather went on. "Back in those days, people just ate whatever grew naturally in the area. Bananas, lemons, alligator pears, none of that grew here."

"Alligator pears?" Aster asked, making a face. "*That* sounds terrible."

"You like avocados, don't you?" her grandpa asked.

"You know I do," Aster said.

"Botanists like David Fairchild—"

"The guy who brought avocados, I mean alligator pears, from Chile," Aster said.

"That's right," her grandfather said. Aster could tell he was pleased that she remembered. "Botanists like David Fairchild traveled the world and brought back plants to see what could grow here. Supposedly, DiSanti gathered a few of the white oranges to see if they would survive the trip back across the Atlantic and grow in his South Florida groves."

"He was already growing oranges, right?" Aster asked.

"Oh, indeed," he said. "The DiSanti family had hotels and orange groves up in the northern part of Florida. Then Flagler had that railway built that opened up the state, built with the labor of Bahamians and other immigrants, of course. Bahamians cleared land and graded the course for the tracks. That's when the DiSantis came south and started eating up land with their orange groves. They built that big old house like they were the Medicis."

"What happened to the Winter Sun orange?" Aster asked. "That's not the whole story, right?"

"Well, that's the story you read in the books," her grandfather said. "But the *real* story, at least according to our family, is that my great-uncle Charles traveled as an assistant to a botanist. And on his last trip before he settled here with his family in 1895, he got a cutting of the Winter Sun tree, which he brought and planted." Her grandfather tapped his finger against the tabletop.

"Our people knew what to do on this land when folks from up north were still just trying to figure out how to travel straight through the state so they could vacation here in the winter," her grandfather said.

"So how did the DiSantis end up being known for the

Winter Sun orange if Charles Douglas was the one who brought it over?"

"That's the mystery," her grandfather said. "Charles planted the cutting on his land and it grew. His wife, Carol Anne, was the DiSantis' cook. Family lore says she's the one who came up with the recipe for that Winter Sun pie, you know."

"They stole that too?" Aster asked, leaning in closer.

"That's what I'm trying to find out," her grandfather said, scraping another cookie onto his plate. "When the hurricane hit in 1915 it came like the Big Bad Wolf. Huffing and puffing and blowing everything down. The trees our family owned were destroyed. But a few years later, lo and behold, the DiSantis were marketing their Winter Sun products, everything from pie to perfume."

"But how did they do that if the trees were gone?" Aster asked. "And weren't there records that showed where the original tree came from?"

"Child, what do you think I'm looking for?" Her grandfather frowned. "The hurricane didn't just destroy trees. It flooded houses too. If we had anything that could have documented the origins of the fruit here, it disappeared. If not for the fact that this house is built from some sturdy pine, it would've been knocked down and washed away too."

"Have you ever tried just asking Mrs. DiSanti?" Aster asked, breaking a cookie in half to let it cool. "Maybe she has information to share."

Her grandfather gave her a look that said *what do you think?*

"Over the years I've called and written letters," he said. "Even tried to use my position as faculty at the university to get to the woman. She's a hard lady to track down, especially after her husband died and she stopped going out in public much."

"Have you ever been to the house?" Aster asked, remembering the palms in grassy hula skirts.

"Once," he said. "The botanical society used to offer tours of the property a long time ago. They have some of the oldest varieties of several tree species in the state. But the tour was limited, and Mrs. DiSanti ended that too when her husband passed."

"Do you think Mrs. DiSanti knows anything about the trees?" Aster asked. "It's been so long. Maybe it's just one of those mysteries that will never be solved, like Amelia Earhart's disappearance."

"My behind, it's a mystery," her grandfather said. "I bet

anything that woman has the answer. She may not know she has it, but it's probably somewhere on that property."

Aster remembered the feeling she had when the DiSanti gate locked behind her. Like she'd had something precious within reach one moment, and then it was gone. She looked at her watch.

"I'm meeting some friends at two, is that okay?" she asked.

"Who are these friends you've been meeting up with?" her grandfather asked. "You know they're welcome here."

"I know," Aster said. She had never had real friends to invite over to the house. The thought of inviting these girls felt strange. "They're just some girls I met at the library."

"You sure you want to leave me alone with these cookies?" her grandfather asked, picking up the cookie sheet with a pot holder.

"I trust you," Aster said.

"Fine, but take my raincoat. It's wet out there," her grandfather said. "And don't forget your mother is calling later."

"As if I could ever forget that." Aster smiled. "Seriously, Grandpa. Don't eat all the cookies."

"No, ma'am," her grandfather responded. "I won't."

But as Aster walked to her room she could hear the scratch of the spatula against the cookie sheet.

She pulled on her grandfather's raincoat and grabbed her recipe box. The little brown glass bottle of sandalwood oil her mom had left behind sat on her dresser next to it.

When Aster tried to remember what it was like to have her mom around, her memories always came from her senses. She remembered her smell; the sandalwood oil was sweet and smoky like campfire and flowers. Sometimes it was peppermint, especially in the summer when she wanted to feel cooler. Aster remembered the way her mom's fingers felt in her hair, the scratch of the comb against her scalp as her mom pulled and twisted her hair into braids. Remembering those things, trying to imagine the smells and the feelings, made her heart ache.

Aster applied a drop of oil and rubbed her wrists together, then behind her ears like she'd watched her mom do many times. She sniffed her wrists. As she placed the recipe box in her backpack, she decided that she would get back on the DiSanti property and help her grandfather find what he was looking for.

CHAPTER 14

Lane waited on the Esther Williams stool at the Frosty Dream. It looked like all the other stools in the ice cream shop with its stainless-steel base and glittery, swimming-pool-blue vinyl seat. But unlike the others, it had a little metal plaque on it that declared ESTHER WILLIAMS SAT HERE IN 1953!

From the yellowed, laminated newspaper clippings that decorated the walls, she learned that the woman had been a competitive swimmer and a movie star who once ordered an egg cream at the Frosty Dream. The egg cream could still be found on the menu as, of course, the Esther Williams.

On that rainy afternoon, Lane ate a bowl of Neapolitan ice cream, taking even amounts of strawberry, chocolate, and vanilla and trying not to look at the clock on the wall. The last time she checked it was 2:01. Everyone was late. Or maybe no one was coming. It had been raining most of the day, and she tried to convince herself that this was the reason the girls wouldn't show. She had almost invited Ofelia to walk to the Frosty Dream with her, but she didn't want to assume that the girl wanted to be a part of the group.

Lane turned at the sound of the door opening. A mom and her young son walked in. Behind them, she noticed a figure had pulled up on a bike. Lane tried not to visibly sigh in relief when Cat entered.

"Am I the only one here?" Cat said, sliding onto the stool next to her. She grabbed a few napkins from the dispenser and wiped her arms.

"I'm here," Lane said. "Want something? My treat."

"Really?"

She could see Cat was considering the offer.

"Sure," Cat said. "I'll pay next time, okay?"

The door opened again and Ofelia walked in, shaking out her umbrella. She squinted, and Cat waved her over.

"You could have walked with me," Lane said, tugging on her crystal.

Ofelia shrugged and sat. "My mom asked me to help her with something. And then I had to beg her to let me come. *And* to give me money, which she didn't. Sometimes being a kid is just one humiliation after another."

"I have money," Lane said. "I can pay for your ice cream."

"No, that's okay," Ofelia said, wiping her glasses with a napkin. "Thanks, anyway."

The teenager working the counter placed a peanut butter shake in front of Cat. There was an awkward silence until a gust of air announced the arrival of a figure dressed in an oversize yellow raincoat. Lane watched Aster walk in looking like Big Bird. The raincoat ended below her knees and the hood draped over her face. She took off the wet coat and hung it on a rack near the door.

"Is this an official meeting?" Aster asked, all business. She looked around the Frosty Dream.

"Hello to you too," Lane said, waving her spoon.

"Hi," Aster said, grabbing a stool. "Why did we have to meet here?"

"For ice cream," Cat said, stirring her shake with a straw.

"I'm not eating," Aster said.

"If you don't have money, it's my treat," Lane said. She noticed Aster roll her eyes and shift in her seat and knew she'd said the wrong thing.

"I don't need your money," Aster said. "I can buy my own ice cream."

"I didn't say you couldn't," Lane said. "I was just offering because I bought Cat's, and Ofelia didn't have money, so—"

"No," Aster said. "Thank you."

"Did I do something wrong?" Lane asked. She looked at Cat and Ofelia who didn't make eye contact. "If someone had offered to treat me, I'd be—"

"Are you trying to buy our friendship with ice cream?" Aster asked, cutting her off.

"No!" Lane said. At least she didn't think she was doing that. "Sorry I offered."

"Good, because you can't," Aster said, propping her elbows on the counter. "So, is this a meeting?"

Lane felt weird eating when two of them weren't. She pushed her dish away.

"I thought we could just hang out," Lane said.

"To see if we like one another enough to be a troop, you mean?" Cat asked, glancing between Aster and Lane.

Ofelia pulled out her notebook and chewed-up pencil from her bag.

"What are you always writing in there?" Aster asked.

"Story ideas," Ofelia said. "I'm entering a contest. The winners get to go to journalism camp in New York City next summer."

"That sounds exciting," Cat said, plucking the stem off the maraschino cherry on her shake.

"It is," Ofelia agreed. "But I still have to persuade my parents to sign the application."

"Why wouldn't they sign it?" Lane asked.

"OCP." Ofelia tapped her pencil on the counter with each letter. "Overprotective Cuban Parents."

"I live in New York," Lane said. "Or at least I will live there at the end of the summer. You could visit me if you go."

"I thought you lived in London," Ofelia said, pointing at Lane with her pencil.

"Who told you that?" Lane asked suspiciously.

"A journalist doesn't reveal her sources."

"I *lived* there," Lane explained. "But I don't anymore."

"I bet New York is amazing," Ofelia said. "Unlike this place. Can you believe I've never even seen snow?"

"It isn't anything like what you see in the movies," Lane said. "Well, it does look like that at first. But then after a day or two it mixes with dirt and leaves and cigarette butts, and dogs pee on it and—"

"But it feels nice coming down, right?" Cat asked. "Like a cashmere sweater?"

"Or a cloud of whipped cream?" added Ofelia.

"Have you ever seen a frozen dog turd?" Lane said.

Aster let out a laugh and swiveled in her stool. The sound

of laughter made Lane feel less nervous, like she could breathe again. She got a kick out of the grossed-out look on Ofelia's face when she burst her snow-globe fantasy. But hearing Aster laugh eased the tension she'd felt hovering between them.

"Eww," Cat said, scrunching her nose.

"You should let me know if you make it," Lane said. "I mean, if we're in touch after I leave."

Ofelia opened her mouth as if she was about to say something but didn't.

"I just had an idea," Lane said. "You know a good way to get to know each other better?"

"You mean, besides just talking like we are now?" Aster asked.

"Truth or Dare," Lane answered her own question, ignoring Aster.

"I don't know if that's such a good idea," Cat said. "No matter which one you pick, someone always ends up hurt."

"Oh, come on," Lane urged. "How are we supposed to be a real troop if we can't tell one another everything? I'll even go first."

"Exposing yourself to physical or emotional harm,"

Aster said. "Sounds like a lot of fun *and* a great way to build friendships."

"I'll even take a dare," Lane said, squinting at Aster, challenging her.

"Really?" Ofelia asked. "Who would do a dare?"

"Someone with secrets to hide," Aster said, squinting back at Lane.

"Come on," Lane said. "Dare me to do something."

"Fine," Aster said. "I dare you to—"

"Nothing dangerous, though," Cat said nervously. "Right?"

Lane watched Aster as the girl looked around the ice cream shop, thinking. She knew Aster would come up with something good.

"I dare you to spin really fast," Aster finally said, pointing to Lane's stool. "One minute. I'll time you on my watch."

"That is so easy," Lane said, sliding off her seat. She lay over the stool on her stomach. "Tell me when."

"Go," Aster said, looking at her watch, then at Lane.

Lane began to push, running her feet in circles.

"Hey, you can't do that," the teenage girl working the counter called out. She shook her ice cream scooper in Lane's direction.

"Someone please stop her before she falls off," Cat said.

"Thirty-four seconds," Aster called out.

Once Lane had enough speed that she could spin without pushing herself, she hung on to the edge of the stool, knees bent under her so that her feet wouldn't hit anything.

"I swear, if there's blood—" Ofelia said.

"Forty-nine," Aster counted.

Lane learned somewhere that the way to avoid dizziness was to focus on one spot so she tried finding the same tile on the floor as she revolved.

"Fifty-four, fifty-five, fifty-six." She heard Aster count somewhere in the distance.

But before she could get to fifty-seven, Lane's left foot hit the stool next to her, stopping her suddenly and sending her flying to the floor where she landed in a tangle of limbs.

Lane could hear voices calling her name. Aster, Ofelia, Cat, the Frosty Dream employee who had run out from behind the counter, and the mother with her young son stood over her.

"Are you okay?" the mother said, holding back her kid.

"Is she dead?" Aster asked, as Cat leaned in. The girls crowded closer.

"You wish," Lane groaned.

"Do I have to call an ambulance?" the teenage worker asked.

Lane tried to stand up. Ofelia grabbed her arms and helped her just in time for Lane to run to the bathroom.

When she returned to the counter a few minutes later, Lane had water all over her shirt.

"Why'd you let me do that?" she whined.

"Are you serious?" Aster said.

"Did you throw up?" Cat asked.

"Strawberry, vanilla, and chocolate," Lane said and held her stomach.

"You could've hit your head and gotten a concussion or something," Ofelia said.

"I'm fine," Lane assured them. "Now, whose turn is it?"

"No one's," Cat said, looking at her phone. "I have to go."

"But I'm the only person who took a turn," Lane whined. "No fair."

"Next time?" Cat asked, backing away from the counter.

"You're like Cinderella," Ofelia said. "Is your bike going to turn into a pumpkin?"

"Possibly," Cat said, pushing open the door. "But I don't want to find out."

"Which way are you headed?" Ofelia asked. "I'll walk with you."

"Me too," Aster said. The three girls stood, leaving Lane at the counter.

As each girl walked out of the ice cream shop, Lane had a feeling that she needed to move fast or she would lose them.

"Hey, wait! I'll go too," she called. "But can someone help me? I'm still a little dizzy."

CHAPTER 15

When Cat saw her mother's car in front of the Floras House, she stopped cold.

"Oh, bird droppings," she muttered, letting her bike fall onto the grass outside the library. She quickly ducked behind the book return.

"Are you okay?" Ofelia asked.

"No," Cat whispered, an urgency in her voice. "That's my mom across the street. In front of the Floras House. Is she still in the car?"

"Which car?" Aster said, looking.

"The black one," Cat said.

"I haven't seen anyone come out of any car," Aster offered. "It looks like the lights are still on."

"Wait," Ofelia said a little too loudly. "You're a *Flora*?"

"Shhh!" Cat hissed.

"Skipping a Floras meeting?" Lane said excitedly. "I knew you had a bad streak in you, bird girl."

"I do not," Cat insisted, despite the fact that she was hiding from her mother behind a book return. "But when my mom finds out I haven't been going to meetings, I will probably be stuck in my room for the rest of my life. I'll never see or hear a bird again."

"I think you're being a little dramatic," Lane said. "I'm sure your mom will let you crack open a window so you can listen to your bird friends."

"This is not funny," Cat said glumly. "You should just leave. I need to figure out what I'm going to do."

She let herself drop to the wet ground in defeat and wrapped her arms around her knees, putting her forehead against them. She could feel tears pushing behind her eyes.

"The car lights just went off," Ofelia reported.

"What can we do?" Lane asked, kneeling beside Cat.

"I don't know," Cat said. She felt her shake churning in her stomach. "What are the chances I can run across the street and go around the back of the house without my mom seeing me?"

"I'm not a statistician," Aster said slowly. "But I'm going to guess zero."

"You might be able to do *something* if you come out from behind that thing and move fast," Lane said. "Oh, wait. Never mind, your mom just got out of the car."

"Nooo," Cat moaned quietly.

She slowly began to stand, resolved to just walk up to her mother and confess everything.

"Why exactly are you hiding?" Ofelia asked, digging through her bag.

"If you pull out that notebook and start taking notes, I don't know what I'm going to do," Lane threatened, glaring at Ofelia.

"*What?*" Ofelia asked.

"This is no time for writing," Lane said. "*That's* what."

Ofelia sighed and stuck her pencil into her ponytail.

"Duck," Aster warned. She pulled Cat back down. "I think she was looking this way."

"Well, I want the truth before I decide if I'm going to be aiding and abetting whatever this is," Ofelia said, motioning toward Cat. "Plus, this is definitely story material, so I'm sorry, but I have to take notes."

"She isn't a criminal," Aster said. Then she looked at Cat on the other side of the book return. "Right?"

"No, I'm not," Cat insisted. "What's she doing now?"

"She walked up to the porch, but she's on her phone," Aster said.

"Why don't you just go tell her whatever you need to tell her," Ofelia advised. "My parents say honesty is the best policy."

"You don't know my mom," Cat said. "Really, you can go. You don't need to get involved."

Cat pulled her Floras bandanna from her bag and waved it like a lavender flag of surrender.

"Give that to me," Lane said, holding out her hand.

"Why?" Cat asked. But she gave the bandanna to Lane.

Lane tied it around her neck and walked toward the curb.

"Where are you going?" Ofelia asked.

"Wait inside the library," Lane said, skipping across the street.

"I don't know about that girl," Aster said, shaking her head. "But come on, then. Let's go inside."

"I'll watch your bike," Ofelia offered.

Cat took one last look over her shoulder at where Lane was already talking to her mother before following Aster into the library.

"You want to know where the best hiding place is?" Aster asked.

"The bathroom?" Cat guessed. "That's where I found Lane's invitation."

"Me too," Aster said. "In a yellow book-club bag. But no, it's not the restroom."

"Where then?" Cat asked.

"There." Aster pointed to an area where several large machines sat on tables.

"What are these?" Cat said.

"They're microfilm readers," Aster said. "No one ever comes back here. Except my grandpa."

"I don't think I've ever been this far back in the library," Cat said, sitting down at a microfilm station. "What do they do?"

"They're projectors," Aster explained. "You wind in these little film reels that have entire issues of old newspapers and magazines on them, and the images are projected so you can read them." She ran a hand across the white screen.

"Could I find articles from the early 1900s?" Cat said, relieved to talk about something that wasn't her mom and the Floras.

"Definitely," Aster said, nodding. "I can show you some time."

"I'd like that," Cat said. She glanced toward the entrance. "What do you think I should do now?"

"Just wait, I guess," Aster said. "I'll go see what's happening outside."

Cat sat at a microfilm station for what felt like hours. She knew she didn't have to live a life of hiding. It had been three weeks since she had run out of the Floras House, and she was exhausted. Why didn't she just tell her mom she didn't want to be a Flora anymore? What was the worst that could happen?

She remembered what Lane had said. *Did* she have a bad streak? She'd been skipping Floras meetings and lying to her mother. She'd given away money that wasn't hers to give. Maybe Lane was right. She was supposed to be the Last Great Garcia Hope. The Last Great Garcia Hope was a Miss Floras, not a scared, rule-breaking kid hiding in the library.

Cat peered out from the side of the microfilm machine when the automatic doors swooshed open. She saw the three girls walking toward her and quickly stood up like the defendant at a trial.

"What happened?" she asked, looking behind them and expecting to see her mom.

"Well," Lane said, removing the Floras bandanna and handing it back to her. "The good news is, your mom seems nice."

"How is that good news?" Cat said through gritted teeth.

"It's good news because I don't think the punishment will be as bad as you imagine it will be," Lane explained.

"Just tell me," Cat said, closing her eyes.

"The bad news is, your mom is waiting for you," Ofelia said, giving her a solemn look.

Cat felt her insides crumple. Her mom was small, but she had a big mouth and she wasn't afraid to use it. It was probably why she made such a good attorney.

"Thanks for trying," Cat said, with a sigh. "I'd better go."

As she walked toward the door, Lane let out a cackle and soon Ofelia joined her in laughter. Aster shook her head but smiled.

"We're kidding," Lane said, shoving Cat in the arm.

"*What?*" Cat looked from face to face. "What do you mean you're kidding?"

"I told her the meeting had let out early and you had run across to the library to grab a book," Lane said. "She said she just needed to make sure you had turned in the brownie money like she kept reminding you to do. I told her I saw you do it and that I'd come get you."

Lane looked proud of herself.

"Oh, double bird droppings," Cat said. She could feel the blood rush out of her face.

"What's wrong now?" Aster asked. "You're in the clear, right?"

"I can't turn in the money because I don't have it anymore," Cat said.

"You lost it?" Aster asked.

Cat shook her head.

"You spent it?" Lane guessed.

Cat shook her head again.

"You stole it!" Ofelia declared with certainty. "I told you we were aiding and abetting."

"No," Cat said defensively. "I put it in the donation box at the nature preserve."

"I think that's still stealing," Lane said.

"But like Robin Hood," Aster added. "Taking from the rich to give to the needy."

Cat gave Aster a half smile. She appreciated her attempt to make her bad situation better.

"This just keeps getting worse," Ofelia said, writing in her notebook.

"Anyway, after I *lied* to your mom for you, Aster started talking her ear off about seeing her in the newspaper," Lane said. "You should've seen it. They were like a couple of law nerds. But it was a great distraction."

"It was an important case," Aster insisted. "It could affect the way people use social media as a business tool."

"Where is she now?" Cat asked.

"Outside," Lane said. "She needs you to come out because she has to get back to work."

"Why'd you stop going to the meetings?" Ofelia asked.

"It's a long story," Cat said. "Thanks for helping me. I guess I owe you."

She hurried for the door but turned back to the girls. Cat put her hands together, intertwined her thumbs, and fluttered her fingers, making her favorite shadow puppet, a bird flapping its wings, before heading out.

CHAPTER 16

"I'm glad to see you reading that," Mrs. DiSanti said.

She walked into the bedroom where Lane lay on the floor looking through the Floras handbook. Lane didn't want to be interrupted. She was busy trying to figure out how you made a group *a group*. Connected. What was the magic? The Floras had been around for a hundred years so they had to know something.

"I haven't changed my mind," Lane said, turning a page.

"Who were those girls on the property?" her grandmother asked, sitting down at the antique rolltop desk.

"What girls?" Lane said, looking up. "Ofelia?"

"And the other two," Mrs. DiSanti said. "Mira said you buzzed them in."

"They're friends," Lane said. "I can have friends visit, right?"

"Of course, you can," Mrs. DiSanti said. "I didn't know

you had friends here. Where did you meet them?"

"I put an ad in the paper." Lane gave her grandmother her flatline smile.

"I don't want strangers wandering around the property," Mrs. DiSanti said, ignoring Lane's joke.

"They weren't *wandering*," Lane said. "They were in the tree house with me."

"Mira saw one of the girls around the back."

Lane didn't see the girls leave after the meeting but assumed they had just let themselves out. Why would anyone want to stay and walk around the property anyway? It was just a bunch of trees and ugly statues. And why did her grandmother care?

"Maybe she got lost on her way out," Lane said, closing the book on her finger to hold her page.

"If you're going to have friends visit," Mrs. DiSanti said, "I would like to know. And they are not allowed to roam around unaccompanied. This isn't a public park."

"I'm sorry, Grandmother," Lane said. "I'll be sure to tell them. If they ever come back."

"I spoke with your father," Mrs. DiSanti said. "He says you haven't answered his calls."

Lane ran her fingers through the rug and thought about

her father. The last time she had seen her parents was at the airport in London a few weeks earlier. Her mom had some final things she needed to do before leaving for New York so her parents had gone together to see her off. They stood next to each other as she boarded, but they might as well have been strangers with the space between them. Her mother had one hand in her pocket, one waving, and her father stood with his arms crossed. Lane cried on the plane, quietly and with her face turned to the plastic windowpane so no one would know.

"I sent him a text," Lane said, opening the book to the Floras oath.

"You should call him," her grandmother continued.

"If he wanted to speak with me, he wouldn't have sent me away," Lane said, not looking up from her book.

When Lane thought about her family, she got a feeling she couldn't name. It wasn't just anger or just sadness or just loss. It was all of those things and something else that Lane felt simmering inside her, threatening to boil to a scream like a teakettle. Sometimes screaming seemed like the only way to let go of that feeling she couldn't name. But she didn't want to scream in front of her grandmother. She knew it wasn't her grandmother's fault that her parents were divorcing or that her mother had moved them to New York or that her father had sent her to Sabal Palms for the summer instead of letting her spend it in London. Making art helped, so did breathing like her mom taught her. She took a deep breath in through the nose and all the way down to her belly, then back up and out through the nose.

"Your *parents* sent you here for the summer because they thought it would be good for you," Mrs. DiSanti said, tilting her head as if pleading for understanding.

"How would being away from my family be good for me?" Lane asked. She sat up and pulled on her sneakers over her bare feet.

"I'm your family too," her grandmother said. "Even if you aren't happy here, your parents need to straighten things out. I know that's not easy for a child to understand because you feel like the world revolves around you."

Lane knew there was some truth in what her grandmother said. She didn't understand. She dog-eared the page and stood up.

"Call your father, Purslane," her grandmother said. "He's worried about you."

"I don't have anything to say to him right now," Lane said quietly. She held her crystal tightly. She didn't have anything to say to either of her parents.

She walked past her grandmother, but the woman stopped her with a hand to her shoulder. Lane's muscles tensed as if her body were preparing for a fight.

"I'm glad you're with me this summer," her grandmother said, her eyes searching Lane's face.

Lane felt her body soften, but she couldn't bring herself to say anything other than, "I'm going to the tree house."

She hurried down the stairs before her grandmother could stop her again. Once outside, she climbed up to the tree house, feeling fortunate she had a place where her grandmother wouldn't follow. If her dad were here, he'd probably climb the ladder easily, trying to force her to talk when she didn't want to.

Lane settled into the hammock and opened the Floras handbook to the oath. An oath was a promise. Maybe if her family had spit into their palms and made an oath, they would have stayed together. Maybe an oath was what made individuals a real group. Maybe an oath was what the girls needed.

CHAPTER 17

Aster tugged on the rope attached to the wind chimes and made her way up the ladder. There had been so much excitement after helping Cat hide from her mom that the girls had parted without any plans to meet again. But she wasn't terribly surprised when Ms. Falco delivered the invitation from Lane to meet at the tree house.

"You came," Lane said, when Aster appeared in the entrance.

"Of course, I came," she said. "I brought cream puffs."

"You don't have to bring food every time," Lane said, looking at the container Aster carried. "Mira made her peanut butter cookies, and they're *the* best."

"It's rude to show up at a gathering without food," Aster said, looking around the tree house. There were small containers of paint on the floor and a few paintbrushes in a jar of water. The afghan hung on the wall like a tapestry.

"Is that where the coven's power rises to its full potential?" Aster asked, pointing to the black circle Lane had drawn on the floor.

"A coven," Lane said. "I like that."

Aster stepped inside the circle. She sat and opened the container, revealing a mess of pastry and cream.

"Or at least they *were* cream puffs," Lane said, joining her.

"It probably wasn't the best idea to put them in the bike basket, but my limo was being cleaned," Aster said sarcastically. "Wait, *does* your grandmother have a limo?"

"Is that a joke?" Lane asked, frowning.

Aster twisted her hair. She knew that when people were nervous they showed all kinds of telltale habits like nail biting, rocking, and hair twisting. She pulled her hand away from her head.

"Limo or no limo, you're lucky you get to live here," she said.

"Yeah," Lane said. "I'm the luckiest. I live in a Florida postcard."

"You live on the west side of the Wall," Aster rolled her eyes. "How bad could it be?"

"What wall?" Lane asked.

Aster stared at Lane. Even if she had been a local, she probably wouldn't know anything about the Wall.

"It's not a real wall," Aster explained. "Gray Kingbird Avenue is where the town splits. East side is poor, mostly Black, west side is . . . different."

"Different how?" Lane asked, raising an eyebrow.

"Look around, Lane," Aster said. "Different mostly white, different mostly not poor."

"Just because I'm not poor or because I'm white doesn't mean I don't have problems too," Lane said defensively. "You think you're so smart because you don't go to school."

The two girls looked at each other for a few seconds before laughing.

"Now *that* was funny," Aster said. "I didn't mean to say you don't have problems, but there are definitely problems you don't have to deal with."

"Like what?" Lane asked. She rubbed unsuccessfully at a smudge of green paint on her forearm.

Clueless Lane, Aster thought and sighed.

"Like coming into this neighborhood and being afraid that people are going to be watching you and wondering what you're up to," Aster said. "Right before I was buzzed in, some nosy old white lady stopped her Mercedes and asked me if I was lost."

"Maybe she was trying to be helpful," Lane offered.

"Right," Aster said, rolling her eyes.

"We could meet somewhere else from now on," Lane suggested. "If you don't want to come here. Somewhere . . . neutral? Like at the Frosty Dream."

"Not everyone has money to spend at the Frosty Dream every week, you know," Aster said.

"What do you want then?" Lane asked. Aster could tell she was flustered. "You wouldn't let me buy your ice cream. You don't want to meet here, so what . . . "

Aster saw the look on the girl's face change. Like maybe a lightbulb had turned on.

"I'm sorry," Lane said. "Maybe we can meet in different places."

"Maybe," Aster said, thinking. If they met at different places, she would have fewer opportunities to explore the DiSanti place for information for her grandpa. "But I like the tree house."

"We could meet at the library? Or at your house?"

"I don't know," Aster said. "I'd have to check with my grandfather."

"Do you live with your grandfather?" Lane asked. She moved in a little closer. "Where are your parents?"

"Where are *your* parents?" Aster asked back.

"I'm only living with my grandmother for the summer," Lane said, sliding her crystal along its piece of yarn. Aster had noticed Lane do this before. It was her sign of nervousness. "It's how my parents get me out of the way while their lawyers take our family apart on paper."

"That's too bad," Aster said. She didn't know if there was something else, something better she should say.

"Thank you for reminding me." Lane sighed. The wind chimes rang, and she got up to look out the entrance.

"It's just Eunice," she said, sitting back down.

"What I meant is, I'm sorry," Aster said. "Maybe it's for the best?" She'd heard adults say that. *For the best.* Also, *everything happens for a reason.* As if either of those meant anything when you lost something important, something that you couldn't get back.

"You sound like an old person," Lane said, confirming her thoughts.

"I know," Aster mumbled. "What I really—"

"Don't worry about it," Lane said. "It's not like anything you say changes it."

"Well, you get to see them, right?" Aster said. "At least you have that."

"My mom and I are going to be living in New York. My

dad and my brothers are staying in London." Lane chewed on her lip. "No, I don't even have that. I'm the only one who didn't have a choice."

They sat in silence for a minute before Lane spoke.

"So, what's wrong with your family?"

"Nothing's wrong with my family," Aster said defensively.

"Then why do you live with your grandfather?" Lane asked.

"Why does living with my grandfather mean something's wrong with my family?" Aster said. "You should know there are all kinds of families."

Aster watched Lane twist the crystal, not making eye contact.

"Besides," she said, grabbing a peanut butter cookie, "my parents aren't around because they're merpeople, summoned by Poseidon."

"They drowned?" Lane asked.

"What? No!" Aster said, shaking her head. "Forget it."

"Nice," Lane said. "I tell you about my family, but you don't tell me about yours. Maybe you shouldn't be here. This is going to be an initiation where you're making a serious commitment to the group. And that means being truthful."

"Are you always this intense?" Aster asked, brushing crumbs off her shorts.

Lane stood up and looked at her phone.

"My dad died in a combat accident a long time ago," Aster said. "And my mom is stationed in Japan right now with the army."

"Oh, okay," Lane said. "Why won't you just say that?"

"I don't know," Aster said. "Sometimes I feel like if I talk about my mom I'll somehow jinx us. That's weird, right? When she's here, I know she eventually has to leave. I try not to think about stuff like what if it's the last time . . . "

Aster sometimes feared that her mother would suffer the same fate as her father. She had never told anyone, not even her grandpa, that she was afraid. Sometimes she thought not talking about her mother would keep her safe.

"It's not weird," Lane said. "When my parents told me they were getting divorced, I would sleep with a photo of my family under my pillow every night. I thought I could dream us back together. Sometimes I still do it."

Aster nodded. She knew the feeling.

"Do you miss your dad?" Lane asked.

"I don't have any memories of him," Aster said. "Sometimes I think I do, and then I realize there's no way I could remember him when I was six because he wasn't alive when I was six. It's like I draw him into my memories."

"I do the opposite," Lane said. "Sometimes when I'm really missing my dad and brothers, I try to imagine that it's always just been me and my mom. It's easier to pretend I can take an eraser and rub them out."

"Does it work?" Aster asked. "Do you feel better?"

"No," Lane said. "I feel worse."

"I have a closet full of my dad's shirts," Aster said, patting down the plaid shirt she wore over a tank top. "Makes me feel like I have a part of him with me."

Aster remembered finding the box labeled MARK'S CLOTHES in her mother's closet and dragging it into her room, placing each shirt on a hanger. When she wore her dad's shirts, she imagined it was like being in his hug. She felt safe.

"I like that," Lane said, smiling. Then she was serious again. "We don't have to talk about your mom if you don't want to." She pretended to zip her lips, then unzipped them to take a bite of a cookie.

"Not as exciting as them being summoned by Poseidon, right?" Aster said.

"Well, no," Lane agreed. "But nothing beats being summoned by Poseidon."

"Unless you're summoned by Zeus, of course," Aster said.

"You are so weird," Lane said and laughed.

CHAPTER 18

"What's all this?" Ofelia asked. Cat trailed behind her, followed by Eunice.

"Initiation stuff," Lane said, waving them in.

"Are those cream puffs?" Cat asked.

"Deconstructed cream puffs," Aster corrected, holding out the container.

"So are we going to talk about what happened after the Frosty Dream?" Ofelia said, pulling out her notebook. "Are you ever going to tell us why you're skipping Floras meetings? I need details."

Lane turned to Cat. They all waited.

"I don't want to be a Flora anymore," Cat said, swiping a finger across the pale yellow cream smeared inside the plastic container.

"So, don't," Lane said. "My grandmother tried to get me to join, and I told her no way."

"It's not that easy," Cat continued. "My mom won't just let me stop being a Flora. It's too important to her."

"Why don't you want to be a Flora?" Aster asked.

Cat told the girls about her school project on the Migratory Bird Treaty Act.

"What does that have to do with the Floras?" Ofelia said.

"The Migratory Bird Treaty Act became a law because people were hunting birds and using their feathers to make hats," Cat explained. "Hats like the one Miss Floras wears. Birds and their feathers were so popular that sometimes women wore entire stuffed birds on their hats!"

"That *is* awful," Ofelia said, a look of disgust on her face. "Those poor birds."

"What difference does it make now?" Lane said.

"It's about what the hat symbolizes," Cat explained. "Birds aren't just things you can kill to make something pretty. People still do that to animals, you know? Hunt them to wear parts of them, or for sport. It's horrible. And *I* don't feel right being a part of any group that can't see why it's wrong to use something that has such an awful history."

"My grandpa says you have to stand up for what you believe in," Aster said. "I don't know if skipping meetings

137

and hiding from your mom would be considered standing up for what you believe in, though."

Cat shrugged.

"Dead birds, a controversial hat," Ofelia said, chewing on her pencil. "This is good."

"Good?" Aster frowned.

"Will you stop writing in that thing?" Lane asked.

"I can't," Ofelia said, shaking her head. "Tell me, Cat, how does your mom not even know you've been skipping out on the Floras? Doesn't she watch your every move like a hawk?"

"I appreciate the bird reference," Cat said. "My parents can get wrapped up in their jobs. My mom works. *A lot*. So does my dad. Sometimes they're gone before I even wake up. Some days they get home really late. And my older sisters have their own stuff going on."

"No adult supervision," Ofelia said to herself, scribbling in her notebook.

"Sometimes it gets lonely," Cat said. "But times like this, it helps to not have anyone asking questions. My mom would never imagine that me or any of my sisters *wouldn't* be Floras. She just assumes I'm doing what I'm supposed to be doing."

"Sounds like you have some stuff to figure out," Aster said.

"Well, speaking of Floras and figuring things out," Lane said, "I've been reading my grandmother's old handbook, and I know we aren't the Floras—"

"And we don't want to be the Floras," Cat reminded her.

"But you *are* technically a Flora," Ofelia said, looking at Cat. "Right?"

"Not in my heart," Cat replied, shaking her head.

"The point is," Lane said, "we're a different group, but we still need to have an oath because that's what bonds a group."

She handed each girl a pencil and tore a sheet of paper into four pieces.

"I think what bonds a group is something else," Aster said. "Not just some words on paper. But okay."

"The oath is our promise," Lane went on. "The code by which we live."

"Did you read a textbook called *Introduction to Groups*?" Aster said with a smirk.

Ofelia stifled a giggle.

"Are you going to be difficult the whole time?" Lane asked. "You don't have to be here, you know?"

"No one's leaving," Cat said, looking around at the group. "Right?"

"Don't worry," Aster said. "I'm not going anywhere."

"Good," Ofelia said. "What are we doing with these?"

"We each write a word," Lane said. She had thought a little about what the oath could be. "A word that represents you, something that is important to who you are and that you want to be important to the group too."

Lane thought about her word. The only sound in the tree house was the rustle of leaves and the occasional scribbling and erasing. When they had all put their pencils down, Lane collected the papers and read their words.

"Truth. Kindness. Justice. Community."

"Those are good words," Cat said. Aster nodded approvingly.

"I can combine them into some kind of statement," Ofelia offered.

"You're the writer," Lane said, handing a pen and the blank book to Ofelia.

When Ofelia was done, Lane took back the four pieces of paper with their individual words. She opened the small canvas bag inside the circle and set out its contents. The girls crowded closer to get a better look at the rock-like items of various lengths and widths and colors she lined up on the floor. Lane picked up a piece that looked like a lumpy red rock.

"What are those?" Ofelia asked, leaning in.

"These are crystals," Lane said. "This one is called zeolite. It's for beginnings. It encourages groups to work together and support each other. Which is exactly what we need, right?"

The girls watched as Lane spread out a black bandanna. She placed the crystal and their pieces of paper on it, gathered the four corners of cloth, and joined them, tying the corners together to make a little pouch.

"Where did you learn about this?" Cat asked, running her fingers gently over a crystal.

"Back home in London. There was a store that sold all kinds of crystals and stones," Lane said. "The owner was an old witchy woman who could tell you what each one was good for. I have some library books about crystals, too, if you want to see those."

"Rocks?" Aster said. "With power?"

"Why not?" Cat replied. "Crystals are naturally formed in the earth. I believe they could have some kind of energy."

"Exactly, thank you," Lane said smugly. "Now, we protect our space."

She picked up four white chunks.

"These are pieces of halite. They protect from bad energy and negative influences. That includes you, Aster."

Aster made a face at Lane.

"We'll each place one at a corner of the tree house," Lane instructed.

She held her hand out and dropped a crystal in the palms of Cat and Ofelia.

"You sure you want to do this?" she asked when she turned to Aster.

"Give me the crystal," Aster said, holding out her hand.

Lane placed the last one in Aster's palm and stood up. Each girl claimed a corner.

Ofelia wrote RITUAL FOR PROTECTING A SPACE on a blank page of the handbook.

"And finally," Lane said. "We take our oath."

Lane picked up the largest crystal.

"This is rose quartz," she explained, holding the pink crystal against her chest. "It inspires self-love and creativity and friendship. It's one of my favorites."

"And it's so pretty," Cat said, admiring the crystal.

"We'll each read the oath while holding the rose quartz," Lane said. "We'll go around the circle. No blood involved."

Cat breathed an exaggerated sigh of relief and grinned.

Aster looked at the crystal and the book Lane held out to her, but didn't move to take them.

"I can start if you don't want to be first," Lane offered. She opened the book to read the oath Ofelia had written.

"We, the Ostentation of Others and Outsiders, swear to seek truth and justice, demonstrate kindness, and create community."

The handbook and the crystal were passed from girl to girl until the items had made their way back to Lane.

"Oath sworn and space protected," Lane announced. "We are officially a troop."

"An ostentation," Ofelia corrected.

"I think this calls for a cookie *and* a cream puff," Cat said, helping herself to one of each.

"Wait," Lane said. "I have a few more things for you."

She unwrapped the white tissue paper that sat among the items in the circle and handed each girl a small round badge made of gray craft felt. On each badge was an embroidered peacock eye in green and blue thread. On the back of each was a small safety pin.

"You made badges?" Ofelia asked, pinning hers to her backpack. "This feels so official."

"Since the Floras have bandannas, I thought we could have our own too," Lane continued, distributing black squares of fabric in the middle of the circle.

Cat tied hers around her neck, replacing her Floras bandanna.

"And we can't forget to sign the membership page," Ofelia said, holding up the book.

After each girl signed, Ofelia finished writing down the details of their ceremony. Lane only saw her take a break from writing to shoo Eunice away from the cream puffs.

"One last thing," Lane said.

She walked to where the afghan hung and carefully lifted the ends from the nails on which she'd hooked it. She removed it to reveal the wall of the tree house. The three girls gasped. Even Eunice seemed excited, fluttering down from the windowsill. Lane had worked hard on the peacock illustration affixed to the wall, and this was exactly the reaction she had wanted.

"It's perfect," Cat said.

"How did you make it?" Ofelia asked, touching the bird.

Lane explained how she drew and painted the peacock

across a few newspaper spreads, cut out the image, then made wheat paste to stick the bird to the wall. It was her first time wheatpasting, and she felt proud of her work.

As they stood together, Lane felt a spark of excitement, as if the tree house was charged with electricity. But something was still missing.

"We need a dead body," Lane announced.

"A what?" Cat turned from the drawing to face Lane with a worried look.

Lane laughed at her reaction.

"Like in that old movie where the four boys go on an adventure to see this body," Lane said. "We need a mission too. A goal."

"But not a *real* dead body," Cat said. "Right?"

"A metaphorical dead body," Aster offered.

"Exactly," Lane said.

Aster said an oath didn't make a group, and maybe she was right, Lane thought. The oath was just a beginning.

CHAPTER 19

The inside of the DiSanti house was spookier than Aster had imagined, especially after talking about a group mission as if it were a dead body. The old mansion was exactly the stuff of ghost stories, the kind of place where skeletons fell out of closets. Now that she was in—under the ruse of using the bathroom—she realized she had no idea what she was looking for. And on top of that, she was afraid of running into Lane's grandmother. She imagined her like Cruella De Vil. Maybe she wore a coat of puppies too.

The floor was covered in worn evergreen rugs that looked like endless forests. Golden dragons peered up with menacing faces. And even though the heavy maroon velvet curtains were pulled open with thick cords, the whole place felt dark.

A large marble staircase led up to the second floor. Aster peered through a doorway where a hall stretched in opposite directions, seeming to continue at the turn at either end. She felt like she was in a choose-your-own-adventure book.

She climbed the stairs thinking how lucky she was that marble didn't creak. The stairwell was lined with gold-framed paintings. At the very top hung a family portrait. The woman in the painting wore a large orange blossom corsage on her wrist. Her husband wore a smaller, matching bouton-niere. One of the two boys looked especially like Lane, the same willful expression on his face.

The portrait made her think of her parents' prom photo—her favorite picture of them together—that sat in a frame on a bookshelf in the living room of her house. In it, her dad had a look that said, *I may be wearing this silly tuxedo, but I'm still cooler than you.* Her grandpa always said she had the Douglas eyes just like her dad, brown and full of wisdom. She wondered if Lane saw her own dad when she looked in the mirror the same way Aster saw hers.

Aster couldn't believe people lived in a house like the DiSanti's. Still, she wouldn't have traded her little cottage for it. Nothing in the house or the property took away from the fact that it all seemed kind of empty and lonely and untouchable. She wondered if Mrs. DiSanti ever ate a sandwich in her bed while watching TV or left toothpaste smudges and stray hairs in her sink.

Aster made her way down the hall, holding her breath whenever she heard a sound.

At the end of the hallway, she opened a pair of French doors. Aster pressed her lips together to hold back the gasp that threatened to escape. The room was lined with books as high as the ceiling. A ladder hung from a track that allowed it to slide along the bookcase so that no matter how high a book was set, you could climb up to reach it. The room was Grandpa heaven. Surely there was something he might find useful among the many books on the shelves in Mrs. DiSanti's personal library.

Aster scanned the titles on the spines. There was a section on Sabal Palms history and one on Florida history. Another area was lined with leather-bound classics. There were books on natural life in South Florida, and a section dedicated to family history. Gold, she thought.

Most of that other stuff her grandfather could probably find at the public library. But not the family bibles, the photo albums, and scrapbooks. She zeroed in on the scrapbooks.

"I wish I knew what the heck I was looking for," she muttered. The spines were embossed in faded gold text indicating years and contents. DISANTI CITRUS, CELEBRATIONS, DISANTI HOUSE, FLORAS HISTORY, TRAVELS, GARDENS, MISCELLANEOUS.

She pulled out a scrapbook and flipped through the yellowed pages of black-and-white photographs of DiSantis posing in front of the house, playing tennis, lounging by the pool, picnicking, waving from sailboats. There was a photo of a DiSanti holding a hunting rifle in one hand and a long white bird in the other. Aster thought of Cat's feathered hat. Some of the photos captured their servants in the periphery. The serious, tired looks on their faces a contrast to the relaxed, happy expressions on the posing DiSantis and their friends.

There was a scrapbook of Floras photographs and newspaper articles. She opened it, curious to see if she could find a photo of the feathered hat, which wasn't hard to do since it was featured prominently in several, perched on the heads of Miss Floras throughout the years.

She closed the book and looked at the spines again, wishing one would shine brighter than the rest, maybe push itself off the shelf and drop at her feet.

Aster opened a scrapbook labeled GARDENS next. Its spine cracked like her grandpa's knees when he got up after sitting for a long time. There were photos of trees and plants and flowers. She could tell they were on the DiSanti property because, although many years had passed, the landmarks were still there—the pools, the naked statue, the wall of lion faces.

Her eyes looked over the photos like she was scanning a microfilm reel when suddenly they stopped on two orange trees. Even in the black-and-white photograph, she could tell that the fruit hanging from them was white. Like a Winter Sun orange, she thought.

She pulled the photograph out of its black corners and turned it over. There was something written on the back in a language that wasn't English. She dug her recipe box out of her backpack and hesitated before filing the photo behind the *D* tab. She wasn't sure how it would help her grandfather, but she would plan to return it.

Aster pushed the book back on the shelf and shoved the recipe box into her bag, then quietly moved to the French doors and peeked out. The hallway was clear. She slipped out of the room and down the hallway to the bathroom. By then, she really did have to go.

As she washed her hands over the sink made from the shell of a giant mollusk, Aster thought about what she knew of research. There's usually a question the researcher was trying to answer.

She dried her hands, making sure to reposition the towel on the rack as perfectly as it had hung before. There was a fancy bottle of lemon verbena lotion on a shelf above the sink. Aster pumped lotion into her hands and rubbed it in, thinking. What was the question that would be most helpful to her grandfather's work? He wanted to prove that the Douglas family was an important part of local history. That they, too, had contributed to making the town what it was. And that they should have been credited for bringing the Winter Sun orange, which people associated with Sabal Palms and the DiSantis, to the area. He never outright claimed the DiSanti family had stolen the tree or the fruit. Had he implied it? And could you even *steal* fruit?

Aster looked at her reflection in the mirror. She remembered reading that old mirrors sometimes had mercury in them. This one looked like something out of *Snow White*. It was cloudy, covered in silver-gray splotches that seemed to move in from the edges like a photo on fire. *Mirror, mirror on the wall*, she thought, *what is the answer to it all?*

CHAPTER 20

Mrs. DiSanti had given Ofelia's mother the morning off, and she offered to take the girls to the beach.

"You don't have to, Ma," Ofelia said. "We're happy to just hang out in the tree house."

"I want to meet your friends," Mrs. Castillo said, shoving bottles of water into a cooler full of ice. "What do we know about them?"

Ofelia hated that her mother was always so suspicious of everyone. Even twelve-year-old girls.

"Hmm," Ofelia said. "*We* think Cat might belong to a biker gang."

"Are you laughing at me?" Mrs. Castillo asked, hands on hips.

"No, Ma, I'm making fun of you," Ofelia said. "Just please promise you won't come at them like a tornado of questions."

"¿Yo? ¿Un tornado? I'm more like a Caribbean breeze," Mrs. Castillo said with a wink.

When Mrs. Castillo finished packing the car, they picked up the other girls at the DiSanti house. Ofelia introduced them and waited for her mom to start with the questions. To her surprise, she didn't.

"I thought we could use a snack for the beach," Aster said, handing Ofelia's mother a container.

"You made this?" Mrs. Castillo asked. Ofelia could tell she was impressed.

"I hope it's more cream puffs," Cat said.

"It's potato and beet salad," Aster said. "My grandpa has a very picky palate so he wouldn't eat any of it."

"And by picky you mean smart, right?" Lane said, cringing at the sight of the pink contents visible through the clear sides of the container.

"What about your parents?" Mrs. Castillo asked. "Won't they want to eat it? This looks like it took a lot of work."

"Maaaaa," Ofelia groaned. She could see that familiar look on her mom's face. It was her I'm-just-making-conversation-but-really-hoping-you'll-share-something-important look. "Don't be nosy. You promised."

"It's pretty easy to make," Aster said. "You just dump

153

everything in a bowl together and mix it up. I can show you if you'd like."

Mrs. Castillo gave Aster a big smile in the rearview mirror and shot Ofelia an approving look. "It's my lucky day, eh? Because I love beets. Right, Ofelia?"

"She does," Ofelia said, holding in a laugh. "*Loves* beets."

The girls giggled. Ofelia watched her mother adjust the rearview mirror. She knew she was trying to get a better look at the group in the back seat.

"Are you going to be cool enough in that, Lane?" Mrs. Castillo asked. Lane's beach gear was an oversized black hat and a black T-shirt that hung down to her knees.

"I'm always cool, Mrs. Castillo," Lane said, causing the girls to crack up.

When they arrived at their favorite beach, Mrs. Castillo parked next to the Eden Roc Hotel, and the girls dragged the cooler filled with ice and drinks while she fed the meter.

Ofelia loved Miami Beach with its bright, Art Deco buildings. The sound of music bounced along with the ocean breeze, fast and jumpy, making her feel like she had ants in her pants that needed to be danced out.

It was midday, and the sun beat down mercilessly. It was sand-that-burns-your-feet hot, frizzy-hair-that-will-yieldto-no-hair-products hot, eyeglasses-sliding-off-your-face hot. Ofelia wiped the bridge of her nose with her beach towel. The occasional breeze that came in over the water made the humidity and heat just a tiny bit more bearable.

"Purple flag," Aster announced, pointing to the lifeguard stand.

"What's it for?" Lane asked.

"It means there's dangerous marine life," Cat answered.

"Sharks?" Lane said hopefully. "Cool!"

"Not sharks," Mrs. Castillo said, walking up to the group. "The lifeguard says a few Portuguese man-of-wars washed up on the beach earlier, so no getting in the water."

"Did you know the Portuguese man-of-war isn't a single animal?" Cat asked the group. "It's not even a jellyfish."

"Pray tell," Lane said, digging a hole in the sand with her big toe.

"It's a group of organisms," Cat went on. Ofelia liked how the girl ignored Lane's sarcasm. "It's several creatures in one."

"A community," Aster said.

"Whatever it is," Mrs. Castillo said, "I don't want to have to tell your adults that you were stung by one on my watch. So stay out of the water, okay?"

"We'll stay out, Mrs. Castillo," Aster assured her.

Lane pulled a washed-out spaghetti sauce jar from her bag and unscrewed the lid.

"Who wants to collect shells?" she asked.

Cat opened an app on her phone to help them identify what they found. While the girls looked for seashells, Ofelia read over the growing list of headlines she'd written since meeting them:

More Than Books in the Book Return.
Librarian Finds Girl Hiding from Her Mother.
　　By Ofelia Castillo

Strange Birds Convene on Horned Lark
Lane Tree House.
　　By Ofelia Castillo

Something shiny among a pile of seaweed that had washed onto the beach caught Ofelia's eye. She moved closer to get a better look.

"Come here," she called to the other girls.

Cat, Aster, and Lane walked over.

A man-of-war's sail glistened pink and purple and

blue, like a big soap bubble reflecting light, threatening to burst.

"It's beautiful," Cat said dreamily. "I feel so sad for it."

"I wonder how they end up on the beach," Aster said, brushing sand off her knees.

"They just drift," Cat explained. "They can't intentionally move so they depend on the wind and currents. It must have just drifted too close to the shore, poor thing."

"Don't you mean poor *things*?" Lane corrected. "Look at all that garbage that washed in with it."

Among the tangle of seaweed and the creature's tentacles was a plastic supermarket bag, a Popsicle wrapper, and a Styrofoam cup.

"People can be so gross and careless," Aster said, a hint of anger in her voice.

"This is why we can't have anything nice," Lane agreed.

"Can we push it back into the water?" Ofelia said, glancing in her mother's direction. "Maybe we can still save it."

"No way," Lane said. "Unless you want to get stung. That thing has to stay right there."

"But it's going to die," Ofelia insisted.

"Everything dies," Aster said, turning away from the creature. She joined Cat, who had begun to pick up trash.

Ofelia watched Lane move closer to Aster.

"It could've been floating along to who knows where by now," Cat said, motioning toward the ocean with an empty bag of chips.

The girls stared at the creature. Their moment of silence for its death and its lack of self-determination was interrupted by Ofelia's mother.

"¡No lo toquen!" she screamed, rushing over. "Do not touch that thing!"

Ofelia shook her head. Her mom sounded like a squawking gull.

"The lifeguard said it can still sting even if it's dead," Mrs. Castillo continued. "Step away."

"We're just looking, Ma," Ofelia assured her.

Everything was so dangerous, Ofelia thought. She felt empathy for the creature that had no control over something so basic as where it wanted to be. She watched her mom hurry over to the lifeguard, pointing to where the man-of-war lay. The girls walked away from the creature and took the collected trash to a nearby garbage can.

"Have you decided what you're doing about the Floras?" Ofelia asked Cat.

"I don't know," Cat said, wiping a shell on her shorts.

"The Miss Floras contest is getting close. I should probably just tell my mom already and get it over with."

"But what about the hat?" Lane asked.

"What about it?" Cat said. "It's not like Mrs. McAllister cares what I think. No one does."

"We care," Aster said, looking at the other girls. "Right?"

"Let's do something," Lane agreed.

"Well, yeah, but—" Cat started.

"But what?" Aster said. "My grandpa says that to bring about social change you need a two-pronged attack."

"What are the two prongs?" Cat asked.

"Actually, it's three prongs. First, you have to get off your butt," Aster said, counting off on her fingers. "You need to change policies. Which isn't happening, right? And you need action because that's what will get people to pay attention and think about changing policies."

"Like Harriet Hemenway and Minna Hall," Cat said, thoughtfully.

"Who?" Lane asked.

"They organized boycotts and sent out flyers and are really the reason why the Migratory Bird Treaty Act even exists," Cat said, standing up.

Ofelia could see Cat was excited. She talked with her

hands, and her eyes widened as she explained how the women worked to protect birds. Ofelia could feel herself getting excited too. Here was an unfolding story about truth and justice right in their own backyard.

"Yes," Ofelia said, losing interest in the jar of shells. "Like *that*."

"So, let's figure out a way to convince people that it's wrong to keep using the hat," Lane said.

"But I can't get into trouble," Cat said quickly. "It's bad enough I'm skipping the meetings, and I gave away the brownie money."

"Who said anything about trouble?" Aster asked, looking at the other girls.

"Not me." Ofelia grinned.

"We can make stickers," Lane said. "Like street artists do. No one would have to know who made them."

"Street artists?" Cat asked. "You mean like graffiti?"

"Isn't graffiti illegal?" Ofelia said, swatting a biting fly.

"What would we do with stickers?" Aster added.

"We put a message on them and stick them up everywhere," Lane said. "To raise awareness about the feathered hat and the mistreatment of birds."

"I don't know about this," Cat said, picking at a scab on her elbow.

"*This* is our dead body," Lane said. "Or is your plan to just keep skipping meetings until you're caught?"

"Could you please stop calling it a dead body?" Cat said, making a disapproving face.

"What else could we do?" Aster asked.

"What about writing a letter to the editor of the *Sabal Palms Sun*?" Ofelia offered, thinking back to Ms. Niggli's unit on the anatomy of a newspaper. This was the section of the paper where they printed letters people sent in.

Cat nodded. "I vote for writing a letter to the editor."

"Why don't we do both?" Lane said. "Stickers and a letter to the editor. Different audiences. And there's no guarantee a letter to the editor will be published, right?"

"Can you write the letter, Ofelia?" Cat asked. "Please?"

"I can, but I'll need more information," Ofelia said, sitting down on her beach towel. "I don't know anything about the hat or the Floras."

"I'll tell you everything, and you write it, okay?" Cat said.

"Sure, okay."

Ofelia tried hard to listen, but she was already thinking

ahead. She remembered reading about Nellie Bly, a journalist who was famous for going undercover to investigate and expose abuses of mentally ill patients in 1887. If she did the same, pretending to be someone interested in the Floras and sitting in on a meeting, she could get a real insider view not just for her letter to the editor, but maybe also for a story about the feathered hat.

"Hey, Cat," Ofelia said. "When do the Floras meet?"

"Thursdays at two," Cat said. "Why?"

"Because I'm going undercover," Ofelia declared. She wrote the day and time in her notebook.

"You really don't have to," Cat said, shaking her head.

"I'm a muckraker, and if there's anything to uncover that can help, I'm on it," Ofelia said.

"Be careful, Ofelia," Lane warned. "I've heard those Floras meetings can get wild."

"Well, there *was* this one time a raccoon climbed in through a window," Cat said. "Mrs. McAllister pulled a cushion off the couch and was swinging it wildly trying to make contact with the raccoon, but she ended up hitting Nia instead. And the raccoon ran off with the pound cake Mrs. McAllister had baked for our meeting."

Ofelia's sides hurt from laughing as she pictured the raccoon going for a touchdown like a football player.

"What about the stickers?" Aster said, wiping tears from her eyes.

"Where can we use a scanner and a printer?" Lane asked. "We don't really need them, but it'll be easier to make a lot of stickers at once."

"The library has both," Aster suggested.

"Then we'll make stickers in the library," Lane said, looking at Aster, Cat, and Ofelia. "Everyone in?"

CHAPTER 21

"Grandpa, can I have a few print cards?" Aster asked, holding out her hand.

The girls had met at the library to work on the stickers. She introduced her grandfather to her friends. But only by first name. She wasn't sure how he'd respond to Lane's last name, and she didn't want him blowing her cover. She had never really had close friends to introduce him to, so she was a little nervous. He shook each of their hands and made corny grandpa jokes that, to Aster's relief, the girls laughed at.

"In my bag," he said. Aster dug around in her grandfather's satchel until she found his little plastic sandwich bag full of cards.

"What is all that?" Lane asked.

"Print cards," Aster said. "To pay with. My grandpa loses one, so he gets another, or he finds one left behind at the printer. Before you know it, sandwich bag full of cards." She held up the bag and shook it.

"What are you gals up to?" her grandfather asked, looking up from his book.

"We're planning a revolution, Mr. Douglas," Lane said matter-of-factly.

"Oh, I like you," he said to Lane and held up a fist.

Aster caught Lane smiling bigger than she'd ever seen.

"Come on," she said, leading the girls away.

"Will you show me how to use the microfilm readers later," Cat said. "Please?"

"Sure," Aster said.

"But important business first." Lane pulled a large envelope from her bag. "Label paper that we'll print the image on."

"Where's the picture?" Ofelia asked.

Lane slid a sheet of paper out of the envelope.

"What do you think?" she said, holding up her drawing. "I tried to draw it like Cat described it."

"That's really good," Cat said, admiring Lane's skill. "It looks just like the feathered hat, but how will anyone know what it means?"

"We should write something on it," Aster said. "Every revolution needs a slogan."

"Like no taxation without representation," Ofelia said, dropping into a chair with her notebook and pencil.

"Give me liberty or give me death," Lane yelled.

Ms. Falco looked over from her desk.

"Shhh," Cat said. "This isn't a revolution. It's just a hat."

"It's not just a hat," Aster said. "You're fighting to change something that has always been. It's a small thing, but it's still a revolution."

"Oh, bird droppings," Cat said. "Fine, what about 'Return the Feathers'? Or 'No More Hat'?"

"Who would they be returning the feathers to?" Ofelia asked, writing.

"It's a symbolic return," Cat said. "Not using the hat would mean returning the feathers to the birds."

"I like that," Aster said. "Return the Feathers."

The girls watched as Lane wrote the slogan in black marker above the image of the hat. At the bottom-right corner, she drew the peacock eye that had become their symbol.

"Where's the scanner?" Lane asked.

The girls followed Aster and watched as Lane scanned the image.

"How many of these do we want to print?" Lane said. "One sheet fits nine stickers."

"A lot," Ofelia said. "Right?"

Lane sat at a computer and pasted the image multiple times onto a blank document, then sent it to print.

"Let's play the guess-which-card-has-money-on-it game," Aster said. She pulled a print card out of the bag and inserted it in the card reader. The card reader shot it back out with a disapproving whir.

"This one's probably damaged," she said, setting it aside and trying another card.

"This one only has five cents on it."

"Are we going to be here all day?" Lane sighed.

Aster finally found a card that worked and printed a test page.

"Now we're ready for the label paper," Lane said, waving a small stack of sheets. "Courtesy of my grandmother."

"Your grandmother knows we're doing this?" Ofelia asked, in shock.

"Of course not," Lane said. "I got these from your mom's office."

She placed the sheets into the paper tray.

"There's another card reader over there." Aster pointed

to the print station at the other end of the room. "Why don't you try some of these and set aside the cards with money."

"I'll do that." Ofelia grabbed a stack of cards.

When Ofelia returned, she had marked the cards with their amounts and thrown away the ones that didn't work.

"I hope Grandpa doesn't freak out that we cleaned up his print card supply," Aster said. She inserted a card with a little more than a dollar on it and printed.

When she lifted the twenty sheets of label paper from the printer, they were warm and smelled of fresh toner. She handed them to Lane. Cat and Ofelia looked over her shoulder.

"How did you learn to do this?" Ofelia asked. "I never knew you could actually *make* stickers."

"You can make anything," Lane said. "Don't you know that necessity is the mother of invention?"

"I think you just channeled my grandpa," Aster said.

"What now?" Cat asked.

"Now we cut them to size," Lane said. "And violà! We've got stickers."

"I think you mean *voilà*," Aster said.

"No, my dad always says—" Lane cut herself off. "Never mind, I know it's voilà."

"I'll get the paper cutter," Aster offered.

She returned and set it on a table where Lane measured the stickers and cut them as evenly as possible. When she was done, she held up the stacks.

"We'll keep them in the tree house until we figure out what we want to do with them," Lane said. "Anyone want to head back with me?"

"I'll walk out with you, but I have my Floras meeting," Ofelia said, picking up her backpack.

"You're really doing it?" Cat asked, wide-eyed.

"Of course," Ofelia said. "Why wouldn't I?"

"But you're too old to join the Floras," Cat said. "Mrs. McAllister will know you're up to something, don't you think?"

"You're a wilted Flora," Aster joked.

"It's worth a shot," Ofelia said and shrugged. "It'll be good experience. What about these?" She motioned to the stack of stickers in Lane's hand.

"Let's put them up this weekend," Lane said. "No time to waste, right?"

"I think my mom is working on Saturday so I can tag along with her," Ofelia offered.

"I can't Saturday," Aster said. "The Bahamas Day Festival is happening."

"What's that?" Lane asked.

"It's a festival that happens every year," Aster explained. "It's this big celebration of Bahamian history and culture. There's food and music and a parade."

"And the Floras will have a booth," Cat added.

"Why?" Ofelia said. "The Floras aren't Bahamian."

"It's a street fair," Aster said. "So, all kinds of local vendors and businesses set up booths. It might even be a good place to put up stickers, come to think of it. There will definitely be a lot of people."

"This has to be discreet," Lane said, glancing in the direction of Aster's grandfather. "We don't want to be seen putting up the stickers. And we can't do it with your grandpa around, no matter how cool he is."

"My grandpa isn't going," Aster said. "He says it's gotten too commercial for his taste."

"I'm supposed to be there anyway," Cat said. "My mom assumes I'll be working at the Floras booth. I could go, but I have to keep a low profile too. I don't want Mrs. McAllister seeing me."

"Let's meet in the tree house," Lane said. "Don't forget your bandannas. We're going to need them."

Mr. Douglas waved to Aster with a microfilm request slip.

"Can you show me how to use the microfilm now?" Cat

asked, after Ofelia and Lane left the library. "I want to see if I can find some information about the hat's origins."

"Sure," Aster said. "I just need to get this reel for my grandpa. I'll meet you at the machines."

Aster collected the microfilm request from her grandfather and walked over to the reference desk.

"Hey, Aster," Ms. Falco said, looking up from her computer. "What have you and your friends been up to? You looked awfully busy."

"Oh, just a project," Aster said. "Grandpa needs this microfilm, please." She placed the slip on the desk. "And I have a question, a reference question."

"Sure," Ms. Falco said, standing. "What is it?"

"Do you know what language this is?" Aster pulled the photograph she'd taken from the DiSanti library out of her recipe box and held it out.

"Wow, that's a great old photo," the librarian said, examining it. She turned it over. "Is this for your grandfather's research?"

"Yes," Aster said, hoping the woman would not ask too many questions.

"Well, that's definitely Italian," Ms. Falco said, reading the back. "DiSanti's Sole dell'inverno."

"Italian," Aster repeated.

"I'm pretty sure the first word means 'sun,'" Ms. Falco said. "Sun of something. I'm not sure what the other word is, but please don't tell my nonna." The librarian laughed and gave Aster a guilty look. "Come on, let's look it up."

Aster followed her to the reference section where Ms. Falco pulled an Italian-English dictionary from the shelf. As the librarian's fingers flipped through the thin pages of the book, Aster repeated the words in her head. *Sole dell'inverno.* The words were familiar, and suddenly, she realized why. It reminded her of Spanish.

Aster felt like she had stopped breathing. She knew what the other word meant before Ms. Falco had even found it in the dictionary.

"Let's see," Ms. Falco said. "*Inverno.* It means—"

"Winter," Aster finished for her.

"That's right," Ms. Falco said. "Sole dell'inverno translates to sun of winter."

"The winter sun," Aster whispered, looking at the photograph.

CHAPTER 22

"I don't want to discourage you, dear," Mrs. McAllister said, sweetly. "It's never too late to be a Flora, but I'm not sure it makes sense for you to join now. This would be your last year. Why, it's too late for you to even enter the Miss Floras contest."

The woman patted her short hair. It was dyed a shade of reddish purple that reminded Ofelia of the wine her mom drank on special occasions. Ofelia thought attending a Floras meeting would be as easy as slipping in and sitting in the back, but when Mrs. McAllister saw her, she motioned for her to follow her to the office. Which is where Ofelia found herself having to make her case and being reminded that she was, as Aster had said, a wilted flower after all.

"Please, Mrs. McAllister," Ofelia said, turning up the drama like an actress on the telenovelas her parents watched. "It's always been my dream, but my parents couldn't afford the membership." She gave the woman her saddest look. "I finally decided to save up for the dues myself. I've been mowing lawns and babysitting. And I know it's a little late, but if I could just sit in on a meeting to see what it's like to be a Flora it would mean so much to me."

"An entrepreneurial spirit is a key Flora trait," Mrs. McAllister said.

"Yes, I know," Ofelia said. "I've read all about your brownie campaign. And it would be an honor to sell the heck out of them. Pardon my language. I'm already thinking of a way to combine them with my existing businesses."

Ofelia could feel her nose growing with each lie.

"A motivated girl," Mrs. McAllister said. "I like you, Amelia."

Ofelia almost corrected her but decided she would let the woman think of her as Amelia. It would be her Floras alias.

"Very well," she said. "You're welcome to sit in."

Ofelia followed Mrs. McAllister to the meeting room where other girls were gathered. So this is what Cat no longer wanted to be a part of, she thought, looking around.

Once the meeting was called to order, Ofelia waited, notebook and pencil in hand, for something to happen. But instead, it was the opposite. She listened as girl after girl gave brownie sale updates. For the rest of the meeting, the girls were instructed to work on signs for the Floras' stall at the Bahamas Day Festival.

The girls broke into groups and went their separate ways with poster board and art supplies. Ofelia watched Mrs. McAllister turn to the display cabinet and remove a gold box. The woman walked over to her.

"Now, Amelia, I'm sorry you won't have the opportunity to be part of the Miss Floras competition, but would you like to see the hat?"

"I would love that," Ofelia said, watching as the woman opened the box and lifted the hat for her to see.

The only hat Ofelia had ever worn was the Marlins baseball cap she'd taken from her dad. This hat was something else altogether. The wide brim was made from a soft, gray material. A purple ribbon encircled its crown and was tied into a huge bow on the side. A row of small amethyst stones ran along the center of the length of the ribbon. Tucked into the big purple bow was a thick spray of feathers: wispy, white and salmon and pink. The feathers looked aged, but they were still beautiful. Lane's drawing did look very much like the hat.

"It's wonderful, isn't it?" the woman said proudly.

"It is," Ofelia agreed. "Thank you for letting me see it."

Mrs. McAllister placed the hat back in the box and closed the lid. Ofelia watched as she set it on its shelf in the display case. After closing the door to the case, Mrs. McAllister sat down at the coffee table where she lifted a little glass figurine of a palm. She dusted underneath it before placing it back on the table.

Ofelia couldn't believe it. Sure, she had seen the infamous hat, but in every other way, she had infiltrated the Floras for nothing. Where were the shocking secrets? The scandals? The controversies? The raccoons? It was a muckraking fail. She jotted down a description of the hat in her reporter's notebook and stuck it back in her bag.

"Does anyone know the whereabouts of Catarina Garcia?" Mrs. McAllister asked.

A group of girls about Ofelia's age whispered and giggled.

"She lives on my street," one girl said, waving a long dark braid in the air.

"Do you know if she plans on returning, Olive?" Mrs. McAllister asked. "I haven't been able to get in touch with her mother by phone."

"I don't know," the girl said. "But I can find out."

"Would you mind delivering this to her mother?" Mrs. McAllister got up and walked over to Olive with a sealed envelope.

"I can do that," Olive said. "A Flora is always helpful."

"Thank you, Olive."

Ofelia watched as the girl took the envelope and folded it into the pocket of her shorts. Then she picked up a tube of glitter glue and struggled to twist off the cap. Ofelia walked over.

"Need help with that?" she offered.

"Yes, please," Olive said, holding out the tube.

Ofelia turned the cap until she broke the glue seal and it came off, but not before getting a squirt of glitter on her hand.

"Here you go," she said, handing it back.

"Thank you," Olive said, turning to her poster board and squeezing out a huge glob of glitter.

"I know Cat too," Ofelia said hesitantly. "I'm walking past Mrs. Garcia's office on my way home. I can deliver the letter for you."

Olive twisted the end of one braid and held it between her nose and upper lip like a long, drooping mustache. She looked at Ofelia for a few seconds before taking the envelope out of her pocket.

"Okay," Olive said, her braid dropping back into place. She handed the envelope to Ofelia. "Thank you."

"It's no problem," Ofelia said, turning to leave.

"Excuse me?" Olive said.

Ofelia stopped, hoping the girl wouldn't ask any questions or want the envelope back.

"What is it?" Ofelia asked.

"Could you please tell Cat I miss seeing her at the meetings?"

"I will," Ofelia said and tucked the envelope into her bag.

CHAPTER 23

"Are you sure you girls will be okay going to the festival alone?" Mrs. Castillo asked. "Who's in charge? Lane seems like a little bit of a loose cannon. And Cat and Astro—"

"*Aster*, Ma. And Lane's not a loose cannon," Ofelia said. "No one is in charge. We're a *collective*."

"Bueno, collectively do not talk to strangers," Mrs. Castillo warned. "Call me if you need me to come get you."

"I will," Ofelia assured her, eager to get to the tree house.

Mrs. Castillo dug in her purse.

Ofelia held out her hand hoping for lunch money. Instead, her mother placed a bright yellow whistle around Ofelia's neck like she was awarding her a gold medal. It was the kind PE coaches used to blow out the eardrums of poor, unsuspecting children.

"Use this if you need it," she said.

Ofelia looked down at her chest, and shook her head.

"And for lunch." Her mother handed her a ten-dollar bill.

"*Ten* dollars?" Ofelia asked.

"Oye, I'm not made of money," Mrs. Castillo said. "Be grateful before I leave you with five."

"Thanks, Ma." Ofelia gave her mom a peck on the cheek before running off.

Cat, Aster, and Lane were already in the tree house when she climbed up. Each girl wore her black bandanna. Cat wore hers like a neckerchief, twisted and tied at the side over the strap of her binoculars. Floras habits die hard, Ofelia thought. Aster tied hers around her bicep. And Lane wore hers around her right wrist. Ofelia pulled hers out of her bag. She took off her dad's Marlins baseball cap and tied her bandanna like a headband with a knot at the nape of her neck.

"This is for you," Ofelia said, handing the envelope from Mrs. McAllister to Cat.

"What is it?" Lane craned her neck to see as Cat opened the letter.

"Mrs. McAllister," Cat said. "She wants to know where I've been and if I'm still entering the Miss Floras contest."

"She said she hasn't been able to get in touch with your mom," Ofelia said.

"That's because I blocked her number on my mom's phone." Cat gave a guilty look.

"You're a genius, Cat," Lane said, patting the girl's back.

"Is that supposed to be a compliment?" Cat said.

"Did you find out anything good at the meeting, Ofelia?" Aster asked.

"Not really," Ofelia said. "Just that. And that glitter glue is a pain to wash off. Oh, and I saw the hat."

"Do you mean, *the* hat?" Aster asked. "What's it like? I've seen photos, but how much does it look like Lane's sticker?"

"A lot," Ofelia said. "The feathers are pink and white."

"Snowy egret and flamingo feathers," Cat explained.

"What about the letter to the editor?" Aster asked. "Did you get a chance to write it?"

"I did," Ofelia said, pulling it out of her bag and handing it to Cat. "Let me know if you want to change anything. I mostly used the information you gave me."

"Will they publish it anonymously?" Aster asked. "Do they even print letters from kids?"

"I looked into that," Ofelia said. "I gave them my mom's name and my number as the contact. And I signed it with a pseudonym."

"A. Castle," Lane read from the paper.

"Mrs. McAllister called me Amelia," she explained. "And my last name is Spanish for 'castle.'"

"It sounds good," Cat said.

"And convincing," Aster added, reading over Cat's shoulder. "Who wouldn't agree the right thing to do is stop using the hat?"

"I'll put it in the mail then," Ofelia said.

Lane lifted a loose plank of wood in the floor.

"Whoa," Ofelia said. "There's a secret compartment? You've been holding out on us!"

The shoebox-size opening was filled with candy from the bulk bins at the Frosty Dream.

"What is all this?" Aster asked, staring at Lane's candy selection.

"Licorice, Bit-O-Honeys." Ofelia picked up pieces of candy and dropped them back in. "And soft peppermints. Where's the real candy?"

"You're all welcome to bring your own," Lane said, pulling out the plastic sandwich bag where she had stored the stickers.

"These soft peppermints aren't bad," Aster said, taking one from the pile. "My grandpa likes them."

"Here's how sticker slapping works," Lane explained. "You have to be sly about it. You can't just slap a sticker on something in full view of everyone."

"Why not?" Cat asked.

"Because even though this is a sticker of truth," Lane said, waving her stack, "it's still considered defacing property, remember?"

"Defacing property?" Ofelia asked. "We could give them out, right? Let other people stick them up?"

"Are you listening? No, we cannot," Lane said, exasperated. "Because then there are faces to connect to them. Got it?"

"Fine, got it," Ofelia said.

Lane looked at Aster.

"Got it," Aster said, rolling her eyes.

"Are we ready to go?" Lane asked. Cat nodded.

Ofelia didn't like the sound of defacing property, but her apprehension was overshadowed by the giddy excitement she felt. She was going to a street festival. With her friends and no adults. They were on a mission. And she had a real story.

The girls ventured out the side entrance of the property.

When the gate closed behind them, Ofelia noticed a sticker had been placed on it.

"Hey, when did you do that?" she asked.

"Just now," Lane whispered conspiratorially. "That's how you do it. So no one sees you."

CHAPTER 24

Cat had only ever been to the Bahamas Day Festival as a Flora, selling brownies. Mrs. McAllister didn't usually let them explore beyond the area where their booth was located. Standing in the middle of the crowd, she soaked in the different experience. The clanking of cowbells and the *rat-tat-tat* of hands against drums was all around them while men and women in colorful costumes danced down the street, joy on their sweat-drenched faces. A band of people in yellow, bright as the sun, marched past.

"Look!" Lane yelled, pointing to a group of dancers decked out in turquoise and green. They wore headdresses and carried fans with peacock feathers. "It's a sign."

"Come on," Aster said, grabbing Cat's hand and pulling her into the parade.

The girls trailed after the parade of peacock feathers. Cat watched as Ofelia reached for Lane's hand to twirl her. Lane managed to laugh after the initial shock. The girls danced and marched and sang along with the band and other festival attendees.

"I love all the feathers and sequins," Ofelia said. "Gotta send this to my mom so she knows I'm okay." She snapped a photo of the musicians and dancers.

"Those aren't real feathers, right?" Lane asked.

"I hope not," Cat said. "That's a lot of birds."

"No, they're plastic feathers," Aster said, leading the girls to a food truck with a picture of a large smiling conch shell on its side. "Grandpa says there's some controversy over the costumes. I guess back in the day they were made with a few basic supplies like cardboard and crepe paper, but now a lot of people are more interested in being dazzling. Lots of sequins and fake feathers. I still think they're pretty."

They placed their orders and sat on a curb to eat.

"Is all Bahamian food this good?" Lane said, biting into a conch fritter. "Where have you been all my life?"

Cat shook her head at the loving look Lane gave her fritters.

"Did you see the Floras booth?" Ofelia asked, glancing in the direction of where it stood farther down the festival path.

"They always get that prime spot at the start of the route," Cat said. "I think they pay extra for it."

"Does anyone else think those brownies are terrible?" Lane said. "I'll eat anything with sugar in it, but even I won't eat those."

"It's true," Ofelia said, laughing. "My mom loves the turtle brownies. They're like little sawdust and caramel cakes. They taste like they've been sitting around in a warehouse from one season to the next."

"You know where these stickers would be great?" Cat said, squeezing a packet of Tabasco sauce on her fries.

"Do we want to know?" Aster raised an eyebrow.

"On those brownie boxes."

Cat felt three pairs of eyes turn to her.

"And how exactly do you propose doing that?" Ofelia asked. "Have you thought about that tiny detail?"

Cat *had* thought about it. She had thought about it so much it kept her up a good part of the night. She had opened her window to the humid evening air and lay in bed listening for birds. And thinking. Not about the stickers themselves, but about the need to do *something*. No one listened to Cat. Not Mrs. McAllister, not the other Floras, not her mom. As the youngest, she was used to not being heard and just going along with what was expected of her. But this was different. It *was* a small revolution, just like Aster said.

"Of course, I've thought about it," Cat said. "I know how the whole space is set up."

"We're listening," Lane said.

"Mrs. McAllister usually brings the boxes in her station wagon," Cat said. "And parks it behind the booth so she can get to it whenever she needs to restock."

"But how likely is it one of us could go back there unseen?" Aster asked.

"I don't know," Cat said, thinking. "There's usually a big Floras banner hanging across the back of the booth that blocks the view of Mrs. McAllister's car. There's at least some cover."

"It's also the start of the route where the festival organizers have a donation table set up at the entrance," Lane added. "So, it might be a little more crowded and less likely for people to notice."

"But you aren't even supposed to be near that booth," Ofelia said to Cat.

"I know," Cat said, thinking. "What if I'm the distraction? I'll talk to Mrs. McAllister. About the letter. Tell her my mom got it. Make up a reason why I've been gone."

"And the three of us will do the stickering," Lane said. "It's perfect."

"If she starts to head to the car, you give us a signal," Aster added. "Shout something like . . ."

"Sawdust brownies!" Lane yelled.

The girls laughed.

"So . . . the boxes?" Cat asked. She was a little surprised at how easily the plan had come to her. And deep down, a part of her hoped her friends would come to their senses.

"One for all," Ofelia said, interlocking her thumbs and flapping her fingers before pulling out her notebook to write something.

Aster and Lane gave Cat the shadow bird sign as if indicating that they were in. Cat gave her own fingers an unenthusiastic flap in return.

At the Floras booth, Mrs. McAllister and a group of Floras chatted with festivalgoers, exchanging money for boxes of brownies. Brownie boxes were stacked neatly by flavor—regular, turtle, peanut butter, and their signature orange—on the two tables covered in pastel floral tablecloths and decorated with mini flower bouquets in glass jars. The Floras banner hung across the back of the booth. The front of Mrs. McAllister's car poked out from behind it.

Cat waited for her friends to disappear around the side of the stand and walked up to the booth, her insides shaking.

"Cat," Olive yelled. The girl bounced up and down like a pogo stick. "Are you back?"

"Hi, Olive," Cat said. She felt a little guilty. Olive was always so friendly.

Mrs. McAllister looked up and slammed the lid of the money box shut. She walked over clutching the metal box under her arm.

"Catarina Garcia," she said. "I thought you'd fallen off the face of the earth."

"Hi, Mrs. McAllister," Cat said quietly. "I just haven't been feeling well, and then my family was out of town. My mom has been meaning to get in touch, but she's really busy with a case and my dad always forgets and—"

"You're rambling, child," Mrs. McAllister said. "And rambling usually means lying."

"She's not a liar," Olive said indignantly.

"Olive," Mrs. McAllister said. "We're running out of our ever-popular orange brownies. Go with Mariana and get a few more boxes, please."

Olive sighed and walked away, giving Cat an apologetic shrug.

"Now, Catarina, I want the truth," Mrs. McAllister said. "What is going on? Are you in the Miss Floras contest or not?"

Cat drowned out the woman's talking as she watched Olive peer behind the banner. Olive turned back slowly, looking at Cat, wide-eyed.

"I don't know, Mrs. McAllister," she said, chewing on a nail. "I don't think so. Not unless the Floras stop using the hat. Couldn't you use something else?"

"Again, with the hat," Mrs. McAllister said, frustrated. "This is not up for discussion. I need to see you and your mother in my office as soon as possible. If I don't hear from her by the end of the week, I'll assume you are no longer interested in the Floras or the contest. Now, I'm very busy so excuse me."

The woman turned and looked at Olive whose head had disappeared behind the banner.

"Olive," Mrs. McAllister said, walking toward the girl. "Where are those boxes?"

"Sawdust brownies!" Cat yelled, as the woman reached the banner.

Startled, Olive stumbled backward and fell, pulling the banner down with her.

Cat saw her friends still at the station wagon. All three had pulled their bandannas up over the bottom halves of their faces.

"What are you kids doing back here?" Mrs. McAllister yelled.

Lane slapped a sticker on the bumper of Mrs. McAllister's car before taking off running with Aster and Ofelia behind her.

Cat watched as Mrs. McAllister kicked into turkey mode. The woman rushed toward the front of the booth, yelling and flagging down a security guard on a bike. She paced and shook her head, waving her hands frantically in the direction of the girls. With the exception of Olive, the other Floras ran out from the booth to see what was happening.

"Give me some stickers, Cat," Olive said eagerly. "I'll put them up for you. And I won't tell anyone it was you and your friends."

"I don't know those kids," Cat said, hoping she didn't look as guilty as she felt.

Olive gave her a look that said she didn't believe her.

"Forget it," Cat said. "You can't get involved."

"Please." Olive pressed her palms together.

"You can't, Olive," Cat insisted. "You'll get in trouble."

Olive gave Cat a pleading, pathetic look in response.

"Fine, here," she said and shoved a few stickers into the girl's hand before running off to catch up with her friends.

CHAPTER 25

Now, *this* was the life of a journalist, Ofelia thought, as she raced through the crowd, following Aster.

The girls found themselves in a traffic jam of people. What had been fun earlier—bands and dancers, people strolling at a snail's pace with drinks and food, kids with balloons bopping into them—were now obstacles to freedom.

"Sorry, excuse me!" Ofelia yelled when she bumped into a couple dancing. She ran under their joined hands like she used to do back in preschool during games of London Bridge.

She watched Aster maneuver around a towering man in an orange-and-purple costume. But the man was too busy playing the drum that hung from a strap around his neck to even notice the girls.

"Security guy coming!" Lane called.

They stopped briefly to regroup.

"One more block," Aster said, panting. "That'll be the end of the festival route."

"I hope you know what you're doing," Lane said.

"Trust me," Aster assured her.

Ofelia worried for a second that Lane would want to go her own way and felt relieved when she saw the girl nod and follow.

"Where's Cat?" Ofelia asked.

"I'm here," Cat said, running up to them. She waved just as a woman with a large fruity drink walked past. Her hand hit the woman's mermaid-shaped plastic cup and blue liquid splashed them both.

"Oh, I am so—" Cat started.

"Do you know how much this drink cost?" the woman yelled.

"We're sure you overpaid," Aster yelled back. She grabbed Cat's hand and dragged her away.

Ofelia smiled at Aster's boldness.

As the four girls wound through the throngs of festival-goers, Ofelia looked behind her to see if the security guard was any closer to them. She spotted his blue shirt. The guard peered over the crowd. Before she could warn the girls, the guard made eye contact.

"He sees us!" she said.

"Left at the corner," Aster instructed.

"Hurry up," Lane urged, pushing Cat.

"I'm going as fast as I can," Cat said, swatting at Lane.

Ofelia could see that the security guard was having difficulty getting through the crowd on his bike. He came to a full stop as a group of dancers dressed in gold and red surrounded him.

"Alley on the right!" Aster yelled when the group reached the end of the festival and followed her onto the cross street. They ran into the alley where they all slumped to the ground.

"I have a cramp," Cat cried. "Go on without me. Save yourselves."

"Stop being so dramatic, and take a deep breath," Lane said.

"You think we lost him?" Ofelia asked. If the security guard found them, it would be the end of her story.

"He just rode by," Lane whispered, pointing to the entrance of the alley and pressing herself against a wall.

"Come on," Aster said. "I know where we can hide."

Ofelia jogged behind Aster with Lane and Cat on her heels until the sounds of the festival had faded, and they came upon a cemetery in the middle of a residential neighborhood. An iron gate with an archway that read MARIAH JEAN MEMORIAL CEMETERY surrounded the space. The rusted gate was open a crack. Aster pushed it open, wide enough for all of the girls to get through.

The ground was covered with rectangular white slabs that Ofelia thought looked like the dominos the old Cuban men played with at the park. Some of the graves had flowers that appeared to have been left recently, but most looked like no one had come to visit in a long time, like maybe no one was alive to visit anymore. Some of the stones were cracked, and from the dates, Ofelia could see that no one had been buried there in a while.

"What is this place?" Cat asked.

"It's where a lot of early Bahamian settlers were buried," Aster said. "See how all the graves are aboveground?"

"Why is that?" Ofelia said.

"It's how they bury people in places that are at sea level," Aster said. "So the graves don't flood. I have ancestors buried here."

She pointed and led the girls in the direction of the graves.

"Some of these are so old it's hard to read the names

and dates." Aster swept dirt off one with her hand.

"Charles Douglas," Ofelia read the name on the stone.

"I'm pretty sure that security guy isn't following us anymore," Lane said, looking toward the entrance.

"Yeah, I figured he wouldn't go too far from the festival," Aster said. "White people don't usually come to this side of the Wall unless they're doing something touristy."

"It's not a real wall," Lane explained to Cat and Ofelia.

"I know about the Wall," Ofelia said. "We learned about it in social studies class." She bent down with a pencil and her reporter's notebook to take some notes.

"I saw a lot of white people at the festival," Cat said.

"Exactly," Aster said. "They come for the music and fritters, but that's about it." She explained how the invisible Wall separated the town's residents.

"How does that happen?" Cat asked. "How do you make a wall that isn't even a real wall?"

"Neglect, racism," Aster said. "My grandpa says the local government gives more money and resources to some areas than others all because of who lives there. The east side of the Wall is where Black families settled. Not a coincidence that it's the area that's neglected."

"That's sad," Cat said, shaking her head.

"It's sad that politicians and business people only think certain people deserve good things," Ofelia said. "Right?"

Aster nodded.

"Why can't people just live together?" Cat asked. "And be treated equally?"

"That's sweet, Cat," Lane said. "But you're being unrealistic. Don't stick your head in the sand like an ostrich."

"Okay, Lane," Ofelia said, looking up from her notebook. "Could you be any meaner?"

"What?" Lane said. "It's true, isn't it?"

"Ostriches don't actually stick their heads in the sand," Cat said. "It's a myth that they do it when they're scared. They bury their eggs, so when it looks like they're sticking their heads in the sand, what they're actually doing is turning the eggs."

Ofelia looked at Aster and Lane and the three girls burst out laughing. It was such a typical Cat comment, Ofelia thought, wiping tears from her eyes.

"Seriously though," Aster said. "My grandpa says people find reasons and ways to oppress other people based on color and language and anything else that makes us different from one another. It's how the rich and powerful stay that way, by dividing people. And there aren't a lot of rich and powerful people on this side of the Wall."

"There aren't a lot of rich and powerful people where I live either," Ofelia said. "Sabal Palms isn't just east and west or Black and white, you know. My neighborhood is mostly people who are immigrants or refugees, like my parents."

"You're right," Aster agreed. "It's not that simple."

"I'm not Black or white," Cat said. "Where do I fit?"

"You're Cuban, right?" Lane asked.

"I'm Cuban American," Cat corrected.

"How is that different?" Lane asked. Ofelia thought she sounded genuinely interested.

"Well," Cat started. "I guess I've never thought about it. That's just what my mom says."

"It's because your mom was born here but her family is from Cuba, right Cat?" Ofelia asked.

"Right. My dad too."

"People from Latin America are everything," Ofelia continued. "I have Black cousins, brown cousins, cousins who are pale-skinned like you."

"Colonialism and slave labor," Aster said, as if it were the most obvious thing in the world. "But people see you for your skin color first regardless of what language you speak. Like, your pale cousins can go to places without thinking twice about how they'll be seen. I bet it's not the same for your Black cousins. Just ask them."

Aster seemed to know about stuff on a deeper level, Ofelia thought. A level that her parents didn't talk about and that her teachers didn't get into.

"Our next small revolution should be doing something about this invisible Wall," Cat declared.

"That's a good idea," Lane said, nodding.

"Except that one would *not* be a small revolution," Aster said. "It's one that has been going on for a long time already."

The girls sat in silence for a few minutes.

"We should get out of here," Ofelia said. She had finished writing down what Aster had said about the Wall and closed her notebook. "I feel like we're intruding on the dead."

"Yeah, let's go," Aster said. She led the group back out the way they came in.

Outside the cemetery grew a mango tree that had dropped some of its fruit onto the sidewalk. Ofelia crouched down and picked up four mangoes that had survived the fall intact, admiring their bright red-and-orange skins. She handed one to each of her friends before they made their way back to the DiSanti house.

CHAPTER 26

"'Vandalism at Local Street Festival,'" Cat's sister Carmen read. "'Floras Seek Eyewitnesses.'"

"Keep reading," Cari urged.

Cat sat at the table with a bowl of cereal, listening to her sisters.

"Look, there's a funny photo of Mrs. McAllister with her hair sticking up," Carmen said, showing everyone. "I wonder if she chased the vandals with her chancla." Cat's older sisters laughed.

"Hey, Cat," Cari said. "You worked the stand, right? Did you see anything suspicious?" She pointed at Cat with her long fingernail where a glittery explosion of red, white, and blue was painted on it as part of her Fourth of July–themed manicure.

"No, I didn't," Cat said, hoping her sisters would drop the subject before their parents appeared.

"Aren't you happy it's your last year working that thing?"

Cari asked. "I hated it every year. Although, I *was* the top brownie seller two seasons in a row."

"Big deal," Clara said. "It was only because you were too much of a wuss to sell them yourself so Mom sold them for you at work."

"Good morning, girls," Mr. Garcia said, walking into the kitchen with Mrs. Garcia behind him.

"Did you hear what happened, Mom?" Carmen asked. "Some kids stickered a bunch of brownie boxes at the Bahamas Day Festival."

Cat slid the paper over to her side of the table to read the story.

"Some people have too much time on their hands," Mrs. Garcia said. "Who would do that?"

"Maybe it was an art project," Cat said, scanning the story for any indication that they had been identified. "Right, Cari?"

"Art project, huh?" Mr. Garcia poured himself a cup of coffee.

"It says the stickers had a message on them," Cari said, reading over Cat's shoulder. "'Return the Feathers.'"

"Oooh, mysterious," Clara said. "I wonder what feathers they're talking about."

"It probably has something to do with that ugly hat," said Cari.

"Return it where?" Carmen asked. "To who?"

Cat lifted her cereal bowl to drink the remaining milk and hide her smile.

"Here, let me see," Clara said, grabbing the newspaper. "It says Mrs. McAllister is trying to sell the stickered boxes as collector's items."

Cat sputtered milk across the table, hitting Carmen's arm with a few drops.

"You're so gross," Cari said, making a face.

"Are you okay?" Carmen wiped her arm with a napkin.

"Yeah," Cat said and let out a cough. "Froot Loop went down the wrong road. Sorry."

"The collector's boxes are being auctioned," Clara continued reading.

"*Auctioned?*" Cat could feel anger rising up.

"I'm glad they were able to make lemonade out of lemons. And I hope they catch whoever did it," Mrs. Garcia said, slicing a banana into her yogurt. "Speaking of Floras, Catarina, what's going on with the Miss Floras contest?"

"There's nothing to tell, Mom," Cat said. "The interview with the committee is the week before the Centennial. That's it."

"Aren't you excited?" her mom asked, shaking Cat by the shoulders. "What I wouldn't do to have the chance to relive that time in my life. So much fun."

"*So much fun,*" Cari said, imitating her mother.

"Oh, Mom." Carmen shook her head.

"Oh, Mom, what?" Mrs. Garcia said. "Don't be mad you three blew your chances."

Clara pretended to fall out of her chair. Cat's sisters laughed. They sounded like a flock of kookaburras.

"Can I take this?" Cat asked, picking up the newspaper.

"Hold on," Cari said. She drew something on the page before handing it to Cat. "Okay, here you go."

Cat took the newspaper. Her sister had drawn horns on the photo of Mrs. McAllister.

"You're such a juvenile," Carmen said.

"We're leaving in thirty minutes, Catarina," Mrs. Garcia said, tapping her watch. "Be ready."

"Have fun, ladies," her dad said before taking his coffee with him out to the garden.

Fun, Cat thought as she placed her bowl and spoon in the dishwasher. *Yeah, right.* The shopping trip had been on the dry erase calendar in the kitchen since the start of the month. *Floras dress*, written in red marker and followed by two exclamation points.

Every day that passed put her closer to the Centennial and forced her to figure out a way to get out of the mess she was in. This would have been the perfect time to put her foot down. Cat imagined the words flying out of her mouth like blackbirds darkening the sky. *I don't want to be a Flora! I'm not nine years old anymore! You couldn't pay me to wear that hat! I'm not sorry I donated that money to the nature preserve!*

Cat walked to her room and stopped at the entrance to the bathroom she shared with her sisters. Carmen was at the sink putting on her makeup. Cat walked in and sat on the edge of the tub, watching with dread as her sister applied eyeliner. Carmen was the oldest and, of her three sisters, always the easiest to talk to.

"Hey, Car," Cat said. "On a scale of one to ten with ten being the most upset, how upset do you think Mom would be if I didn't do the Miss Floras contest?"

Carmen put down the eyeliner and gave her a what-in-the-world-are-you-talking-about look.

"Having second thoughts about doing it?" she asked. "Because if you are, you should say something now. There's not a whole lot of time left before the Centennial."

"I guess," Cat said. "I'm just not really sure I want to be a Flora anymore."

"I totally understand," Carmen said, leaning against the sink. "It gets old. People change."

Cat felt relief telling another family member. If Carmen had her back, maybe she could find the courage to tell her mom.

"Think about it this way, you've almost aged out of the group," Carmen went on. "Why don't you just see it through? You know it'll make Mom happy. This Miss Floras thing means a lot to her. Not that Mom would ever let you get out of it, of course."

"Yeah," Cat said, disappointed. "You're right."

"And who knows," Carmen said. "You might be the Garcia girl who finally wins that tacky hat and makes Mom the happiest woman on earth." She nudged Cat with her foot and grinned.

Cat forced a smile and shrugged. Her dad always took her mom's side, but she didn't expect her sisters to do the same. If she considered what Carmen said even taking a side. She wished Carmen would have offered to talk to their mom for her.

If only she could figure out a way to make her mom happy, make herself happy, *and* convince Mrs. McAllister to get rid of the feathered hat. Why was that so hard to do?

There was no way Mrs. McAllister would ever allow her to participate in the Miss Floras contest now. She hadn't been to a meeting in more than a month. She had lied, and Floras don't lie. There was also the matter of the brownies money. She was, officially, in too deep. Besides, the group was on an anti-hat mission because of her, and it meant too much. They were there for her, and there was no way she'd turn her back on them now.

CHAPTER 27

On the third Saturday of every month, Ofelia's mother went to the salon for a manicure and pedicure and to get her hair color touched up. On the third Saturday of every month, Ofelia's father, who collected and sold stamps, set up a stand at the Sabal Palms flea market. And on the third Saturday of every month, Ofelia was forced to choose the lesser of two evils.

"Can I please stay home alone today?" she'd asked. "I'm just going to be reading."

"How about your first mani?" Mrs. Castillo said, wiggling her fingers.

"No thanks," Ofelia mumbled.

The good thing about the third Saturday of the month was that her dad would get up extra early and come back home with a white bakery box full of pastelitos de guayaba, still hot from the oven, and three cups of café con leche. Ofelia grabbed a pastelito and her coffee and went to her room.

"Meeting today at the . . . flea market?" She sent Cat and Lane a text. Then she dialed Aster's home phone.

"I love the flea market," Aster responded. "Count me in."

One pastelito later, her phone buzzed.

Lane responded in typical Lane style with: **Sure. I have nothing else to do.**

Cat was helping her dad in the garden but said she would ask him to drop her off when they were done.

After breakfast, Ofelia helped her father load his boxes of stamps into the car and dropped her backpack on the floor of the front passenger seat.

"Pa, what is going on with the Qwerty Sholes application?" she asked. "Just tell me the truth."

"Ay, it's too early for this conversation," her father said. "Plus, I need your ma here because if I say the wrong thing, she will kill me."

"Okay, how about this question," Ofelia said. "When are you two going to trust me enough to stay home alone?"

Her father sighed.

"Hey, you want me to tell you a story?" her father said. "It's been a little while."

"Are you changing the subject in the middle of an important conversation?"

"No, no, but remember how much you liked my stories when you were little?" her father asked wistfully. "I miss those days."

When she was younger, her father told her stories that he'd learned back in Cuba when he was a boy. They were stories about the saints. Now that she was older, Ofelia thought it was weird that her dad knew all the stories of the saints even though her family didn't go to church.

Her father had explained that these were stories his own grandmother had told him when he was a boy. He said that when he came to the United States, he had to leave a lot behind on the island, including his abuela, who was too old to make the treacherous journey. But he had his memories and stories.

Whenever Ofelia's parents talked about Cuba, they agreed that it felt like another life, that sometimes it felt like something they'd imagined. Like a dream.

"No thanks, Dad," she said, trying not to hurt her father's feelings. "I'm too old for those stories."

"What? You're never too old for stories," Mr. Castillo said

with a frown. "You're a periodista, right? You should know that. Your bisabuela would be proud that you write. She never learned to read, but she had her stories."

"Speaking of me being a periodista, I need to *see* and *do* things if I'm going to be a real journalist," she said. "Wouldn't my bisabuela want that for me too?"

Ofelia felt a little guilty invoking a great-grandmother she'd never even met, but her parents didn't seem to be budging.

"Before you know it, Ofelia, you will be an adult," Mr. Castillo said. "Take it slow, okay?"

"But the Qwerty Sholes application has a deadline," Ofelia said. "And that deadline is before I'm an adult!"

"Your mom and I have been talking about it, and we aren't opposed to it," her dad said.

"'Aren't opposed to it' doesn't mean you're for it either, Pa."

"Do you know how dangerous it was, *is*, for journalists in Cuba?" Mr. Castillo said. "In a lot of countries in the world. It's still dangerous to write the truth."

"Yes," Ofelia said. Inside she groaned and screamed, NOT ANOTHER STORY ABOUT CUBA! "I know, Pa. Ever heard of freedom of expression and freedom of the press?

I thought you left Cuba to be free, to live in a place where people *can* write the truth."

"We did, we did," her father said. "You're a smart girl, Ofelia."

"So, will you sign the application?" she asked hopefully.

"We need to talk about it a little more, okay?" her dad said. "We know the deadline and how important this is to you."

They pulled into the parking lot of the flea market grounds. Ofelia hitched on her backpack and grabbed a box of stamps while her father unloaded his table and chairs. She helped set up, then opened her notebook. She wrote:

> Parents Leave Oppressive Country,
> Ironically Form Oppressive Household
> By Ofelia Castillo

When Lane and Aster showed up a few hours later, she introduced them to her dad.

"Are you girls here alone?" Mr. Castillo asked.

"No," Aster said. "My grandfather is around here somewhere. He's a junk collector. No offense, Mr. Castillo. Your stamps are nice."

Her dad laughed.

"I'm here alone," Lane said, her arms crossed. "No one cares where I am."

"We care," Ofelia said, elbowing Aster. "Right?"

"I suppose," Aster said with a straight face.

"As do I," Mr. Castillo said. "I want you girls to check in."

"Dad . . ." Ofelia heard her voice rising.

"Send me a message, Ofelia, please," he said. "And stay together."

Ofelia turned away before rolling her eyes at Aster and Lane, but she knew she had to play it carefully now that her dad might be coming around to the application.

"Will do, Mr. C," Lane said.

"I'll be checking my phone," her father said. "Here, for you girls to get something to eat."

He handed Ofelia a twenty-dollar bill.

"Really?" she said. "Thanks, Pa! Come on, I'll take you to the food cart with the best media noche sandwiches."

"Cat's here," Lane said, looking at her phone screen.

The girls found Cat waiting for them next to a stall selling beach hats.

"Smell my hands," Cat said, offering her palms.

"Is this a trick?" Aster asked, leaning in anyway.

"No," Cat said. "I helped my dad plant lavender. It's supposed to attract bees."

"Sounds dangerous," Lane said.

"But smells nice," Ofelia added.

"It's good for the bees," Cat said. "Planting flowers they like provides them with nectar. And bees are important to the environment. *And* I saw a woodpecker! Well, I heard it, the sneaky thing."

"My stomach is growling," Lane said. "Let's eat."

"We should check in with Ofelia's dad first," Aster suggested.

"What are you talking about?" Ofelia asked. "It hasn't even been twenty minutes."

"Just do it," Aster said. "It'll show him that you're listening and being responsible. Isn't that what you want?"

"Well, yeah, but how do you know it'll help?" Ofelia asked.

"Adults aren't that complicated," Aster said.

Ofelia sent her father a text before taking the girls to her favorite food cart. They all ordered the lunch special—a media noche sandwich made of baked ham and roast pork,

Swiss cheese, pickles, and mustard pressed in a sweet, eggy bread, and pineapple sodas—and sat on a patch of grass.

"Did any of you see this?" Cat dug in her backpack and pulled out a newspaper.

The girls gathered around her to read the article about the festival incident.

> Martha McAllister, the director of the Floras of Sabal Palms, said the stickering was a blessing in disguise.
>
> "It's a wonderful illustration of our feathered hat," McAllister said. "And with this one hundredth anniversary, we do intend to follow the message and return the feathers to their original glory. The hat is older than our organization, and it is definitely showing its age."
>
> McAllister stated that the stickered boxes are being sold as collector's items, and the Floras organization intends to use the additional funds to send the hat to a textiles preservationist for, as Mrs. McAllister described, "a cleaning up" and possibly temperature-controlled storage.

"I dare say I'm almost grateful to those hooligans," McAllister continued. "We're auctioning the brownie boxes, and one is up to one hundred dollars, if you can believe that!"

In the meantime, McAllister and on-duty security are looking through video footage and photographs of the festival in an ongoing attempt to identify the vandals."

"They're making money off our sticker?" Lane said. "No way."

"Can you believe it?" Cat said. "It's like the stickering had the complete opposite effect. This is terrible."

"Video footage? Photographs?" Ofelia said. After the car ride to the flea market, she sensed that she had at least her father close to her side. Being found out would ruin any chance of her parents agreeing to let her enter the contest.

"Forget about that," Lane replied. "Even if they find out who did it, what are they going to do? Send us to Alcatraz?"

"Alcatraz isn't an actual prison anymore," Aster said.

"You know what I mean."

"They're probably dusting those boxes for fingerprints

and DNA as we speak," Cat said and took a sip of her soda.

"Come on," Lane said. "We're okay. Does anyone need a crystal to hug?" She pulled a pickle slice from her sandwich and popped it into her mouth.

"Not funny," Ofelia said, though she would not have turned down a crystal if it helped calm her nerves.

"I don't know about you," Aster said. "But I don't like that Mrs. McAllister thinks she got the best of us."

"Agreed," Lane said. "We need to do something else."

Ofelia watched as Cat broke off little pieces of bread from her sandwich and threw them toward a few pigeons that had gathered nearby.

"You think we should let this blow over a little, Cat?" Ofelia asked. She wasn't sure if she was asking out of concern for Cat, who looked worried, or for herself.

"I don't know," Cat said. "I have to think about it."

When the girls finished eating, they threw away their trash and walked around the flea market. Ofelia spied Aster's grandpa looking through used books, but Aster steered the group in the opposite direction.

"Gnome," Cat said, pointing to a stall. "Let's check that out. I want to see if there's something my dad might like for his garden."

The girls followed her and found themselves surrounded by all kinds of plastic lawn ornaments.

"Let me know if you need any help," a woman in a big sun hat called from where she sat.

Ofelia watched as the woman filled a glass globe with layers of rocks and dirt and tiny plants.

"It's a terrarium," the woman explained, as she placed what looked like moss across the bottom.

"That's so cool," Ofelia said. "Like a parfait. Except not food."

"Exactly." The woman laughed.

"Ofelia, come," Cat said, hurrying over and grabbing her elbow. Cat motioned to Lane and Aster and led the girls to an area of discounted items.

"What's the emergency?" Lane asked.

Cat pulled something from a pile of plastic reindeer and snowmen.

"What do you think?" She held out a faded pink plastic flamingo. The three-foot-tall bird sat on top of two wire legs.

"For the tree house?" Aster asked.

"Not exactly," Cat said, a smile creeping across her face. "For the lawn of the Floras House."

The girls stared at the pink flamingo. Ofelia thought it

seemed to stare back at them from the plastic eye on the side of its head.

"Mrs. McAllister thinks she got the best of us," Cat said. "But she won't get the last laugh."

Ofelia was afraid to ask what Cat had in mind. But she knew this wasn't the time to get nervous about their anti-hat agenda. She swallowed, suddenly aware of the overpowering sweetness of the pineapple soda that coated her tongue.

"You're devious," Lane said, throwing an arm around Cat's shoulders.

"You girls like that?" the woman called out to them. "I named him Frankie Flamingo." The woman left her terrarium work and walked over. "No one wants to buy these guys anymore. Can you believe it? I have more of them than I know what to do with."

Ofelia and Lane looked at each other. Lane gave her an odd little smirk and raised her eyebrows. By now, Ofelia knew the grin meant no good.

"How many more?" Lane asked.

"And do you offer a bulk discount?" Cat added.

CHAPTER 28

"Are you sure this is okay, Aster?" Cat asked. The girls sat on the front steps of the little green house waiting for the delivery.

"Don't worry," Aster said. She draped her upper body across the handle of the old shopping cart she'd found in her grandfather's shed. "My grandpa is at the library, and he won't be back anytime soon."

This was the first time she'd had friends over to the house. She crossed her fingers that Hurricane Hendricks wouldn't make an appearance and muck things up. She could hear them in their backyard, their shrieks carrying across the street.

"Can you please stop hitting that thing?" Ofelia said to Lane.

Lane was tapping lightly on the old capstan head attached to the house, just to the left of the front door, with the little wooden mallet that hung next to it. Across the top of the darkened metal was etched the name ISOBEL. Every time Lane hit the round bronze object, Aster noticed Ofelia wince, as if she heard the sound deep in her ear canal and it was going straight to her brain.

"What is this thing anyway?" Lane asked, knocking on it with her knuckles.

"It's from a wrecked ship," Aster said. "Wrecking used to be a way a lot of people earned a living in this area. They'd get rewards for salvaging cargo from shipwrecks. Some of Grandpa's family were wreckers a long time ago."

Lane tapped it one more time, then dropped the mallet, letting the ring vibrate.

Mrs. Thomas from down the street was pushing her elderly mother in her wheelchair. Aster knew Mrs. Thomas liked to take her mom by the water every day. She waved and smiled to the women. When the women waved back, she noticed Lane lift a hand and wave at them too.

"I don't even know who lives in my grandmother's neighborhood," Lane said. "Everyone just stays inside. It's like a ghost town."

Aster watched as a pickup truck came down the street and stopped in front of the house. A baby blue pickup truck

222

full of pink flamingos. Not at all obvious, she thought.

"Anyone order twenty-five flamingos?" the flea market lady yelled out the window and chuckled.

"Yes, ma'am," Lane said eagerly. "That would be us."

The girls had pooled all of the money they had saved between them and negotiated a discounted price for taking twenty flamingos. The woman had even thrown in a few extra birds for free.

Aster pushed the cart up to the truck, and the woman helped the girls arrange the birds in the shopping cart. Those that couldn't fit would have to be carried.

Aster handed her the money and thanked her.

"I read somewhere that there are more plastic flamingos in the world than real live ones," the flea market lady said. "Can you believe that?"

"I can," Cat said.

"All right, well, you girls have fun with these, and if you need more, you know where to find me."

The woman honked her horn and drove off. The girls waited for the truck to turn the corner before starting their journey.

"What are we going to say if someone sees us?" Ofelia asked, hitching on her backpack.

"Why would we have to explain anything?" Lane asked. "Who would find four kids with a bunch of plastic flamingos strange?"

"We won't get caught," Aster said, locking the front door. "We'll take the back way through the nature preserve."

As the only one without a bike, Ofelia was the designated cart pusher. The other girls walked their bikes, carrying flamingos that didn't fit in the shopping cart. Aster lay one across her handlebars since her basket was occupied by the blackberry clafoutis she baked. Cat placed two in her bike basket, their wire legs poking through the bottom on either side of her front tire. Lane carried one under her arm.

"I feel like we're in the woods," Lane said. The group followed Aster along a dirt path lined on either side with ancient trees whose gnarly roots crept over the ground and looked like they could reach up and grab them at any moment.

"Heading straight to the witch's house," Ofelia added.

"These are live oak hammocks," Aster explained. "This land belongs to the state so developers can't come in and destroy it all like they do everything else."

The sun was shining, but in the shadows of the trees it seemed later in the day. The girls walked in silence. Aster felt at ease and content despite the fact that they were smuggling plastic flamingos.

Besides the rattling of the cart and the flamingos bouncing against one another, the only sounds were the crunching of their footsteps and the occasional slapping of hands against arms and legs as they fended off mosquitoes. Every so often a birdsong would ring out high above in the trees, and Cat would try to identify it for them.

They were nearing the DiSanti house when Ofelia stopped and grabbed Lane's arm.

"Did you hear that?" she asked, looking around.

"What? Don't *you* ever fart?" Lane said, shaking off Ofelia's grip.

"I'm not joking," Ofelia insisted. "I heard something."

"Hey, Cat, is there a bird whose song sounds like—" Lane started.

"A growl?" Ofelia finished for her.

Cat laughed nervously.

"Let's just keep going," Aster said. "We're almost there."

But before Aster could continue pushing her bike, a growl rolled out from somewhere among the trees.

"You heard that, right?" Ofelia whispered, her hands gripping the cart. The only answer was the crackling of someone or something walking on fallen leaves, through branches, in their direction.

"It's probably just a squirrel," Cat said.

"That is the biggest squirrel I've ever seen," Lane said, pointing to the dog that hopped out. It hopped, Aster noticed, because it only had three legs.

The brindled dog was medium size and so skinny the outline of its ribs showed on either side of its body. It didn't look like a menacing monster. Until it bared its teeth and let out another growl.

"Poor doggy," Cat said gently. "Good doggy."

"I think we're okay," Lane said. "Do you think it can run?"

Aster gave Lane an incredulous look.

"Bikes," she said quietly, as the dog emerged fully from the wooded area and looked at the group from squinty eyes.

"What about me?" Ofelia, the bikeless, asked in a near panic.

"Get on," Lane said.

Aster mounted her bike and watched as Ofelia moved slowly toward Lane's bicycle and settled on the piece of metal above the back tire, holding on to the seat.

"What about the flamingos?" Cat asked.

The dog let out a ferocious bark. Aster saw the dog bare its canines. It didn't look harmless, and she wasn't waiting to find out if it could run.

"Forget the flamingos," Aster said. "Go!" She pressed down on her right pedal and took off.

The motion of the bikes caused the dog to come out of its lowered stalk and rush the girls. Aster was impressed by how quickly it moved for having only three legs.

Cat screamed as the dog pounced, just barely missing her.

The girls tore through the path as quickly as they could pedal over rocks, avoiding branches.

Lane had fallen behind, slowed down with the extra weight, and Aster took the lead toward the DiSanti property. Aster looked behind her. The dog's ears flapped as it ran after the bikes as quickly as its three legs could go. She felt a little sorry for it, even though it didn't look like it planned on stopping. Aster wondered what would happen once they reached the DiSantis and had to stop their bikes when she heard a crash.

Cat had pulled out one of the two flamingos from her bike basket and thrown it back toward the dog.

"Sorry, pup!" Cat yelled.

The flamingo missed the dog, but it worked as a distraction. The dog stopped running to inspect. When the girls reached the DiSanti gate, Lane skidded to a sudden stop, just barely missing the back tire of Aster's bike. Ofelia jerked forward and toppled off the bicycle.

"My glasses!" Ofelia yelled. "Watch where you step."

Aster climbed off her bike. Her insides quivered like an aspic, but she couldn't help laughing.

Ofelia picked up her glasses and placed them on her face.

"What's so funny about that?" She brushed dirt off her knees and rubbed her sore bottom. "We almost became lunch for that feral dog."

"Come on, that *was* fun," Lane said, opening the gate. They wheeled the bikes into the yard.

"Less fun for me from now on, thank you," Ofelia muttered.

"What now?" Cat asked. "We have three flamingos."

"We'll go back and collect the rest," Aster said, in between fits of laughter. It was nervous, scared-witless, and relieved laughter, but it felt good.

"I'll find something for the dog to eat," Lane said. "In case it's still out there."

After parking their bikes and dropping off their bags,

Lane led the girls back down the road, armed with a leftover chicken breast and a package of bacon they'd snuck from the refrigerator when Mira was out of the kitchen. There was no sign of the dog at the site where they'd abandoned the cart.

"Looks like we have a casualty," Aster said, picking up the flamingo Cat had thrown at the dog. Its head was covered in bite marks.

"Poor guy," Cat said sadly.

"The dog or the flamingo?" Ofelia asked.

"Both," Cat replied.

"I hope Rufus likes low-sodium bacon," Lane said, placing the meat on the ground.

They collected the abandoned flamingos, and Aster pushed the cart to the DiSanti house where they parked it behind a banyan tree just outside the property. As the girls gathered fallen palm fronds to layer over the bright pink birds, Aster couldn't help smiling. She liked the feeling of having friends.

CHAPTER 29

"¿Y qué hacen?" Mrs. Castillo asked.

"Not much," Ofelia said into the phone. "Just playing a card game."

She ran her fingers over the second embroidered badge Lane had given them. Lane had gotten the idea to make the badges from watching her grandmother. Ofelia tried to picture Lane alone in her room at night embroidering. The latest badge was decorated with a rectangle. Inside was a simple line drawing of a hat with feathers to represent the sticker.

"We're going to roast some hot dogs in a little while," she went on.

Ofelia could not tell her mother that they were sitting on the floor of the tree house with the day's newspaper spread open to her printed letter to the editor, eating the now-cold blackberry clafoutis Aster had baked. And she certainly couldn't tell her mother that they were preparing for that night's outing. Just getting permission to stay overnight had been an ordeal. She had begged and made so many promises she was afraid of the day her parents would want to collect on them.

"How are los mosquitos?" her mother asked for the millionth time. "You know you have that sweet blood, como un merengue."

"I sprayed myself," Ofelia said. Her parents were obsessed with mosquitoes and disease. "I'll be fine, Ma."

"Bueno," Mrs. Castillo said. "Your father wants to say hi."

"Oye, no entiendo sleepovers," she heard her mother say in the background as she handed the phone to her father. "Why would anyone want to spend a night sleeping away from home and in a tree?"

"Ofelia," her father said. "Be good and be careful, okay?"

"I know, Pa," Ofelia said. A twinge of guilt shot through her.

"We'll see you tomorrow," he said. "Don't stay up late and come home cranky. Un besito."

"Pa, I can't," Ofelia groaned, glancing at the girls.

"I'll send you one and one from your mom." Her father made two kissing sounds before hanging up.

When Ofelia rejoined the group, they were busy working.

Aster had the idea of attaching information to each plastic flamingo. Cat and Aster were writing facts about bird extinction, the Migratory Bird Treaty Act, and the history of the plume trade on bright-orange sticky notes. Eunice sat in her usual spot, this time facing out the window as if she were the lookout.

Women who opposed killing birds wore bird-friendly hats called Audubonnets.

The Migratory Bird Treaty Act of 1918 (MBTA) protects all species native to the United States and its territories.

The MBTA's list of protected species includes the American flamingo (Phoenicopterus ruber) and the snowy egret (Egretta thula).

Most threats to bird species are due in part to humans.

Under the MBTA, a migratory bird doesn't have to be a bird that migrates, just a bird that is native to the US.

Hatmakers (also known as milliners) had such a big demand for feathers and bird skins that as many as 15 million American birds were killed every year in the last decades of the 19th century.

One in eight bird species are threatened with extinction. That's more than 1,300 species!

About 150 bird species have gone extinct.

"Wow," Ofelia said, after reading from one of the sticky notes. "They killed a lot of birds for a lot of hats."

"Can you imagine entire species disappearing?" Cat asked. "Right now there are about thirty-two threatened or endangered bird species in Florida alone."

"Poor defenseless animals," Aster said, shaking her head.

"Don't worry, Eunice," Lane called over to the bird. "We've got your back."

"Well, technically, Eunice isn't a native bird and peafowl aren't endangered," Cat said. "But we still have her back."

The girls nodded in agreement. The peahen was as much a member of the group as any of them, Ofelia thought.

"Hey, did you realize the bird act is celebrating a centennial too?" Lane asked, from where she worked on a stencil.

"All the more reason to persuade the Floras to stop using the hat," Aster said.

"Here, read this one," Cat said, handing Ofelia a sticky note.

"If I'd known about the Audubonnet when I wrote my letter to the editor, I would have suggested it as an alternative to the hat," Ofelia said. She returned the sticky note to where Aster and Cat were placing them.

Lane had cut a stencil out of a piece of cardboard and was carefully painting white letters onto a black bandanna like the ones the girls wore. Ofelia held down the bandanna as Lane peeled the cardboard stencil away.

"Should we hang it up to dry?" Ofelia asked.

"That's a good idea," Lane said. She handed the bandanna to Ofelia, who placed it on a windowsill.

"I think that's it," Aster said, when the last sticky note was done. "Now we wait?"

"Now we eat," Lane announced, wiping ink on her shorts.

In the kitchen, Mira piled hot dogs, buns, and vegetable kabobs on a tray. Mira caught Lane as she tried to sneak the kabobs back into the refrigerator.

"No vegetables, no sweets," Mira said, returning the kabobs to the tray.

"Yum," Cat said. "Yellow peppers and red onions."

Lane made a face.

"And your grandmother said your father called *again*," Mira continued, a more serious look on her face. "Call your papa, Lane, okay?"

Ofelia looked between the woman and Lane. Lane nodded slightly before picking up a box of graham crackers.

"Someone grab the bag of marshmallows and the chocolate bars," Lane instructed.

"Henry lit the firepit for you," Mira informed the girls. "Go on now, have fun."

"Thank you, Mira," Lane called out as she pushed the screen door open with her foot.

"Hold this," Lane said, handing Ofelia the tray as they walked through the backyard. She pulled pieces of peppers off the kabob sticks and threw them into the bushes. "Animals gotta eat too."

"Hey, so do I," Cat whined. "Save some for me. I don't eat hot dogs."

"Pit's burning," Henry called to them from where he was bent over adjusting sprinklers on the lawn. "You gals look like a pack of crows."

The girls eyed one another, puzzled.

"Because you're all dressed in black," he explained and chuckled.

The girls had agreed it would be a good idea to dress in black for that night's activity.

"Murder," Cat said, out of the blue.

Ofelia and the others turned puzzled looks on Cat.

"Excuse me?" Henry said, alarmed.

"A group of crows," Cat explained. "It's called a murder."

"Okay, then," Henry said, backing away. "Y'all have fun."

"Let's go," Lane said. She pushed Ofelia in the back with the tray of food, urging her to move.

They gathered thin branches and followed Lane to the firepit.

"How long are we supposed to cook these?" Ofelia asked, stabbing a branch through a hot dog.

"Hot dogs are precooked," Aster said. "Not long."

"I'm going to let mine blister like a bad sunburn," Lane said.

The firepit and a few citronella torches had been set up on the edge of the backyard looking out onto the bay where several real flamingos slept. Ofelia held her hot dog over the fire until it was nearly charred, then pulled it away and ate it right off her branch.

"That looks exhausting," Lane said, standing on one leg like the birds. "Time me."

"Did you know that scientists haven't figured out why flamingos sleep standing on one leg?" Cat asked.

"What I want to know," Ofelia said, "is how they don't just fall over."

"They adjust their bodies so that the leg they're standing on isn't off to the side but right under them," Cat said, sandwiching pieces of chocolate and gooey, melted marshmallows between graham crackers. "For better support."

The birds turned their necks and tucked their heads into their bodies while they slept.

"In the Floras handbook, they call s'mores *Some Mores*," Lane said. "Isn't that cute? Can someone please make me a Some More? And when I'm done, I will want some more Some More."

"Sure," Cat said, stabbing two marshmallows with a stick. She put together a s'more and handed it to Lane.

"The Floras handbook also says you should only indulge in *one* Some More because a young girl must watch what she eats," Lane said, in a snooty voice. She finally put her foot back down and sat on a lawn chair. "Just because it's called a 'some more' is not an invitation to gorge on them."

The girls laughed and jostled one another for the bag of marshmallows.

"Anyone have a scary story?" Aster asked.

"The Floras handbook says you should only tell scary stories that are in good fun," Lane said. "Nothing that can give you nightmares."

"That handbook sounds like a drag," Ofelia said. She

licked melted marshmallow from her fingers and remembered her one Floras meeting.

"This place is definitely haunted," Lane whispered. She pointed toward the house with her stick. "I hear things at night when it's just supposed to be me and my grandmother."

"Like what?" Aster asked.

"Creaks and footsteps," Lane said. "Once I heard the water running in the bathroom in the upstairs hallway . . . and no one was there. I think it's the ghost of my grandfather. He died in the house, you know."

"Ghosts aren't real," Aster said matter-of-factly.

"Is that why you have goose bumps?" Lane asked. She poked Aster with a branch. Aster swatted the branch away.

"I have a story," Ofelia said. "I'll tell one of my dad's saint stories."

"Like Joan of Arc?" Cat asked. She smacked her neck and inched closer to one of the torches.

"Yeah, like that," Ofelia said. "Once there was a very wealthy man who had a beautiful daughter."

"This sounds like a fairy tale," Lane interrupted.

"Shush," Aster said. "Let her tell the story."

"The wealthy man wanted to marry her off to some guy who had money and could make him richer. Also, this was before Christianity started to spread in Europe, when people still worshipped different gods," Ofelia said, searching her memory for the details her dad included. "The maiden's father didn't want her getting involved with these new ideas, so he locked her up in a tower."

"Like Rapunzel?" Lane asked, peeling the charred skin off a marshmallow and throwing it on the ground.

"I guess," Ofelia said. She gave Lane a look that meant her interruptions were not welcome.

"This isn't scary at all," Lane complained. "Sounds like history class."

"*Anyway*," Ofelia went on. "The maiden was learning about these new ideas, even locked up in a tower. She believed in the messages of being kind and helping the less fortunate."

"I like that," Cat said. Ofelia could see her smile in the light of the fire.

"Wait, how was she still learning if she was locked away in the tower?" Aster asked.

"Use your imagination," Ofelia said, flustered. "It's a story."

"Maybe Rumpelstiltskin was bringing her books," Lane suggested.

Lane and Aster laughed.

"Okay, I'm done," Ofelia said, crossing her arms and sitting back. "Someone else can tell a story."

"No, finish, please," Cat pleaded. "I want to know how it ends."

"I'm sorry," Aster said. "We won't interrupt again. Right, Lane?"

"Yeah, finish the story," Lane said.

"Okay," Ofelia continued. "When her father brought a suitor to be her husband, she refused to marry him and told him that she was dedicating her life to her new beliefs. This made her father angry. He didn't want to lose face in their village. He told her she had to give up her new ideas or suffer the consequences."

"But she wouldn't, right?" Cat asked.

"No," Ofelia said.

"Now it's about to get good," Lane said, scooting closer to Ofelia. "What happened?"

"First, her father had her tortured," Ofelia said, looking at each girl. "But her wounds were always miraculously healed. So then, he sentenced her to die."

"Wait, back up," Lane said. "Tortured how?"

"Again, use your imagination," Ofelia said.

"What a monster," Cat said sadly.

"The maiden had long, beautiful hair—"

"*Like* Rapunzel," Lane interrupted, as if to confirm her earlier suspicion.

"The father grabbed the maiden by the hair, and—" Ofelia went on, ignoring Lane, "chopped off her head!"

"What?!" Aster yelled. "That's not how Rapunzel ends, right?"

Ofelia picked up the aluminum tray they had carried out their food on.

"And just as he did, her hair went up in flames and a bolt of lightning came down from the sky and struck the father, killing him instantly." Ofelia shook the tray so that it rattled like thunder.

The girls all held their hands to their ears.

"That's the story of Saint Barbara," Ofelia said, putting down the tray. "She's the saint that protects against lightning."

"That was pretty good," Lane said. "Not super scary, but scarier than Rapunzel."

Ofelia rolled her eyes.

"I think the scariest part was her father trying to marry her off," Aster said, holding a marshmallow over the fire.

"Yeah," Lane said. "I don't plan to marry anyone ever. Especially not someone my parents picked out for me. Like they know anything about love or marriage."

Ofelia noticed a look of sadness cross Lane's face before she threw a branch into the firepit.

"What if you fall in love?" Cat asked. "Why wouldn't you want to get married?"

"Because marriage is just a financial arrangement, a contract," Lane said, making a face. "Besides, I'm going to be an artist and travel the world. I can't be attached to anyone."

"What about friends?" Cat asked sullenly.

"What about them?" Lane said.

"Well, if you travel the world, will you still be in touch with your friends?" Cat asked. "Or would you just disappear on them?"

"Friends are different," Lane said, thinking. "That's not a paper contract."

"But we have a paper contract, don't we?" Ofelia asked. "Our oath, right?"

"Yeah, I guess you're right," Lane said. She rubbed her crystal.

"All relationships require some kind of agreement," Aster said. "Written, spoken, unspoken. It's how we survive.

I think romantic love just sets you up for disappointment and heartbreak, but I'm not against marriage."

"But sometimes it's worth taking risks, right?" Ofelia asked, not quite understanding the look that passed between Lane and Aster.

"Well, I may or may not fall in love, and I may or may not ever marry, but I'll always have friends," Cat said. "And birds too. Friend love and bird love forever." She took a bite of her Some More with satisfaction.

The sky had begun to darken, but the flames of the firepit illuminated the faces of the girls. Ofelia could tell from their expressions that they all agreed. Friends and birds were, in fact, good things to love.

CHAPTER 30

Aster could hear Mira cleaning up in the kitchen. She took a deep breath and kept climbing. She had held off going to the bathroom when the other girls went after dinner just so she would have an excuse to come into the house alone. She patted her pockets to make sure the blank recipe cards and her little folding reading light were in them. The question she had as she made her way back to the DiSanti library was how and when did the family get the Winter Sun orange trees? Had the trees in the photo been on the DiSanti property?

She imagined running into Mrs. DiSanti in the dark. Maybe the woman was like the girl in that one story who wears a green ribbon around her neck and when the ribbon is removed her head falls off. None of them had yet seen the woman. It *was* possible. And Lane wouldn't even know, because how could she with the green ribbon holding her grandmother's head in place? Or maybe Lane did know, and that's why she wouldn't introduce them to her grandmother. Aster imagined the old woman's head rolling down the staircase toward her like a bowling ball. She stopped. Her grandpa would think she was being ridiculous and letting her imagination run wild.

From the top of the stairs she could see a light on in the library. She crouched down and peered around the banister to see if there was any movement in the room. A few minutes passed before the lamplight went out and one of the French doors opened. A dim light shone from the sconces that lined the hallway, and she watched as a figure in white seemed to float toward her.

All the muscles in Aster's body tightened as she waited for the ghostly apparition to reach her. She wanted to turn and run, but even in her fear she had to weigh falling down the stairs against coming face-to-face with a ghost. Fortunately, the figure went into a room and closed the door behind it.

It's not a ghost, *you dummy*, she thought to herself. She knew it was Mrs. DiSanti. It had to be. But she sure looked like she was floating. Aster took off her flip-flops, sprinted from her crouching position, and didn't stop until she got to the library at the end of the hall. She slipped inside and closed the door carefully.

The room was pitch-black with the exception of the bit of moonlight that came in through the window. She unfolded and flicked on her reading light and felt her way around the desk, moving toward the shelves that held the family scrapbooks. She pulled the one with TRAVELS—1880 TO 1900 printed on a spine.

She opened the scrapbook full of photos of DiSantis on trips to Europe. Aster stared at a photo of Anthony DiSanti posing with the Eiffel Tower in the background. The structure looked nothing like the pictures she'd seen of it. In the photo, the Eiffel Tower was mostly just a base, still in the process of being built. How cool it must have been to see history before it was history, she thought, as she flipped through the pages. The Eiffel Tower was completed for the World's Fair in 1889, so she knew the photo had been taken before that, when construction had just started.

Her grandpa had told her the written history said that Anthony DiSanti traveled to Italy in 1902 and that was when he supposedly brought back the orange. He had tracked down the earliest newspaper ads for Winter Sun products back to 1910. She had gone too far back.

Aster closed the book and placed it back in its spot, moving on to another shelf lined with a row of thin volumes. These had nothing on the spines. She pulled one out. DIARY was printed on the green clothbound cover. Aster opened it. The name Charlotte DiSanti and the year 1897 were written in a delicate cursive inside. Aster pulled out the next book. It was the same except with the next year written in it.

She heard the screen door to the kitchen slam shut downstairs. She knew she had to move faster. She grabbed the first three diaries and stuck them in the back of the waistband of her shorts, underneath her dad's too-big shirt. Aster kept her light on until she was at the door, then turned it off before slipping out. She hurried down the hall and took the stairs as quickly as her shaky legs allowed.

"Aster?" she heard Lane call.

"I'm coming," she said.

She rushed toward the entrance to the kitchen, almost bumping right into Lane.

"What are you doing?" Lane asked. "What's taking you so long?"

"Sorry," Aster said.

"Purslane?" a voice called from the second floor.

Aster looked up and saw a shadow moving along the

wall, growing as it made its way closer to the top of the staircase.

"It's just me," Lane answered.

"Is everything okay?" the voice asked.

"Yes, Grandmother," Lane said, grabbing Aster's arm.

"Did you call your father today?" the voice asked before they could escape.

"I didn't get a chance," Lane said. "I will tomorrow. Good night, Grandmother!"

"Come on," Lane whispered.

Aster looked back hoping to get a glimpse of the woman, but Lane had already pulled her toward the kitchen.

"She's like a parrot with that question," Lane muttered, heading into the office where Ofelia's mom worked. "'Did you call your father yet?'"

Aster watched as she opened the door of a small switch box in the wall. Lane looked closely trying to find what she needed. Aster pulled out her reading light to help.

"Why won't you call your dad?" Aster asked.

"I'm not speaking to my dad *or* my mom. And this is not the time to talk about them," Lane said, flipping down switches. "We have stuff to do."

"Well, I think you should call them," Aster said. "Even

if you're mad. You never know when . . . when things will change."

"I will, okay?" Lane said. Aster couldn't see Lane's face in the darkness, but she could sense from the way she answered that she was thinking about it.

"Don't let me forget to turn these back on," Lane said, closing the door to the box.

"What are they?" Aster asked.

"Outdoor motion-sensor lights," Lane said. "Let's go."

CHAPTER 31

"The lights have been off for a while," Ofelia said, looking toward the house.

"My grandmother should be in bed by now." Lane got up from the hammock.

Even Eunice was asleep on her window perch, her head and neck lowered into the feathers of her chest.

"Are we ready?" Cat asked.

"Not so fast," Lane said, opening her canvas pouch. "You'll need this."

"Do you have a few teeny-tiny cans of pepper spray in there in case that dog appears again?" Ofelia asked. "Because that's probably the only thing we could use."

"Then you don't want this?" Lane dropped a small crystal into Aster's and Cat's hands.

Ofelia opened her palm. Of course, she wanted the crystal. She still wore the azabache, the little black stone, that was bought for her when she was a baby. It was supposed to ward off el mal de ojo. She wanted all the help she could get.

"It's black tourmaline," Lane said. "For calming fear and for protection."

Lane tied her bandanna over the lower half of her face, then pulled it down around her neck.

Ofelia was excited but also wished the whole thing was over already. This was her big story, and there was no way she was missing out on the opportunity. Still, Ofelia's parents had finally trusted her enough to let her sleep away from home. She couldn't blow it.

She tied the bandanna like Lane had done.

"I've got the bags." Cat held up a few trash bags.

Ofelia double-checked that she had her phone and tested her flashlight.

Lane patted the pocket of her shorts and pulled out a key.

"Have to make sure we aren't locked out," she said, before leading them down the ladder.

"You could use some lights out here," Ofelia said, as the girls crept across the yard. "It's so dark."

Lane stifled a laugh.

"What's so funny?" Ofelia asked.

"There *are* sensor lights out here," Aster said. "But she turned them off."

When they reached the groundskeeper's cottage, Ofelia could see the glow of a television. An announcer's voice was rattling off stats for the player at bat. Ofelia imagined her father was probably still up watching the end of the game. The girls slipped past quietly.

Once outside the gate, they uncovered the cart of flamingos from its hiding place.

Cat distributed the bags, and they worked together, stuffing the flamingos in headfirst before starting toward the Floras House.

"What if the dog is still out there?" Ofelia asked. "Did anyone think to bring something to feed it?"

"I thought you could just sacrifice yourself for the good of the cause," Lane said.

"Very funny," Ofelia said, shifting the bag of flamingos from one hand to the other.

Ofelia imagined the dog coming back for them. What if it bit her? And she couldn't tell her parents because if she did, they would never trust her enough to go to New York. And then she got rabies? And started frothing at the mouth one day at breakfast? Her mom would say, "Ofelia Castillo, *this* is why we don't do sleepovers!"

She imagined the headline:

> Sabal Palms Seventh Grader Succumbs
> to Dog Bite. Special Pulitzer Prize Awarded
> Posthumously.

"Ofelia," Lane said. "Are you listening?"

Ofelia snapped out of her nightmare. "What? Yeah."

"How are we going to do this?" Lane asked. "Should we all just head out onto the Floras lawn together?"

"No," Aster said. "I think one person should go out, make sure the coast is clear, and signal to—"

She didn't have a chance to finish her statement because their discussion was interrupted by the sound of a neigh. Ofelia edited the headline in her head:

> Sabal Palms Seventh Grader Succumbs
> to Nighttime Horse Trampling. Special
> Pulitzer Prize Awarded Posthumously.

"Dogs *and* horses?" Lane asked, looking around as if expecting them to appear.

The high-pitched neighing answered her.

"Not a horse," Cat said, excitedly. "It's an Eastern screech owl." She flicked on her flashlight and pointed it overhead into the trees.

"Turn that thing off," Lane said.

Cat sighed and everything went dark again.

"We have other birds to deal with," Lane reminded her, shaking her trash bag.

"As I was saying," Aster continued. "One person can head out first and be the lookout. Sound okay?"

"Rock-paper-scissors?" Lane asked, holding out a fist.

"Not rock-paper-scissors," Ofelia complained. "I'm terrible at rock-paper-scissors."

"How can anyone be terrible at a game of chance?" Aster laughed.

"Paper beats rock by covering it?" Ofelia asked. "Really? That makes no sense to me."

But the girls rock-paper-scissored until only one was left.

"Guess you were right," Aster said when her rock crushed Ofelia's scissors.

"Great," Ofelia muttered. She handed her bag of flamingos to Aster and lifted her bandanna over her nose to cover the lower half of her face.

"You've got this," Cat reassured her. "You can always just run back."

"Two thumbs-up will be my signal to come out," Ofelia said, adjusting her braid. "Frantically waving my arms and running for cover means stay put."

The girls giggled and patted her on the back as she turned to head toward the house.

Ofelia's heart raced as she walked out from the trail. She had never been out past ten, much less out alone. The streets were quiet except for the chirping of bugs and the occasional car in the distance. The Floras House was silent. All the lights inside were off, but the fixtures at either side of the front door—lightbulbs made to resemble old gas lamps—flickered. She could see moths fluttering in their glow.

A car drove by, and Ofelia dropped to the ground, making herself as flat as possible. When it had passed, she slowly stood up. She brushed off her shorts and gave the thumbs-up. Her heart still raced, but now with excitement. She felt like a spy on a mission.

The three girls came out of the darkness like nocturnal forest creatures and got to work.

Aster and Lane stabbed the metal legs of the flamingos into the lawn while Cat stuck the orange sticky notes onto the birds. Every time a car sounded near, the girls all dropped to the ground.

When all twenty-five birds had been planted in front of the Floras House, the lawn looked overgrown with pink flamingos.

"Someone's going to have to weed tomorrow," Aster said, looking at the birds approvingly.

"Here," Lane said to Ofelia. "You do the honors since you were our brave lookout." She held out the bandanna she had stenciled earlier.

"Pick a bird, any bird," Cat said.

On the black bandanna, Lane had painted a peacock eye and the message: RETURN THE FEATHERS.

Ofelia looked at the birds and picked the one closest to the porch steps. She grinned as she tied the bandanna around its neck, imagining Mrs. McAllister walking up to it and reading the message. She couldn't believe they had done it. And she couldn't wait to get back to her notebook to write about it.

Ofelia dropped onto the bottom porch step in satisfaction. As soon as she did, she found herself in a flood of brightness as lights on the porch turned on.

"Time to go!" Lane yelled, grabbing her hand.

The girls took off running and disappeared back into the dark trail.

CHAPTER 32

Cat was still tired from the late-night excitement as the girls walked to the bakery for cinnamon rolls the next morning. Mira had insisted on making some, but Lane pushed them all out the door before the woman could open the container of flour.

As they neared the Floras House, Cat saw a crowd of people gathered on the sidewalk.

"Holy smokes, there's a news truck," Ofelia said. She stood on her tiptoes trying to get a look at the reporter.

"I hope Mrs. McAllister is there," Lane said. "I want to see the look on her face." She clapped her hands gleefully.

"They sure look pretty in the morning light," Aster said, admiring their work.

Cat thought the flamingos did look especially pretty. Their pink plastic bodies seemed to shine in the sunlight. She watched as the reporter, a man with big sweat stains on the armpits of his nice button-down shirt, headed up the walk. Mrs. McAllister had come out of the house, and the two met halfway. The camerawoman hurried over and turned her equipment on the pair.

"Look at that," Ms. Falco said, walking over to the girls, a ring of keys jingling in her hand. "I wonder if this is part of the Centennial celebration."

"It's not!" Olive ran up, breaking away from her parents, who were among the crowd of people gathered. "We were on our way to breakfast and saw Mrs. McAllister get out of her car and scream. It was really funny."

Ms. Falco tried to give Olive a stern look, but Cat could tell her lips were threatening to break into a smile.

"Cat," Olive said, out of breath with excitement, "Mrs. McAllister called *the police*."

Cat tried not to let her panic show.

"Did they come?" Lane asked. "The cops?"

"They did," Olive said, her eyes getting bigger. "They were here. Mrs. McAllister told them she would review the surveillance camera—"

"There's a surveillance camera?" Ofelia said.

Cat ignored the look Ofelia shot her.

"Didn't you know?" Olive asked.

"Guess not," Aster said.

Cat couldn't remember ever noticing cameras anywhere on the property. But she also never had a reason to. She glanced at her friends guiltily.

A couple of women out for a morning walk stopped in front of the girls.

"Who would do that?" one said, blocking the sun with her hand to get a better look at the lawn.

"I don't think it's a funny prank," the other woman replied. "Not funny at all."

"Well, I think this neighborhood could use a little more color," Mr. Foreman, the mail carrier, said. He pushed his cart up to the group, a detour from his usual delivery route on Orange Blossom Road. He pulled out his earbuds. "I think the birds are a nice touch."

The two women sighed and walked on.

"I agree," Aster said, before Cat poked a finger into her side.

Mrs. McAllister ripped sticky notes off the plastic birds, showing them to the reporter.

"Does anyone know what's on the sticky notes?" Ms. Falco asked. "I'm so curious."

"I do," Olive piped up. "Bird facts, Ms. Falco. And stuff

about how the Miss Floras hat shouldn't be used because birds were *killed* for their feathers. Right, Cat?"

"Who are you?" Lane said, looking at Olive suspiciously. "And why are you here?"

"It's okay," Cat said. "This is Olive. She's a Flora."

Olive grinned at Lane.

"That's another thing this place could use," Mr. Foreman said. "Someone to shake up this old dusty town." He put his earbuds back in and continued on his route.

"Interesting," Ms. Falco said. "Sounds like there's an activist in Sabal Palms."

"Or maybe activists," Olive suggested.

"Yes," Ms. Falco said. "Maybe *activists*."

Cat could feel the woman's look directed at her and her friends. There was no way Ms. Falco knew anything, she thought.

"Well, this is all exciting, but I have to go open the library. Let me know if Mrs. McAllister is giving away those birds, okay? I can use them for a display." The librarian crossed the street to the library.

"Let's get closer so we can hear," Lane said.

"But not too close," Ofelia warned.

"What's with the kid?" Lane whispered to Cat, motioning toward Olive with her head.

"Olive is harmless," Cat whispered back, but then she turned to Olive. "We have to go. See you later, Olive."

"Oh, okay," Olive said. Cat noticed the look of disappointment on the girl's face as she walked back to where her parents and little brother took in the action.

Cat and the girls inched forward and watched the exchange between the head of the Floras and the reporter.

"And what about the messages on the sticky notes, Mrs. McAllister?" the reporter asked. "Do you think this is just a prank or were the Floras targeted?"

"Steve, intentional or unintentional, I see this as an opportunity," Mrs. McAllister said. She waved her arms, orange sticky notes balled up in her fists, motioning to the flamingos around her. "Floras make the best of situations, and that's what I plan to do. The flamingos will continue to stand on the lawn, and I invite local businesses to . . . sponsor a bird!"

"Tell us more," the reporter said, holding the microphone in front of the woman.

"As you know, we're raising funds to have our Miss

Floras hat restored by professional preservationists," Mrs. McAllister said. "It isn't cheap to take good care of this important part of our history. Right now, we keep it on display in the house for all visitors to enjoy, but we'd like to eventually have the hat stored in a temperature-controlled space where it won't continue to deteriorate. That costs money, of course."

The reporter pushed the microphone a little closer to Mrs. McAllister, encouraging her to continue.

"So, in addition to our brownie box auction—which is still happening, by the way—I would like to invite local businesses to get in touch about sponsoring a bird with an ad. We'll leave them up through the end of the Centennial celebration. It's a wonderful opportunity for us *and* for local businesses looking to get the word out about their services, don't you think?"

"You heard that, Sabal Palms," the reporter said, turning to the camera. "Get your business ad on a bird right here on the Floras lawn and help this great organization take care of a piece of their history."

Cat watched as Mrs. McAllister beamed a big coral pink smile at the camera. They had been foiled once again.

CHAPTER 33

"Grandpa," Aster called. "I made cookies."

"*My* cookies?" Grandpa asked. Aster could hear him get up from his chair.

"I thought there was no 'my' in this house," Aster said, sliding a spatula under a still-warm cookie and placing it on a plate just as her grandfather appeared in the doorway.

"Except for these cookies," her grandfather replied.

"Grandpa," Aster said. "Tell me about back in the day when you were an activist."

"What do you mean when I *was* an activist," her grandpa said, sitting down. "Being an activist isn't like moving from one job to another or changing shirts. It's something you always are."

"I meant, when you were out doing stuff," Aster clarified, pouring two glasses of milk and setting one in front of her grandfather.

"I'm still doing stuff," her grandpa said. "What do you think this book I'm writing is about?"

"I know, Grandpa. I mean—"

"You mean when I was out there getting dirty," her grandpa said.

"Yeah," Aster said, chewing on a cookie. "When do you know it's time to give up? How do you know what you're supposed to do next?"

"When it's time to escalate, huh?" her grandfather asked.

"Right," Aster said. "Especially if people aren't listening and things aren't changing?"

"Well," her grandfather said. "Knowing when to stop depends on how much you've done, how much you care, and how much you're willing to risk."

"But what if that means getting in trouble?" Aster asked, dipping her cookie into her glass of milk.

"Then you have to figure out how much something means to you," her grandfather said, grabbing another cookie, "and what getting in trouble means for you."

"Were you ever scared?" she asked. "To do something you knew could get you in trouble even if it was for something that mattered to you?"

"No one ever said activism isn't scary," her grandpa said. "Most things that matter carry some risk."

"Like Dad's work?" Aster asked.

"Sure," her grandpa said sadly. "He and I may have had a difference of opinion about his being in the military. He knew it was risky, but it was important to him. Same as your mom."

Aster picked up a potato chip crumb with the pad of her thumb and ate it.

"Now, as far as activism goes, usually by the time you get to the point where you're doing something that could, as you say, 'get you in trouble,' it should mean you've tried other things," her grandpa said. "You've made other attempts to be heard, right? You don't just go from zero to a hundred."

Aster thought about the stickers, the letter to the editor, and the flamingos. She thought about Cat and the whole group feeling unheard. She nodded.

"What's the most trouble you've gotten in, Grandpa?" Aster asked.

"We have had to demand and struggle for everything we have," her grandfather said, looking her in the eye. "My becoming the first Black professor at Sabal Palms University was something people had to fight for, even die for. It hasn't just always been."

"You're not answering my question," Aster said, sliding another cookie onto her grandfather's plate.

"Well, you know I was arrested when I was a student at Sabal Palms University," he said.

"You never told me that," Aster said.

"Of course, I did. Or were you not paying attention when we did our unit on civil disobedience?" her grandfather asked. "Might have to go back and change that grade."

"Tell me what happened," Aster said.

"A group of us had a sit-in in front of the president's office. This was when I was a student. They had finally, grudgingly, integrated the school, but it was just integration on paper because, for the most part, things were business as usual. The president of the school wasn't doing much to make sure anything changed. We had demands, and he wasn't listening. So, we had to force him to listen."

"And you were arrested," Aster said, thoughtfully. "What happened? Did he listen?"

"Well, it got a lot of media attention," her grandfather said. "It was on the national news. One kid in our group kidnapped the university's prized mascot and held it hostage. Thought that might get the president's attention."

"The panther?!" Aster yelled. "Someone kidnapped the *panther*?"

"It was a wild time," her grandfather said, laughing. "But between the sit-in and the panther and all the media, they started to listen."

"And things got better?" Aster asked.

"One of the most challenging things about being an activist and really caring about things and wanting to see them change," her grandfather started, "is accepting that change rarely comes as quickly as we'd like and as quickly as it should. But that doesn't mean we give up the fight. Sometimes the fight changes, takes a different appearance, but we keep at it."

Aster bit into her cookie and waited for her grandfather to continue.

"That said"—her grandfather looked at her seriously—"you also have to understand that the consequences for everyone in a group aren't always the same. Or fair. Taking a stand is riskier for some."

"What do you mean?" Aster asked.

"Well, for example," he said, "in our group, there were white kids and Black kids. All protesting the same thing. But

269

if you have money and other privileges, like being white is a privilege, it's easier to get out of trouble than if you're poor and not white."

Aster thought about her own group of friends and how the consequences might be different for each of them. She knew she didn't have the money or the influence of a DiSanti. All she had on her side was what was right and true.

"So, you think it's important to fight for what you believe in even if it means getting in trouble," Aster said, looking her grandpa in the eye.

"Sometimes it just can't be helped," her grandfather said. "Sometimes the desire for change is bigger than anything else. It has to be."

Aster nodded.

"You doing okay?" her grandfather asked, peering over his glasses. "Anything you want to tell me?"

Aster appreciated her grandfather asking. Still, she wasn't ready to say anything about the group's activities. That might lead to talking about Lane and the DiSanti house, and she wasn't ready for that yet either.

"Yeah, Grandpa," Aster said. "I'm doing great."

She took one more cookie and went to her room to continue her nightly readings of Charlotte DiSanti's diary.

CHAPTER 34

"Steal the hat?" Cat squeaked. "But that's breaking the law."

"It's civil disobedience," Aster said. "We won't harm it, we'll just hold it hostage until Mrs. McAllister is ready to listen."

The girls sat in the tree house listening to Aster's idea.

"Do you really think she'll listen to us when we steal her precious feathered hat?" Ofelia asked. "Or do you think she'll—oh, I don't know—be enraged and send us to prison forever!"

"Mrs. McAllister is never going to listen," Lane said. "In fact, she's *benefiting* from all the things we've tried."

"We have to make her listen," Aster said.

Cat knew they were right. Mrs. McAllister was completely closed to the idea of losing the hat. She watched as Aster pulled a page from the newspaper out of her bag and began reading.

To the editor,

As the head of the Floras and as a lifelong citizen of Sabal Palms, it is my duty to respond to the very misinformed letter to the editor from one A. Castle.

"She wrote a letter to the editor?" Ofelia asked, jumping up to see the newspaper. "I cannot believe that woman."

Aster and Ofelia took turns reading from Mrs. McAllister's letter aloud.

I ask A. Castle and all of Sabal Palms who care about our history this question: where does one draw the line?

If we do away with our feathered hat today, what will we be expected to do away with tomorrow?

The letter mentioned tradition, leaving the past in the past, people being products of their time, and what Floras represent today.

"A product of their time?" Cat asked. "What does that even mean?"

"It means that people did awful things in the past

because they didn't know any better," Aster said. "Because it's just what people did in those days."

"Well, that's not an excuse for still using the hat today when we *do* know better," Cat said. "Unless they really don't care."

"Right," Ofelia agreed.

"You know what this is like?" Lane said. "It's like the story of Rapunzel."

"Rapunzel?" Cat asked.

"Yeah," Lane said. "How she wouldn't give up her beliefs no matter the consequences and her dad had her beheaded and then he got struck by lightning."

"That's Saint Barbara," Ofelia said, shaking her head.

"As I was saying, it's like the story of Saint Barbara," Lane said. "Have *we* drawn the line? Are *we* done?"

"Stealing the hat, though?" Cat said, still feeling unsure.

"Well, I'm in," Lane said, from where she sat in the hammock finishing the new badges she was making.

"Of course, you're in," Ofelia said. "You have nothing to lose. My parents will never sign the contest application or let me do anything else ever if we get caught."

The girls looked at one another.

"Ofelia's right," Aster said. "This is next level. And we should think about what could happen if we're caught. Will some of us be in more trouble than others?"

"What do you mean?" Lane asked.

"You, Cat, even Ofelia," Aster said. "All three of you have some kind of privilege. Family connections. I don't."

Cat could see that Lane had stopped embroidering to think about what Aster had said.

"I still think we should do it," Aster said. "But I just want everyone to know that the stakes aren't always equal. And that some of us have more to lose than others."

"We're in this *together*," Lane said. "I promise."

Cat watched as a look passed between Lane and Aster. She knew Lane meant what she said. But she also somewhat understood what Aster was telling them too. What did she herself have to lose? What kind of trouble would she get in?

"Aren't you afraid of getting caught?" Cat asked Aster. She knew Ofelia was out for a story, and Lane was up for anything exciting. Aster always considered every angle, and even though she had been the one to propose the risky idea, Cat thought Aster might reconsider it.

"My grandpa says an activist knows when it's time to

escalate things," Aster said, thoughtfully. "Do you have other suggestions that you think would get Mrs. McAllister's attention, something she can't turn in her favor?"

The girls sat in silence. Cat looked at her friends, each one in her own thoughts.

"Look, I'll steal the thing," Lane announced. "My parents won't care. They're busy living their own lives. I'll say I did it all by myself. No one has to get in trouble but me."

"No way is anyone doing anything alone," Cat said. "We're a troop, an ostentation."

"We do this together," Aster agreed. "Or not at all."

Cat watched Eunice jump down from the window into the tree house. The bird walked cautiously toward the open packet of sunflower seeds Lane brought to share.

"How would we steal it?" Ofelia asked. "We can't just walk in and take it."

"Why not?" Lane said. "Henry does work for the Floras so he has keys to the house."

"And the hat is in the display case in the meeting room," Cat said, before she could stop herself.

"Which is just kind of dumb," Lane continued. "I mean, I don't know how much it's worth, but you'd think they would keep it somewhere that's not just out there in the open."

"It probably has an alarm on it," Ofelia said. "A trap. Like the sensor lights on the porch."

"Maybe," Aster said. "But we won't know unless we try."

"Should we vote?" Lane asked, looking at the group. "All in favor?"

Lane and Aster raised their hands.

"Think of the story," Aster said to Ofelia.

"Yeah," Lane added, "this is your chance to be like that lady you told us about."

"Nellie Bly?" Ofelia asked. "Ida Tarbell?"

"Yeah," Lane said. "That one. Sticking it to the Man."

Aster rolled her eyes.

"You realize *you are* the Man, right?" she said.

"No, I'm not," Lane argued.

"Okay," Ofelia said and raised her hand. "I'm in."

"Cat?" Aster asked. "This is *our* cause now, but it was originally your cause, so if you don't want to do it, we won't. I think we should all be in, as long as we're aware of the consequences."

Cat thought for a moment. The consequences she'd face couldn't be any worse than the ones that awaited her once her mother found out she'd stopped going to the Floras meetings. She looked at her friends' serious faces and sighed.

"I'm in," she said.

There was no fanfare after the decision had been made. The girls climbed down from the tree house and walked to the DiSanti kitchen. Cat noticed each girl seemed distracted. She wondered whether they were having second thoughts.

In the kitchen, Mira fixed them a snack of sandwiches and grapes that they carried back to the tree house, where they ate in almost complete silence until, from below, Cat heard Mira calling to them. She stood and looked out a window.

"Someone left a shirt in the upstairs bathroom," she yelled, holding up a plaid men's button-down shirt.

"It's your dad's shirt, Aster," Lane said, joining Cat. "You don't want to leave that behind."

"Your dad's?" Cat asked.

"Why do you wear your dad's shirts?" Ofelia said, chewing on a grape.

"To remember him by," Lane said.

"Your dad is dead?" Cat and Ofelia said in unison.

"Why didn't you tell us?" Cat asked. She had wondered about Aster's oversize men's shirts that were like the ones her own dad wore. And she wondered why, if they were a group of friends, Aster didn't feel like she could tell them about her father.

"I'm sorry, Aster," Lane said nervously. "I figured you'd told them, too."

"Is that why you live with your grandfather?" Ofelia asked. "Is your mom . . . ?"

"Her mom is in Japan," Lane said, glancing at Aster. "Now, stop being nosy."

"Could all of you just be quiet and stop talking about my dad?" Aster asked, flustered.

"Sorry," Cat said quietly.

She watched as the girl made her way down the ladder to retrieve her shirt, a look of anger and betrayal on her face.

CHAPTER 35

"Oye, there's a storm coming," Mr. Castillo said, motioning toward the television. The screen behind the meteorologist looked like it had been hit with multiple paint guns. Purples and reds swirled and moved across the ocean toward Florida.

"This is Sabal Palms," Ofelia said, settling in on the couch next to her father. Outside, the sun shone like no storm was any match for it. "There's always a storm coming."

"Those hurricanes toss these poor little islands around like they're just pebbles in the way." Mr. Castillo shook his head as the meteorologist talked about Hurricane Cara, churning in the Caribbean.

Ofelia's dad said that next to coming from Cuba, Hurricane Andrew was the scariest thing he'd ever been through. Her mom said she hoped to never see something like it again. She said Hurricane Andrew was so strong the sign from La Vaquita ended up in the middle of their street. La Vaquita was a convenience store. It was really called Farm Stores but everyone called it La Vaquita because their logo was a black-and-white cow. Ofelia imagined looking out her window to see a big metal cow on her street.

"No problem, Mrs. DiSanti," Ofelia heard her mother say. "Thank you, yes, I can work from home."

"Work from home?" Ofelia asked her mother when she'd ended her call.

"Mrs. DiSanti said no sleepover tonight," Mrs. Castillo said. "I'm sorry."

"What?!" Ofelia cried, jumping up from the couch. "That's not fair."

"And what is so unfair about it?" Mrs. Castillo asked. "Look at the news, niña."

What was unfair, Ofelia thought, was that it was going to ruin everything. They were supposed to slip out of the tree house once Mrs. DiSanti had gone to bed, just like the night of the flamingos. But this time they were taking the feathered hat.

"The weather lady just said the heaviest rain isn't supposed to start until late tonight or tomorrow morning," Ofelia said. "I don't understand why we can't have a sleepover."

"I don't think you want to argue about this," Mrs. Castillo warned.

Ofelia sank back into the couch. She could hear in her mother's tone that she was pushing her luck. She looked at the three statues that sat on the bookshelf next to the television. Saint Barbara, la Caridad del Cobre, and the beautiful wood-carved Lady of Regla looked back at her with their sad, serene faces.

"Vieja," her dad called to her mom. "Do you want to give her the you-know-what? Maybe it will put her in a better mood."

"What's the you-know-what?" Ofelia asked, looking from her dad to her mom.

"No se," her mom said. "Se está portando como una baby about this canceled sleepover."

"No, I'm not," Ofelia said, even though she knew she *was* pouting. "Tell me what the you-know-what is."

Her mom picked up a manila folder from the coffee table and held it out to her. Ofelia opened it. Inside was the Qwerty Sholes application with her parents' signatures.

"Really?" she screamed.

Her dad winced and placed a hand over his ear.

"I'm not going to say that I feel one hundred percent okay

with you being away from home for that long," her mom said. "But you've been helping me at the DiSanti house this summer, and you have shown us that you can be responsible when you're out with the girls."

"Ma looked up the contest and was impressed," her dad finished. "And you know impressing your mother is hard to do."

"Thank you, thank you!" Ofelia hugged her mom, careful not to wrinkle the application, then hugged her dad.

"Bueno," her mom said, picking up her laptop and glancing at the television. The meteorologist was talking about hurricane winds now. "Storm or not, I better get to work."

Ofelia carried the folder with her application to her room. She opened the folder and closed it. Then opened it again to make sure the application was actually there, with her parents' signatures. It was. She set it on her desk with the envelope she had already addressed to mail her application packet.

Her phone buzzed with a text from Lane.

Meet at library at 10:30.

Ofelia placed her phone facedown. It buzzed again.

p.m.

Another message came through.

Unless there's a hurricane, of course.

Lane couldn't be serious, Ofelia thought.

She opened the manila folder one more time. It suddenly felt like a ticking bomb. Sneaking out meant possibly getting caught. Getting caught meant disappointing her parents, and it definitely meant no application. But not stealing the hat meant her whole story about the girls' fight wouldn't have an ending. *The* ending. Not having a good ending meant no story. No story meant no application and no chance at winning a spot anyway.

Ofelia picked up her phone and looked at the screen.

Are you in?

She imagined the three faces of the saints in the living room. Our Lady of Regla and La Caridad saying, sadly, *accept your fate. Be a good niña.* And then Saint Barbara in her red cape, lifting her sword into the air valiantly, not going down without a fight.

Ofelia groaned. She typed a response and hit the send button.

CHAPTER 36

Ofelia tucked her glasses into the front pocket of her over-alls and slipped the black trash bag over her head.

"So stylish," Lane joked, twirling in her own garbage bag poncho.

The rain had started to come down.

"Could someone remind me why we had to do this tonight?" Ofelia said. Her hair whipped around in the wind as she struggled to collect it and roll it into a bun.

"Because we're out of time," Lane said. "The Miss Floras contest is next weekend."

"Do you really think we're going to be able to do this?" Cat asked.

"Are you sure *chicken* isn't your favorite bird?" Lane said. "Because you're both acting chickeny."

"Chickeny isn't a word," Aster said, shaking out her poncho.

"I'm not scared," Cat insisted. "I'm worried. There's a difference. I think."

"I cannot believe we're even here," Ofelia said. "How did you manage to get out of your houses?"

"My grandpa goes to bed early and he sleeps *hard*," Aster said. "He can't hear anything over his own snoring."

"I was at Lane's," Cat said. "My dad dropped me off earlier because no one sent him the memo that the sleepover was canceled."

"And by 'no one' she means herself," Lane said, pointing her thumb at Cat.

The streets were empty of cars. The leaves on the Bailey palms made an eerie *rattle-rattle-rattle* like fold-out fans swaying in the wind. To Ofelia, it felt like they were the last people left in Sabal Palms, reminding her that she wasn't safe in her bed at home. She blamed her sudden boost of courage on Saint Barbara. It was just after ten thirty, and the four girls stood outside the library, under the covered porch, watching the Floras House through a curtain of rain.

"Did you bring the map?" Aster asked Cat.

Cat pulled out the map she had drawn of the inside of the Floras House, and Aster flashed her light on it.

"Obviously, we can't go through the front, but if we try

around back we'll be in the kitchen," Cat pointed. "We just need to head down this hallway and then to the right, and it's the last room."

"Are we ready?" Aster asked.

"I can't believe you are doing this for me," Cat said, stuffing the map back in her pocket.

"It's our mission," Lane said. "It's not just about you. We care about what's right, too."

"Ofelia," Aster said, looking at her seriously. "Are you ready to give up the possibility of going to New York?"

"I'm here, aren't I?" Ofelia said, not especially caring for the reminder of her potential consequences.

The girls looked at one another. Cat made a shadow bird with her hands. Aster intertwined her own fingers and did the same, followed by Lane. A nonverbal all for one and one for all, Ofelia thought, making her own shadow bird.

The girls followed Cat and made their way across the street and onto the Floras' lawn. The ground beneath them had turned into a mud pit. Ofelia felt her flip-flops squish and sink into the ground. When she tried to pull her right foot out, her flip-flop pulled back, causing her to fall forward.

"Are you okay?" Aster asked, holding out her hand.

Ofelia grabbed it, pushing herself off the ground. Her pants were soaked. She wiped specks of mud off her face with the back of her hand.

She searched under her poncho, and felt for her glasses in the front of her overalls. She breathed a sigh of relief when she found that they were still in one piece.

"Come on," Lane urged.

Ofelia played tug-of-war with the mud and yanked her flip-flop back. She followed the group until they finally made it around to the back door. Lane turned the knob to check if the door was unlocked.

"Did you get the keys?" Aster said.

Lane pulled a large key chain from under her poncho and shook it.

Ofelia turned her flashlight onto the keys as Lane tried one after another, looking for the one that fit the door's keyhole.

"Aha," Lane said, when one finally turned.

She looked up at the girls and grinned. Ofelia couldn't believe it had been that simple. They slipped into the kitchen. It was a relief to be out of the rain. She put her glasses back on.

"Where now?" Aster asked.

Cat turned on her flashlight and led the group to the Floras' meeting room.

"There it is," Cat said, shining her light on the display case.

Lane rushed over. She grabbed the knob on the glass door and pulled.

"It's locked," she said.

"Maybe there's a key on that key chain?" Aster said.

Lane tried the smaller ones that might have fit in the lock of the display case door. The seconds felt like hours to Ofelia as the girls waited, their ponchos dripping onto the wooden floor.

"Still think this was a good plan?" Cat asked, exasperated.

"Shush," Lane said. She flipped through the keys angrily. "Anyone have a bobby pin?"

"Let's relax," Aster said, pulling a bobby pin out of her hair and handing it to Lane. "No sense getting agitated with one another. If we can't unlock it, we leave."

"That's it?" Ofelia had to keep herself from shouting. "Do you know how hard it was to sneak out of my house? Chucho started crowing like a maniac and set off half the dogs in the neighborhood. My parents might be looking for me right now."

"We aren't leaving without that hat," Lane said, wiggling the bobby pin in the keyhole. "If I have to break the glass, I will."

Aster and Cat looked at each other nervously while Lane tried the handle of the case again.

"At least there's no alarm on it," Cat whispered.

Ofelia took off her poncho and sat down on the couch. The folding chairs from the Floras' meeting were stacked against a wall. A pile of Floras history books sat neatly on top of the coffee table in front of her. Next to the books was the little glass figurine of a palm. She remembered that Mrs. McAllister had sat down on the couch while the Floras worked on their Bahamas Day signs. After she had placed the hat back in the cabinet, the woman had made a point of picking up the little palm figurine, brushing around it as if she were wiping off the table.

"Wait," Ofelia said. Lane growled in annoyance.

Ofelia lifted the palm. The glass fronds wobbled. She pulled them off. The palm was a container. She tilted the palm's trunk. A little silver key dropped into her hand. Ofelia held it in front of her with both hands like a sword, and did her best lightsaber hum as she walked it over to Lane.

"Is that what I think it is?" Cat asked.

Lane slipped the key into the keyhole, seemingly sucking all the air out of the room as the girls waited. The lock clicked open.

"Music to my ears," Lane said.

"Holy bird droppings," Cat said. "How did you know?"

"Just my keen observation skills," Ofelia said proudly.

Lane lifted the gold hatbox off the shelf and handed it to Cat.

"I have room for it in my backpack," Aster offered.

She kneeled and opened her bag, removing the wooden recipe box and placing it on the floor next to her.

"That's cool," Lane said, bending down to pick up the box. "What is it?"

"Leave it alone," Aster said. "It's just my recipes."

"Well, I hope you have a cake recipe in here," Lane said, opening it. "Because we're going to have to celebrate."

"Hey, I said leave it alone," Aster said, more forcefully this time. She attempted to grab the box but instead knocked it out of Lane's hand and sent its contents scattering everywhere.

Ofelia realized that as much as they had talked about getting caught and possible consequences, she hadn't considered that they might be the ones to trip up their own plan.

"We have to get out of here," Ofelia urged. She crouched to help Aster pick up the cards.

"I've got it," Aster said, scooping up what she could into her backpack.

Lane plucked a card from the floor.

From the look on Aster's face, Ofelia could tell—whatever it was—it wasn't something Aster wanted anyone to see.

"DiSanti's Sole dell'inverno." Lane read the back. It was a photograph.

"That's not a cake recipe," Cat said, shaking her head slowly as she placed the hat box inside Aster's bag.

"Where did you get this?" Lane asked Aster. "It looks like one of my grandmother's old photos."

"Can I see?" Ofelia asked, curious now.

Aster looked from Lane to Ofelia.

"We have the hat," Cat said. "Remember? The hat? Let's go."

But Lane wasn't budging.

"Is this from my grandmother's scrapbooks?" she asked, holding up the photo.

"We should go," Aster said. "I'll tell you about it when we're out of here."

"What else is in there?" Lane asked, snatching Aster's backpack from Cat.

Aster grabbed at the bag.

Ofelia and Cat watched as the other two pulled the bag in either direction until it opened, sending items flying. The hat tumbled out of its gold box. Lane and Aster raced to pick up a thin book that had fallen out. Aster got to it first.

"Let's go," Cat pleaded. "We can deal with whatever this is somewhere else."

Lane stared at Aster. She lunged and yanked the book out of her hand.

"Charlotte DiSanti's diary?" Lane asked, reading the inside cover. "Why do you have this stuff?"

The girls waited for Aster to say something, but she stood in silence, avoiding their stares.

"Are you spying on my grandmother?" Lane asked.

Suddenly, Ofelia felt betrayed as well.

"You were spying and didn't tell me?" Ofelia asked, turning to Aster. "And you knew I was looking for something juicy to write about!"

"I wasn't spying," Aster insisted. "Can we please leave?"

"Is it because I told Cat and Ofelia about your parents?" Lane asked. "Were you looking for dirt on my family?"

"What?" Aster said. "No!"

"I don't believe you," Lane said.

For a few seconds, they stood in silence. Ofelia felt like they were all waiting for someone to make a move, to say something. Suddenly, Lane turned and ran out of the room clutching the photograph in one hand and the diary in the other.

"Come back!" Aster yelled, taking off after her.

"Where the heck are they going?" Cat said, following Ofelia who had picked up Aster's backpack and the hat and hurried after the other girls.

Ofelia chased Lane and Aster through the backyard. Lane had stopped at the edge where the rusted chain separated the Floras yard from the bay. There was nothing but darkness beyond the property. The rain was now coming down harder. Ofelia's mom told her that her grandmother back in Cuba would spank her with a wooden spoon when she misbehaved. Ofelia imagined the harsh pelting of rain felt something like that.

The girls inched closer to Lane.

"You took this from my grandmother's house?" Lane yelled, waving the diary.

"Yes!" Aster responded. "I took it, okay?"

"Why?" Lane asked, backing closer to the edge.

A crack of lightning and thunder rumbled overhead. Ofelia had a bad feeling in her gut.

"You're going to fall," Aster called to Lane.

"Why are you snooping on my family?" Lane asked.

Ofelia took off her glasses and put them in her pocket to keep them from getting wet. She moved closer to hear what was happening. She was now standing next to Aster, just a few feet from Lane.

"For my grandfather," Aster said. "He's writing a book."

"Your grandfather put you up to it?"

"No," Aster said. "He doesn't know anything about it."

"So, you did it all on your own?" Lane asked. "You used me to get into my grandmother's house?"

"I didn't!" Aster yelled. "Honest!"

Ofelia could make out that Lane was shaking her head from side to side.

"We have to get out of here before someone sees us!" Cat yelled. She started to pull Ofelia away.

Neither Lane nor Aster seemed like they had any intention of budging. Ofelia knew they couldn't leave Aster and Lane behind.

"Okay, maybe at the beginning I did just want to get into your grandmother's house, but then I wanted to do both," Aster said. "I wanted to help my grandpa with his research.

But I kept coming back because I liked all of you and because I care about what we're doing."

"Then you won't mind if I get rid of these," Lane said.

Ofelia watched as Lane turned her back to Aster and faced the bay. In one quick movement, she flung the photograph and the diary into the darkness. Lane had been standing close enough to the edge that the force of her throw caused her to lose her footing. Her arms flailed in the air cartoon-like, Ofelia thought, as if she were trying to grab the rain or the wind to stop herself from falling. Lane fell over the rusted chain and tumbled off the edge, disappearing.

"Lane!" Aster yelled. She stepped over the chain and looked down to where Lane had fallen.

Ofelia's insides shook as she and Cat joined Aster.

"How far is it?" she asked.

"The drop is about six feet," Cat said. "But there are a bunch of mangrove roots, so probably not that far."

The drop seemed steeper to Ofelia, the darkness a black hole to nowhere.

"What do we do?" Ofelia asked.

Aster turned on her flashlight, waving it below. Ofelia put her glasses back on. She was going to have to ask for contacts. She could now see that Lane had landed on the mangrove roots. She thought she heard a muffled cry.

"I'm going to call my mom," Cat said, moving away from the edge. Ofelia noticed the scared look in Cat's eyes.

"Are you sure?" she said.

"She needs help." Cat nodded.

Ofelia looked to see if there was any sign of movement from Lane.

"Lane!" Aster yelled, but her voice seemed to be carried away by the wind. If the girl heard, she didn't respond.

Ofelia fought the urge to jump in after Lane. She knew that her swimming skills were embarrassing. Ofelia imagined herself being washed out into the bay, away to the ocean, along with the photo and the diary that were now long gone.

In that moment, Ofelia thought of everything her parents tried to protect her from. There were real dangers like being aware of oncoming traffic when crossing the street and, of course, watching out for alligators on the loose. But there were also harmless things like other people, adventures waiting to be had, life. She thought of journalists who reported on dangerous stories from dangerous places. If they could do that, she could help her friend.

There were words her parents used when they were mad or frustrated. Words that she knew she wasn't supposed to repeat, but as she made her decision to act, they all came tumbling out of her mouth, in Spanish and in English. She felt inside her pocket for the crystal Lane had given her that night. It was a piece of carnelian to protect from harm. She rubbed it the same way she'd seen Lane do so many times with the crystal she wore around her neck. Then she began the descent.

"What are you doing?" Aster yelled.

"I'm going down there," Ofelia said. "Shine the flashlight, okay?"

"Why?" Aster said, grabbing her arm. "It's not like you can help her."

"I know," Ofelia said. "But I want to make sure she knows we're getting help."

"Can you even see through those wet glasses?" Aster asked.

Ofelia could see all right, just not clearly. She walked onto the old pier and lowered herself over the side, hanging on to the edge until she could find her footing. She didn't need Ms. Lugo, her PE teacher, to tell her that her upper body strength was not in peak twelve-year-old condition.

She took a deep breath, stretching her bare foot to touch the nearest root. Her soaking-wet clothes made her feel like she was carrying someone on her back. For once, she wished she'd participated in PE more often.

When her feet touched a surface, she wobbled for balance before turning and crouching. She crawled across the mangrove roots, clutching them like she was on the spiderweb climber at the playground. Ofelia preferred the slide.

As the rain danced down on her head, she imagined it was like walking across the hands of monsters rising up from the bay. Any wrong step and she'd be snatched away. She made it to where Lane lay slumped over. She could see that one of her arms had fallen through an opening in the roots. Just like it happens on the spiderweb climber when you lose your footing, Ofelia thought. With the beam of Aster's flashlight, she could see water shining below them. The roots had been a net for Lane's fall.

A flash of lightning lit the sky, and she could make out her friend's face.

"Lane," she said, pushing dark hair off the girl's face with one hand. "Are you stuck?"

"I can't move my arm," Lane moaned. Ofelia could tell from the sound of her voice that she was crying.

She leaned in, putting an arm around Lane's waist to pull her, but Lane let out a scream. There was no way she was going to be able to help her out. So, Ofelia grabbed Lane's hand, and waited.

"Cat's getting help," she said, trying not to sound scared. "Aster's here too. You'll be okay."

Lightning flashed again like the bulb of an old-timey camera. Ofelia counted. One, two, three, four, five, six, seven, eight, nine, ten, eleven. The sky crackled.

Her science teacher had explained that the longer the time between the flash of light and the sound of thunder, the farther away the lightning was. To figure out the distance, you count the seconds from when the lightning flashes to when you hear thunder, then divide that by five. The number you get is the number of miles away the lightning has struck.

"It's about two miles away," Ofelia whispered to herself.

It felt like hours before the backyard lights came on and voices neared.

"My dad is here!" Cat called down to the girls.

Mr. Garcia lowered himself onto the roots. When he realized he wasn't going to be able to lift Lane out by himself, he pulled out his phone and called 911. Then he helped Ofelia back up onto the pier.

Ofelia walked to where Aster and Cat stood shivering next to Cat's mom. Soon the sounds of a siren broke through the rain and two paramedics rushed past them. They disappeared over the side of the pier. Ofelia could hear Lane scream as they pulled her away from the roots. When they were finally able to lift Lane out and had settled her onto a stretcher, Ofelia could see her right arm was twisted at an odd angle.

As the paramedics lifted Lane into the ambulance, Mrs. Garcia turned to Aster and Ofelia.

"I need you girls to call your parents right now," she said.

Ofelia looked at Aster and Cat.

"I am in so much trouble," she said.

CHAPTER 37

Aster wasn't used to being in Mrs. DiSanti's library when the curtains were drawn open, letting sunshine illuminate the room. She could see things without her little reading light. Her grandpa shifted uncomfortably on the green velvet chair that looked like a throne. She knew he still couldn't believe he was inside the DiSanti house. When she had called him the night of the accident and told him where she was and who she was with, he had hung up on her thinking it was a prank call. By the time she dialed the house number again, he had checked her room and knew it wasn't a joke.

Cat sat staring at her shoes. Her dad sat next to her. Mrs. Garcia stood behind her like an angry shadow.

Ofelia stood between her parents, chewing on a finger-nail with a somber look on her face. And across the room, Lane slid a pencil into the space between her cast and her arm, trying to scratch an itch. When she looked up at Aster,

Aster gave her an unsure smile. She was relieved when Lane smiled back.

The whole thing felt like a game of Clue, Aster thought, and they were all suspects, everyone holding their breath while they waited for Mrs. DiSanti. She had gotten a quick look at her the night of the accident, but the woman had been shrouded in a rain cloak, under a huge umbrella, so all she saw was a dark, mysterious figure being helped into the ambulance with Lane. She hoped the woman wouldn't choose this moment to remove the green ribbon from her neck. Although it would be a good distraction from whatever trouble they were in.

The tarte aux pommes she baked and sliced at home sat on its plate on the desk, untouched. Grandpa told her this wasn't a social call, but she needed to make something anyway. Cooking helped calm her nerves.

Finally, the door opened. It was Mira carrying a tray loaded with cups and a teapot.

"Mrs. DiSanti is on her way," she told the group. "Please help yourselves to tea."

Aster saw her give Lane a sympathetic look before leaving the room.

"Maybe you were right to bring that thing after all," her

grandfather said, getting up and pouring himself a cup of tea. He dropped a cube of sugar in and walked back to his seat.

A minute later, an orange-scented breeze flowed into the room, and Mrs. DiSanti walked in accompanied by Mrs. McAllister. Aster stared at the woman as she made her way to the desk. She didn't wear a green ribbon around her neck or a coat made of puppy fur. She was tall and thin like Lane, her white hair pulled up in an elegant twist. She wore no makeup. Her rosy cheeks gave her face a sweetness that surprised Aster. In her cream-colored blouse and pants, Aster thought she looked delicate, like an orange blossom.

"Thank you for coming, everyone," Mrs. DiSanti said, standing behind her chair at the desk. "For those of you I haven't met, I'm Elizabeth DiSanti, and this is Martha McAllister, the head of the Floras. Please make yourselves comfortable."

"Impossible," Aster heard her grandfather mutter as he shifted again in his seat.

She felt warmth spread across her face, but no one else in the room seemed to have heard him. And no one else looked comfortable either.

"Lane has had quite a busy summer running around with the girls, and it's nice to finally meet all of you," Mrs.

DiSanti continued. "Although perhaps these aren't the best of circumstances. In speaking with Mrs. McAllister after Friday night's incident, it came to my attention that there have been a few pranks, instances of vandalism in the area. Mrs. McAllister thinks the girls might be able to shed some light on this for us, yes?"

"Excuse me, Mrs. DiSanti, I'm Benjamin Douglas, Aster's grandfather." Aster watched her grandpa slowly stand from his seat. "I knew Aster was spending time with these girls, but this is all coming as news to me."

"Well, imagine *my* surprise when I get a call from my frantic child, who I think is here at a sleepover," Mrs. Garcia said, looking down at the top of Cat's head.

Aster saw Cat gulp as her mom's fingers pressed into her shoulders.

Mrs. McAllister came out from behind the desk and laid out a few items. The adults got up from their seats and crowded closer.

"You can come over too," the woman motioned to the girls.

Lane was the first to move forward. The other girls followed.

Mrs. McAllister had spread out what looked like a dossier

of their summer activities: the bandanna left on a flamingo's neck when they planted the plastic birds outside the Floras House; a newspaper clipping of Ofelia's letter to the editor; a box of brownies where their sticker had been slapped; and two photographs.

The girls leaned in close to look at the photos. Aster could see that one was taken at the street festival. It was a shot of the crowd, but the thing that drew her eyes was the pair of purple-and-blue unicorn socks in the distance. It was a pair of socks her mom had brought back for her from Japan the last time she was on leave. Aster had worn them that day. It was all that was visible of her in the photo, but next to her were the backs of familiar heads—Lane's dark hair, and Ofelia's Marlins baseball cap.

The other photo was dark and grainy, but not so dark that you couldn't just make out four figures in black surrounded by the outlines of flamingos on the front lawn of the Floras House.

"Ofelia?" Mr. Castillo asked, crossing his arms, waiting. "Habla, por favor."

Ofelia looked down at her bare toes.

"I'll explain," Mrs. McAllister said. "And perhaps the girls can fill in the missing details. It appears they have been on some kind of . . . mission to sabotage the Floras?"

The girls looked at one another. Aster wondered if she should speak first or let someone else take the lead.

"That's *not* what we were doing," Lane said indignantly.

"So you admit it was you." A smug look spread across Mrs. McAllister's face.

"Purslane, is this true?" Mrs. DiSanti asked.

Aster could tell from the look on Mrs. DiSanti's face that she was surprised. That she had hoped whatever Mrs. McAllister theorized wasn't true.

"It's not about sabotaging the Floras," Ofelia spoke up. "It's about that awful hat."

"What hat, niña?" Mrs. Castillo asked.

"Catarina goes to her Floras meetings, the library, and the nature preserve. That's it," Mrs. Garcia said, holding up three fingers. "I've allowed her to come here for sleepovers under the impression that she's *here*. I don't know when she'd have an opportunity to do—" She pointed to the items on the desk.

Aster found it interesting that a lawyer was ignoring the evidence laid out before her.

"Mrs. McAllister is right, Mom," Cat said quietly. "They were helping *me*."

"We were helping one another," Aster corrected.

"It's nice to see you again, Catarina," Mrs. McAllister said. "And very disappointing to know you were involved in these pranks."

"Why?" Mrs. Garcia said. "Why would you do all of this?"

"They weren't pranks," Cat said. "They're statements. Direct action, right, Aster?"

Aster gave her grandfather a sheepish look. Her grandfather covered his face with the palm of his hand and shook his head.

"Social commentary," Lane added.

"That resulted in a broken arm," Mrs. DiSanti said, pointing to Lane's cast.

"My arm had nothing to do with this, Grandmother."

"Can we let the girls explain?" Mr. Garcia said.

While the adults listened, Cat explained. Aster was glad to see Cat hold her ground and speak passionately about the feathered hat and its symbolism, the history of hunting birds for feathers, the Migratory Bird Treaty Act, the importance of conservation of local species, and the Floras' role in it all.

"The Floras are hunting birds?" Mr. Douglas asked, frowning.

"No, Grandpa," Aster said and sighed.

"They aren't hunting birds *now*, Mr. Douglas," Cat said.

"But they're using a hat made of the feathers of birds that were hunted."

"That hat is more than a hundred years old," Mrs. McAllister said. "You're doing all of this to protest something you cannot change."

The adults looked at the girls, waiting.

"Don't you see that by using the hat it's like you're—" Ofelia started, "it's like you're saying this thing that was done in the past wasn't so bad."

"This is still not making sense to me," Mrs. Castillo said.

"It's like this, Mrs. Castillo," Aster said. "The Floras use the hat, and the hat is a symbol of the Floras, it represents the group, right?"

"Yes, it does," Mrs. McAllister said proudly. "It has for more than a century, and it will continue to do so if I can help it."

"But don't you care that it also represents something ugly from the past?" Aster asked. "Even if the Floras organization today doesn't agree with it. Even if hunting birds for feathers was something people just did back in those days. When you continue to use the hat today, it's like saying history and legacy are more important than the fact that what people did was wrong."

"Right," Cat said. "Using the hat makes a statement that the Floras are ignoring how it was made. And if they were okay with it then, who's to say they wouldn't be okay with it happening again?"

"Catarina, you should know better. You've been a Flora since you were seven," Mrs. Garcia said. "Do you really believe they would condone the killing of animals?"

"My grandpa taught me that even though history is in the past, and we can't do anything about what happened then, we can try to make it right today," Aster said. "Shed light on the dark parts of it instead of pretending it didn't happen. Right, Grandpa?"

She looked at her grandpa, relieved when he nodded in response.

"The Floras could make a statement, Mrs. McAllister," Ofelia suggested. "By deciding to no longer use the feathered hat, they could say that they don't agree with how it was made, even though it is a part of their history."

Aster saw Mrs. Castillo shake her head in disbelief.

"And what do you propose they do with the hat?" Mrs. DiSanti asked. "Even if the Floras agreed not to use it?"

"They could donate it to a museum," Cat said. "And use something else."

"They could start using an Audubonnet instead," Lane added.

"While I respect that you girls feel strongly about this, what the Floras do or don't do with that hat is not for *you* to decide," Mrs. DiSanti said. "And it's certainly not for you to take matters into your hands, damaging property."

"We *didn't* damage property," Lane said.

"You stickered more than a hundred dollars' worth of brownie boxes," Mrs. McAllister said. "The stickers couldn't be removed without damaging the boxes."

"And you're auctioning off those boxes," Lane reminded her. "Making a lot more than a hundred—"

"Purslane! *That* is not the point," Mrs. DiSanti interjected. "I can understand what you girls are standing up for. That's admirable, but you might have gone about making your point in a more constructive way."

"I'm most disappointed by you, Catarina," Mrs. McAllister said. "It's one thing to stop coming to meetings, but conspiring to steal the hat?"

"Stopped going to meetings," Cat's mom said, looking confused. "Catarina hasn't . . . "

Aster watched as Mrs. McAllister and Mrs. Garcia turned to Cat.

"I quit the Floras," Cat said softly. "I haven't gone to a meeting in more than a month."

"YOU WHAT?!" Mrs. Garcia yelled.

Aster cringed. If the look on Mrs. Garcia's face was any indication, she was about to go off like a pack of fireworks. Mr. Garcia took her hand as if to calm her down.

"Where should we begin?" Mrs. McAllister asked. "She ran out one day in a huff about the hat and never came back. It was quite disruptive. I had a hard time getting the girls, especially the younger ones, to focus after that scene. Is there anything you'd like to add?"

"Catarina?" Mrs. Garcia said between gritted teeth.

"I'm sorry," Cat said. "And I'm sorry I gave away the brownie money."

"You gave away the brownie money?" Mrs. Garcia asked, closing her eyes and rubbing her temples. "Unbelievable. Who are you? Is it these girls who have been influencing you to act out like this?"

"Now, wait a minute," Grandpa said.

"It's not their fault," Cat said. "I donated the money. And I quit before I even met them. This is all because of me. I'm sorry, everyone. I'm sorry, Mrs. McAllister."

Aster walked over to Cat and put an arm around her.

Ofelia and Lane joined her. Aster looked at her friends. No matter what punishment was coming their way, they were still a united front.

"I accept your apology," Mrs. McAllister said. "It may not be part of our written laws, but it's important for a Flora to take responsibility for her mistakes."

"I accept responsibility," Cat said. "For all of it."

"Me too," Lane said.

"All of it," Aster agreed.

Ofelia looked at her parents. "I do too."

"So, what are we going to do about this?" Mrs. Castillo asked, looking from the adults to the girls.

"For starters, Catarina is grounded," Mrs. Garcia said. "And she is going to work to pay back the money. Mrs. McAllister, I know you have a difficult decision to make, but I would like to respectfully request that you allow her to participate in the Miss Floras contest."

Cat looked at her mother like she couldn't believe what she was hearing.

"Virginia, you know this puts me in such an awkward position," Mrs. McAllister said to Mrs. Garcia. "Catarina should be an example. She's one of the older girls. What are we supposed to do now that she's broken Floras' laws? Catarina?"

Cat shrugged.

"Floras don't shrug," Mrs. Garcia said, nudging Cat's shoulder. "Speak up. Now's your chance to say what you need to say."

"I don't know what should happen," Cat said.

"Skipping meetings doesn't sound like something a person does if she wants to be a Flora," Mrs. McAllister said. "Much less a Miss Floras."

"Let her participate in the Miss Floras contest and show that even when a girl makes a mistake, she can make it right," Mrs. Garcia said. "Even if she is no longer in the running for the title."

Aster saw the look of disappointment in Mrs. Garcia's face and understood why it had been so hard for Cat to say anything.

"I do believe in giving girls second chances," Mrs. McAllister said, looking at Mrs. Garcia. "You and your girls have been exemplary Floras. But does *she* want to have the experience?"

Mrs. Garcia and Mrs. McAllister waited for Cat to say something.

"I do, Mrs. McAllister," she said.

"What are you doing, Cat?" Lane asked. "You don't want this."

Cat looked down and didn't respond.

"Mrs. DiSanti, Mrs. McAllister, I don't know what to say. I am so sorry Ofelia was involved," Mrs. Castillo said. "Ofelia, how are we supposed to trust you to go to New York alone?"

"I'm sorry, Ma, Pa," Ofelia said. "I wasn't trying to make trouble, and I wasn't trying to lose your trust in me."

"So, what were you thinking?" her mom asked. "Were you thinking about how it would look to my employer that my daughter is running around with her granddaughter doing all kinds of locuras?"

"I was just trying to write a story," Ofelia said. "And I wanted to help my friends do something good."

"Ofelia, you have to know how to think for yourself," Mr. Castillo said, tapping on his head with his index finger. "Don't get swept up in group mentality."

"It wasn't like that," Ofelia insisted. "I believe in what we were doing. It's important to me."

"I'm glad you at least believe in it strongly because your papi and I have some talking to do about consequences," Mrs. Castillo said.

"I understand," Ofelia said.

"Mrs. McAllister has agreed not to press charges against the girls," Mrs. DiSanti said. "Thank you, Mrs. McAllister."

"Charges?" Aster's grandfather asked, a look of concern on his face.

"Breaking and entering," Mrs. McAllister said. "Attempted theft, vandalism. You're lucky the hat wasn't damaged or it would have been destruction of property as well."

Aster looked at her friends and shook her head.

"Mrs. DiSanti," Ofelia's mother said, "we could use some extra hands at the Miss Floras event. There are plenty of things for them to do."

"Put them to work," Mr. Garcia said.

"What?" Lane and Aster gasped in unison.

Aster saw her grandfather nod.

"Well, girls," Mrs. DiSanti said. "It sounds like you'll be working off your shenanigans."

"Ofelia will be there," Mr. Castillo said.

"Thank you for coming, everyone," Mrs. DiSanti said, motioning to the group. "It's good to see young girls being passionate about important things. Perhaps they just need a little help channeling that fervor."

"Let's go, Catarina," Mrs. Garcia said. "We'll talk about this at home. Goodbye, Mrs. DiSanti, everyone."

Ofelia left with her family, followed by Mrs. McAllister, who walked out with her box of evidence.

Aster watched as Mrs. DiSanti picked up a slice of her apple tart and bit into it. She could swear the woman's eyes lit up as she nibbled on the pastry.

"Let's go, Grandpa," Aster said, helping her grandfather out of the chair he'd sunk into. To her relief, the photo and the diary hadn't come up, and she hoped to keep it that way. But instead of heading for the door, her grandfather walked toward Mrs. DiSanti.

"Where are you going, Grandpa?" Aster whispered.

"Where do you think I'm going?" he said. "I've tried to get in touch with this woman for years, and here we are in the same room."

"Really? Now?" Aster said. "Don't we need to go home so that you can punish me?"

"Don't worry," her grandfather said. "I'll deal with you later."

Aster watched her grandfather walk to where Lane's grandmother stood behind her desk.

"Mrs. DiSanti," he asked, "may I have a word with you?"

"Of course. I was hoping to speak with you before you left," Mrs. DiSanti asked. "What can I do for you, Mr. Douglas?"

Aster didn't like the sound of what Mrs. DiSanti said. She sat down next to Lane.

"Hey," Lane said. "Working those Centennial events is going to be fun, right?"

"I'm really sorry," she said. "About everything: sneaking into your grandmother's house, taking the photo and the diaries. Not being honest."

"Diaries?" Lane asked.

"Yeah." Aster shrugged, pulling the two other volumes out of her bag and handing them to Lane. "Could you please not tell your grandmother about these?"

"I'm sorry too," Lane said, taking the books, "that I threw it all into the water and that I accused you of not being my friend. I thought you were using me or that you were mad because I mentioned your dad to the other girls. I didn't know they didn't know."

"It's okay," Aster said. "I should have told them. I haven't had a lot of real friends, in case you couldn't tell."

Aster watched the exchange between her grandfather and Lane's grandmother, wondering whether she should say anything. Her grandfather was telling Mrs. DiSanti about his book, and Mrs. DiSanti was listening. She wondered what would have happened if her grandfather had been able to get in touch with the reclusive woman on his own. Maybe she never would have met the group because she wouldn't have wanted to get onto the DiSanti property so badly.

"What are you accusing my granddaughter of now?" she heard her grandpa say. He looked from Mrs. DiSanti to Aster.

Aster's ears perked up.

"Oh, bird crap," Lane muttered.

"My granddaughter told me Aster has been snooping in my library," Mrs. DiSanti said. "I thought I would leave that part out of the conversation with the larger group."

Aster turned to Lane, shocked.

"I'm so sorry, I don't even remember telling her," Lane said. "I was in so much pain that night, and I was so mad, and she wanted to know why we were out there."

"What are they talking about, child?" Aster's grandfather asked.

Aster sighed. She stood up and walked over to where

her grandfather and Mrs. DiSanti stood. She told her grandfather about sneaking into the library and about what she'd found there.

"It was wrong of me to snoop and take those things, Mrs. DiSanti," Aster said. "I'm sorry."

"First that hat, now this?" her grandfather said. "What would your mom and pop say?"

Aster's stomach dropped. She felt Lane walk up next to her and squeeze her hand.

"I just wanted to help you," Aster said, feeling hot tears well up in her eyes. "I wanted you to find what you needed."

Her grandfather sighed deeply and put his hand on her shoulder.

"What exactly are you hoping to prove by finding a connection?" Mrs. DiSanti asked Aster's grandfather.

"I care about people knowing that both our families were part of building this town, even though that invisible Wall divides us," Mr. Douglas said. "My legacy is about truth."

"And what do you believe to be the truth?" Mrs. DiSanti asked.

Aster sensed the woman wasn't asking in a defensive manner. She seemed genuinely interested.

"My family always said that white orange tree—the

one your family is known for—came over with a Douglas," Aster's grandfather said. "But you read the biographies and listen to the locals tell it, all you hear about is Anthony DiSanti bringing the orange back from Italy. I'm looking for the real story. Who planted it first? How did your family get the tree?"

"I have no idea," Mrs. DiSanti said. "But I assume you have a theory."

"As a matter of fact, I do," Aster's grandfather said.

"You have a theory, Grandpa?" Aster asked. "You never told me."

"I do, and you never asked," he said, peering at her over his glasses. "I believe the DiSantis got it from Carol Anne Douglas, my great-uncle Charles's wife. She was the family's cook."

"But how?" Aster said.

"I don't know," her grandfather said. "Might've been an orange, a seed. She's also the one people in our family claim came up with the Winter Sun pie. Might've been Charlotte DiSanti took a liking to it."

"Wow," Aster and Lane said together.

"And you, young lady?" Mrs. DiSanti said to Aster. "Did you at least find something in all your detective work?"

"No," Aster said, looking down guiltily. "But I only got through the first two years of diary entries, after the DiSantis came to Sabal Palms."

"I want an accurate history to be known," Aster's grandfather said. "But I suppose you have to protect your legacy too."

"Well, you're in luck, Mr. Douglas," Mrs. DiSanti said.

"What do you mean, Grandmother?" Lane asked.

Aster and Lane looked at each other. Aster shrugged.

"You make assumptions about me, Mr. Douglas, when you think I care more about a legacy than the truth," Mrs. DiSanti said. She picked up another slice of the apple tart and smiled. Aster saw Lane's eyes widen.

"I'm not afraid of finding out the truth," the woman continued. "So I will help you."

CHAPTER 38

Like the other girls, Aster was grounded for a week. She babysat Hurricane Hendricks, helped her grandfather with his research, and, as agreed on, helped Mrs. Castillo with preparations for the Floras Centennial. Mrs. Castillo had scheduled the girls for different jobs and separate shifts so that they would not have an opportunity to be together during their grounding.

Grandpa also took her back-to-school shopping. She got everything on her school list, and he even told her to pick out some new outfits. She should have been more excited about the offer of new clothes but decided she didn't need them. She liked wearing her dad's old shirts.

Meanwhile, her grandpa had scored big. He went to the DiSanti house where Mrs. DiSanti opened her library to him. He started by walking the entire property in search of any sign of the trees Aster said she saw in the photo. But if they once existed, they were nowhere to be found now.

Her grandfather discovered the recipe for Winter Sun pie tucked in one of Charlotte DiSanti's diaries, written in pencil on a yellowed piece of paper. Mrs. DiSanti hadn't allowed him to take the original, but he was able to scan it and email it to Aster, who printed it out. She had it up on the refrigerator with a plan to make it soon. She and her grandfather both noticed the same thing—the handwriting on the paper wasn't the same as the handwriting in Charlotte's diaries.

"Grandpa!" Aster yelled. "I'm making a celebratory dinner now that my grounding is over. How does fish sound? I want to try the recipe for sole in white wine sauce."

"Sounds good," her grandpa said. He got up from his desk and walked over to where Aster was gathering her things. "Is there anything I can help with?"

"Do we have white wine?" Aster asked.

"I'll see if any of the neighbors do," her grandpa said, taking a few bills out of his wallet and handing them to her. "If not, I'll buy some."

"Thanks, Grandpa," Aster said, stuffing the bills in her pocket.

"Anything else?" he asked. "Preheat the oven?"

"You know how to preheat an oven?" Aster feigned shock.

"Oh, give me a little credit," he said. "I can chop garlic too. How about I de-sole my shoes?" He chuckled at his own joke.

"Thanks for offering, Grandpa," Aster said. "But I've got it. I'm stopping by the library for the recipe before I head to the market, is that okay?"

"Market and library," he repeated. "I heard you."

When she arrived at the library, Aster made a beeline for the reference shelf, but *Mastering the Art of French Cooking* wasn't in its usual place. She checked the reshelving carts. It wasn't there either.

"Hi, Ms. Falco," she said, approaching the librarian's desk.

"Aster, hi." Ms. Falco put down her barcode scanner and rubbed her eyes.

"I'm looking for the cookbook," Aster said. "Do you know where it is? Making some fish for dinner tonight."

"Oh, yes, right," Ms. Falco said, opening a desk drawer. "I'm glad you stopped by to ask for it because I didn't see you come in."

"Why are you keeping it in your desk?" Aster asked.

"Cat came by yesterday," Ms. Falco said, pulling out the cookbook. "She said she couldn't call your house, so she left something for you and wanted to make sure you got it if you came in. Here you go."

"What is it?" Aster asked, her curiosity bubbling over as she took the book.

"I put it inside the book so I wouldn't forget," Ms. Falco said.

Aster carried the book to a table and sat down. She flipped through the pages until she found one of the free Frosty Dream promotional postcards they kept on the counter. It was supposed to look like a vintage Florida postcard with happy kids at the beach eating ice cream. She turned the card over. In the space for a message, there was a date, a time, and the phrase PLAN B.

Aster glanced over at Ms. Falco and caught her looking. She tucked the card into her backpack and photocopied the recipe she needed, then returned the book to its place.

"Thank you, Ms. Falco," Aster said, as she left the library.

"No problem," the librarian said and smiled. "I love a good mystery."

At the market, Aster purchased the shallots and two sole fillets she needed for dinner, then walked home, thinking about the postcard in the cookbook. As she turned onto Whistling Duck Avenue and neared her house, she realized she was being followed.

Aster looked over her shoulder and saw that it wasn't one of the neighborhood dogs trailing her, but a familiar floppy-eared, three-legged dog. She thought about running.

"Go away, you," she called to the dog. "Shoo!" She waved her canvas bag toward it.

The dog flinched, but as soon as she turned around, it continued to follow.

Aster stopped again and sighed.

"You remember me?" she asked, feeling less fearful now that she'd reached her house. "Are you hungry?"

The dog sniffed the air. It slowly began to move toward her again.

Aster crossed her front yard. The dog stopped on the sidewalk as if waiting for an invitation.

She kept her breathing steady as the dog approached the house. Up close, he didn't look scary or ferocious. She opened the front door wide enough to poke her head in.

"Grandpa," she yelled. "We've got company!"

CHAPTER 39

The Saturday of the Floras Centennial was a beautiful day with clear, blue skies and sunshine. But the early afternoon heat hung heavy like a wool blanket, and droplets of sweat trickled like little bugs crawling over unreachable parts of Cat's body. She thought the salmon-colored linen dress her mother had bought her for the occasion made her look like a flamingo.

"Where have you been, Nerdy Birdy?" Emma called over to Cat from where she stood onstage. "I didn't think we'd see you here."

"Leave her alone," Alice whispered to Emma.

Cat ignored them and rubbed the crystal in her dress pocket as they waited for Mrs. McAllister to begin the ceremony.

Olive bounded up to the front of the stage with another Flora.

"Hi, Cat," she said, smiling big. "We just wanted to wish you good luck."

"Thanks," Cat said weakly.

"And to tell you that we care about the birds too," the other girl said. She giggled, and Olive stepped on her toes and glared.

"Ow!" the girl yelped.

"Okay, well, bye," Olive said. She pulled the other girl away with her.

"Bye," Cat said.

She knew she would never be Miss Floras, *everyone* knew she would never be Miss Floras. The contest, the itchy dress, were all part of her punishment. If nothing else, her mother would get to see a Garcia sister on the Floras stage one last time. Her mother had been so mad after the meeting at Mrs. DiSanti's house. But her sisters had supported her which made dealing with her mother a little easier.

Cat scratched her hose-covered legs and scanned the crowd for her friends. When she spotted them, she flapped her shadow bird wings. Seeing her friends was the only reason she'd been looking forward to the day. Aster, Ofelia, and Lane flapped their fingers back at her.

Mrs. McAllister took the microphone at the podium. The

golden box with the feathered hat inside sat on a pedestal waiting to be claimed by the girl who would wear it that year.

Cat felt embarrassed for her friends. They looked like penguins in their uniforms of black shorts and white short-sleeve button-down shirts with bow ties. And it was all her fault they were stuck there working instead of enjoying one of their last days of summer.

She saw Mrs. Castillo walk up behind the girls and separate them, sending Aster and Ofelia to their assigned tables where they were tasked with keeping a steady supply of finger sandwiches and little desserts, and Lane, who only had use of one arm, to the drinks station to pour glasses of lavender agua fresca.

Cat watched Aster walk into the kitchen. When she came back out, she had a tray of the special cream puffs she had made. She saw Aster motion for Ofelia to come over. Ofelia took the tray and began to place the cream puffs on her tables. As Mrs. McAllister went on about the Floras, Cat watched Aster bring out another tray of cream puffs and take them to her own assigned tables.

The cream puff plan wasn't exactly stealing the hat, but it would have to do, Cat thought. They wouldn't let Mrs.

McAllister win. She watched a woman in a big purple hat take a bite of her cream puff. She moved the pastry away from her mouth and examined it. Then she pulled a small roll of paper out of the filling and showed it to the woman next to her.

"And now," Mrs. McAllister announced into the microphone, "the moment we've all gathered to witness. Who will be this year's Miss Floras?" She waved an envelope in the air with excitement.

The girls on the stage smiled at the audience. All except Cat, who felt like she had a hairball stuck in her throat. A quiet murmuring made its way through the crowd as more guests bit into cream puffs to find small scrolls tucked inside the delicious orange cream filling.

Cat glanced in Aster's direction. Aster smiled, then quickly went back into the kitchen. As she passed Lane at the drinks station, Cat saw the girls give each other a fist bump.

"We have a special guest this year who will announce the winner," Mrs. McAllister continued. "We're so honored since this is the first time she's joined us in a number of years. Please welcome, a member of our founding family, Elizabeth DiSanti."

Applause and whispers filled the space as the audience watched the woman step up onstage in her white summer dress.

Cat heard a little boy seated at a table close to the stage ask his mother what Mrs. DiSanti had found. His mother looked confused by the question. "She's from the founding family," he said. "What did she find? Was it one of these?" He showed her the little scroll of paper he had just pulled out of his cream puff.

Mrs. DiSanti stepped up to the microphone.

"Thank you, Mrs. McAllister," she said. "It's a pleasure to be here celebrating one hundred years of the Floras of Sabal Palms. My grandmother Charlotte would be proud to know the organization she founded is still going strong."

Mrs. DiSanti went on to give a brief history of the Floras before moving on to the part of the event everyone was waiting for.

"While all of this year's candidates are worthy of being Miss Floras, only one can wear the hat," Mrs. DiSanti said, placing a hand on the gold box.

Cat noticed Mrs. McAllister gave her a quick side-eye that indicated she thought otherwise. She sighed and tried to scratch her armpit discreetly. She searched the crowd for her parents and sisters. She knew her mom would disapprove of an armpit scratch. Meanwhile, the real entertainment was watching the guests unroll the pieces of paper found in their cream puffs.

They had each played a part in making it all come together. Cat came up with the information for the flyer, a call to action to stop the use of the feathered hat. Lane had designed it, Ofelia had written it, and Aster had baked it into cream puffs.

Mrs. DiSanti described the merits of the winner, her excellent grades, her community service, but Cat could see that she was looking out into the crowd in concern. People were spitting out paper, unrolling chewed scrolls, scraping the cream out of their puffs to find the small flyer intact.

"This year's Miss Flora," Mrs. DiSanti announced. "A true friend to nature who started several butterfly gardens at her school, is . . . Alice Vargas!"

Mrs. McAllister rushed over to congratulate Alice. The girl beamed as she made her way to where the gold box sat. Cat felt relieved. She was happy for Alice, her former best friend, because she knew that being Miss Floras meant something to her. She couldn't wait to take off the itchy dress.

All eyes were on Mrs. McAllister as she lifted the lid of the gold box.

"What in the world!" the woman yelled in a most un-Flora-like manner. What she pulled out of the box wasn't the hat, but a sheet of paper. Alice crowded next to her to read what was written on the sheet.

The already-confused rumblings over the cream puffs turned into full-volume conversations. People expressed shock at the missing hat and held up cream puffs and unrolled papers.

Cat heard glass shatter and looked in Lane's direction. Lane had dropped the glass of agua fresca she had just poured. She looked back at Cat onstage, mouth open and eyes wide with shock. Cat felt her own eyes bug out and a huge grin spread across her face. She located Ofelia in the crowd, who gave her a where-is-it look. Cat shook her head and mouthed back, *Gone!* Ofelia ran over to where Aster leaned against a table, eating a finger sandwich, and pulled her toward the stage.

"This year, the Floras have made a donation to the Aves Society in the name of our winning Miss Floras," Mrs. DiSanti announced. She held up the paper she had pulled out of the box, smiling, then handed it to Alice with a hug.

Alice looked confused, but she waved to the audience.

"Yes, surprise!" Mrs. McAllister cried out into the microphone, a big, fake smile on her face. "Our beautiful hat has been sent off to a textiles preservationist for evaluation, all thanks to your support! Be sure to check our website for updates."

Cat was impressed with how well Mrs. McAllister seemed to roll with the punches.

Mrs. McAllister thanked everyone for coming and invited them to enjoy the food and the rest of the afternoon. Then she collected the empty box and ushered Mrs. DiSanti and the Floras, including Cat, offstage.

Cat found her mother waiting for her as she descended the stairs leading off the stage.

"Where is it?" Mrs. Garcia demanded.

"At a preservation place?" Cat said, puzzled.

"This is not a joke," Mrs. McAllister said, stomping over like a turkey ready to fight. "I'm going to round up your friends and get to the bottom of this."

"Cat?" Mrs. Garcia said.

"Mom, I have no idea what happened to the hat," Cat said. "I swear on the endangered Everglade snail kite."

Ofelia and Aster made their way to where Cat stood with her mother.

"Is it really gone?" Aster asked.

"I can't believe it," Ofelia added. "It's like the universe heard us."

Mrs. Garcia glared at Ofelia, and Ofelia gave her a guilty smile.

"Here comes your mom," Cat said to Ofelia, as Mrs. Castillo hurried toward them.

"What happened to the hat?" Mrs. Castillo asked.

"We don't know, Mrs. Castillo," Aster said. "Honest to goodness."

"Think about it, Ma," Ofelia said. "Why would we take it if we knew that you're all going to suspect us?"

Mrs. Castillo shook her head.

"I don't know what the four of you would or wouldn't do," Ofelia's mother said. "But if I find out you were involved with this, you will be punished for the rest of your life."

"I know, Ma," Ofelia said.

They watched as Lane and her grandmother approached. Cat noticed Lane didn't look like she was in any kind of trouble.

"You'll never believe it," Lane said, grinning.

"Did they find it?" Ofelia asked.

"No," Lane said. "But we know who did it."

"It didn't take long to get a confession," Mrs. DiSanti added.

"I'm confused," Cat said, looking at her friends. "We didn't confess to anything."

"We know *you* didn't take the hat," Mrs. DiSanti said.

"Then who did?" Mrs. Garcia asked.

Lane turned and all eyes followed to where Mrs. McAllister spoke with Olive and her parents. The girl stood with her arms crossed against her chest, an indignant look on her face.

"Who knew that hat had so many enemies," Mrs. Castillo said, watching the commotion.

"*Olive?*" Cat said.

The girls looked at one another, their expressions going from shock to glee.

"I can't believe Olive pulled it off," Ofelia said.

"Small but mighty." Aster grinned.

The girls watched as Mrs. McAllister parted with Olive and her parents. Olive's mother took the girl by the arm and practically dragged her toward the exit.

"Olive Padilla, you tell us where that hat is," her mother said, angrily.

"Not until Mrs. McAllister agrees to stop using it," Cat heard Olive say. As the younger girl passed the group, she waved to Cat.

"Feathers are for birds!" Olive yelled, as her parents pulled her out of the celebration. "Return the feathers!"

"I hope she isn't in a lot of trouble," Cat said. She had never meant for Olive to get involved and take up the cause too.

"Do you see now, Catarina, how much influence an older Flora can have on a younger one?" Mrs. McAllister asked, walking up to the group. "Olive was so swayed by your impassioned outcry at the meeting and your other *activities* that she decided to do something about it. You should be using your influence for positive things."

Mrs. McAllister hurried off in a huff. Like a wild turkey, Cat thought.

"Well, *I* think this was pretty positive." Aster slung an arm around Cat's shoulders.

"Now that we know you didn't have anything to do with the hat disappearing," Mrs. Castillo said, "I have another question for you girls."

Cat watched Ofelia's mother walk over to a table and return with a plate. On it sat a cream puff, its orange filling oozing out onto a piece of paper.

"Does anyone know anything about this?" Mrs. Castillo asked.

Cat and her friends looked at one another. Ofelia began to laugh, Lane joined in, and soon the four girls were laughing so hard tears streamed down their faces.

CHAPTER 40

"In Cuba, people didn't ground their children," Mrs. Castillo said, pulling into her parking spot. "Because children knew better."

"Okay, Ma."

Ofelia twisted her black bandanna and tied it in her hair. She wanted to ask her mom why they left Cuba if things were so good there, but she had a feeling she would be grounded for the rest of the summer if she asked that question. She knew not to push her luck.

She had had a long talk with her parents after the hat incident about responsibility, about seeking the truth through stories, about her future, and about not being afraid. She knew they still didn't understand some things about her, but she thought that maybe they understood some of the more important things. Or, at least, they were trying.

As soon as her mother parked the car, Ofelia grabbed her backpack and ran for the tree house.

"Behave yourself before Mrs. DiSanti bans you from coming here," Mrs. Castillo called after her.

As Ofelia climbed the ladder and listened to her friends' voices, she realized how much she would miss them when the summer ended.

"Ofelia!" Cat yelled when Ofelia appeared in the doorway. She greeted Ofelia with their shadow-bird gesture from where she sat cross-legged.

"I thought for sure your mom was going to keep you locked up the rest of the summer," Lane said, not looking up from her work.

"Like Saint Barbara, right?" Aster added.

"Don't even joke about that," Ofelia said.

She sat down on the floor where Aster cut out the image Lane had drawn and painted over several newspaper spreads that were taped together. Next to the drawing sat Cat's Audubon book, open to Plate 242 for reference. Against the wall were a small yellow bucket, a gallon of water, a bag of wheat flour that Eunice was inspecting, and a large house paintbrush. It was their last project for the summer.

"I still cannot believe Olive swiped the hat," Ofelia said.

She took the piece of cardboard Lane handed her and began carefully cutting out the letters written on it with the X-Acto knife.

"Olive gets the stealing the hat badge." Cat laughed.

"Speaking of badges," Lane said. She dragged her bag over and pulled out an envelope. She handed each of the girls two small felt circles.

On one was an image sewn with pink thread. Ofelia smiled at the recognizable line drawing of a flamingo. On the other badge, Lane had sewn the words TRUTH, KINDNESS, JUSTICE, COMMUNITY.

"My grandmother helped me with these," Lane said. "It was actually kind of nice working on them with her. I'm going to make a cream-puff badge when my arm is out of this thing." She lifted her cast.

"These are great," Aster said, admiring her badges.

"Does anyone know what happened to the hat?" Ofelia asked, pinning a badge to her bag. She pulled out her notebook and flipped it open. "It's the one piece of my story that's missing. Did Olive give up its whereabouts?"

"My mom said she had it in her backpack," Cat said. "She helped set up at the Centennial and swiped it while no one was paying attention."

"That kid's not so bad," Lane said.

"What about us?" Ofelia said, writing. "Are *we* done with the hat?"

"Not if I can help it," Cat said. "There's a Floras board meeting coming up at the end of the month."

"You think we should attend?" Aster asked, uncovering the Winter Sun pie she baked for the group.

"No," Cat said. "I think we should protest. We can enlist Olive. I know there are other Floras who would be interested in joining us. Ofelia, I'm recruiting you to come up with some catchy slogans and messages for our signs."

"I'm in," Ofelia said. "I'll even cover it for the school paper."

"I'd be in too . . . " Lane said sadly.

Ofelia patted her shoulder sympathetically. It had been easy to forget that Lane was leaving, but now the reality loomed in the tree house. What would things be like when she was gone? Would the group continue? Would they stay in touch?

"We'll call you," Cat said, interrupting Ofelia's thoughts. "It'll be like you're there with us." She smiled at Lane.

Lane nodded and stuck a fork in the pie. She stopped before putting the bite in her mouth.

"Do we need to watch out for paper?" she asked. Aster laughed.

"People were really reading the scrolls you stuck in the cream puffs," Cat said. "I could see them from the stage. But more important, I heard people talking about it after. Maybe this is just the beginning."

"How's your grandpa's research going?" Ofelia asked Aster. "Anything good come up?"

"He's reading through Charlotte DiSanti's diaries," Aster said, carefully cutting along the outline of Lane's drawing. "He's also excited because he's looking at property maps now. He's even talking about writing another book about the Wall. I'll be busy with school, so I'm glad he'll have something to keep *him* busy too."

"Wouldn't it be amazing if you two were actually related?" Cat said, looking from Aster to Lane. "What if Aster's grandpa finds there's a blood connection? You might be fifth cousins twice removed or . . . something!"

Aster and Lane looked at each other and cringed.

"Well, you're both the biggest know-it-alls I've ever met," Ofelia said. "I would not be surprised."

"Did your parents make a decision about Qwerty Sholes?" Cat asked cautiously.

"I was surprised when they said I could mail in the application," Ofelia said, thinking back to her conversation with her parents. "Maybe they're actually loosening up. Though it could also just be because they know there aren't any alligators roaming the streets of New York."

"Is the story done?" Aster asked.

"And more important," Lane said, raising an eyebrow. "Are we in it?"

"You," Ofelia said, counting off on her fingers, "and peacocks, cream puffs, wild three-legged dogs. Pretty much everything under the sun is in it. I'll send it to all of you when it's finished."

Ofelia thought her headline was pretty good:

The Strange Birds of Sabal Palms: A
Story of Friendship, Truth, and Subversive
Cream Puffs.
    By Ofelia Castillo

"I'll have you know that Hank is *not* a wild dog," Aster said. "He is the sweetest."

"Wait, I thought you named him Tiny Tim," Ofelia said.

"I *did*," Aster said. "But the Hendricks kids have taken

ownership and they've been calling him Hank. He's very confused."

"I still can't believe you reunited with the dog from the nature preserve," Lane said, shaking her head.

"Is he living with you?" Ofelia asked.

"He's sort of become the neighborhood dog," Aster explained. "Everyone feeds him, but unlike most dogs, he doesn't seem to fear Hurricane Hendricks so he usually sleeps in their yard."

"I can't wait to meet him. *Again*," Cat said and laughed. "I'll bring treats."

While the girls finished cutting out the drawing and its accompanying stencil, Lane explained how to mix the wheat paste in the bucket.

"But we won't do that part until tonight," she said.

"I hope that when people see it, they'll wonder about it," Cat said, carefully rolling up the drawing and setting it on top of the stencil. "And maybe they'll want to find out more."

"What now?" Aster asked.

"Now, I have to call my dad," Lane said. "And then my mom."

"You're finally going to do it?" Aster asked.

"Yeah," Lane said with a shrug. "It's time. Besides, my

dad's coming here in a few days and flying to New York with me. We should probably talk before that."

"Why don't you want to talk to your parents?" Ofelia asked. "And don't worry. I won't put that in my story."

Lane shrugged.

"Because maybe if I don't talk to them, when the summer is over, they might tell me they aren't getting divorced," she said, rubbing her crystal. "They'll tell me they worked everything out and it was all a mistake and we are going to stay together like always."

The girls looked at one another solemnly. Ofelia got up and sat next to Lane with an arm around her shoulders. Soon Cat and Aster joined her.

"Okay, okay," Lane said, giving them a smile. "We need an end-of-summer ritual before we go back out into the world." She motioned toward the doorway of the tree house.

"We need to release our fears," Cat said. "And seek protection."

"Fears?" Ofelia said. "After this summer, I have no fears."

The girls laughed as Lane handed out a strip of paper and a pencil to each of them.

"Do we have to share these?" Aster asked.

Lane gave her a what-do-you-think look.

"Had to ask," Aster said, bending over her piece of paper.

"Ofelia, will you write these into some kind of . . . incantation," Lane asked, when they had all put their pencils down.

"I'd be honored," Ofelia said.

She collected the papers and read over them, thinking. On the back of each she wrote the fears and requests for protection as incantations for the girls. Then she handed them back to Lane. Lane looked at the top paper and smiled before reading.

"For the protection of Aster's mom and Grandpa and Hank, the three-legged dog. For the protection of Aster when she starts school, because school can be tough. For vanishing fears, for courage," Lane said, handing the slips of paper to Aster. "Now you read Cat's."

Aster smiled and gave Lane a little bow before turning to Cat.

"For the protection of Cat's heart in the face of demanding adults. For the protection of the birds and the natural environment we love. For vanishing fears, for courage," Aster read and passed the papers to Cat.

Cat turned to Ofelia.

"For the protection of Ofelia from danger, real and imagined. For Ofelia to always seek the truth through stories. For vanishing fears, for courage."

Ofelia took the papers from Cat and turned to Lane.

"For the protection of Lane as her family changes and she starts her life in a new place. For vanishing fears, for courage," she read.

Lane collected the papers, then held them out to Cat.

"Can you please roll them?" Lane asked. "Can't roll with one hand."

"Yeah," Aster said. "I had to hold the ladder for her to climb up. It wasn't a pretty climb."

Cat rolled the papers, then passed them back to Lane. Lane handed Aster a box of matches. Aster struck a match, and Lane held the roll of papers to the flame. She dropped them in an empty jar and blew out the match. The girls watched them burn slowly until all the embers had gone out. When the papers were just ashes, Lane turned the glass over on the floor by the doorway and blew them out.

"What should we do with the handbook?" Ofelia asked after documenting their end-of-summer ritual. "You want to take it back to New York? You started it, so you should keep it."

"No, we should leave it here," Lane said. "For next time."

Lane lifted the floorboard and moved the few pieces of remaining candy. She placed the handbook inside. No one spoke of the fear they shared in that moment, the one no one had written down. Their summer together was ending, and they all wondered if there would ever be a next time.

That night, after the lights had been off in the DiSanti house long enough, after the baseball game playing on the television in Henry's cottage was over and the blue light of the TV had disappeared, after Eunice the peahen had fallen asleep with her head burrowed in her feathers, the girls put on their black bandannas and backpacks and slipped out. They walked the familiar route to the Floras House and stopped at the sign on the front lawn.

"Too obvious," Lane said. "It has to be unexpected, something people stumble across."

"A place where the people who see it will feel rewarded for finding it," Aster added.

"Yeah." Lane smiled. "Like that."

They went to the side of the house that faced traffic coming down the one-way street. Lane put down the bucket of wheat paste. Aster dipped the paintbrush in and painted a layer of paste as tall and wide as Lane's drawing. Cat and

Ofelia unrolled the paper slowly and, with Lane's help, smoothed it out against the wall. Once it was attached, Aster dipped the brush in the bucket again and painted another layer of wheat paste on top of the drawing, securing it to the wall.

Lane opened a small can of purple paint. "Spray paint is easier, but no one will sell spray paint to a kid."

Ofelia and Aster held up the cardboard stencil above the drawing while Lane painted across each word. When she was done, they carefully peeled off the stencil to reveal their message, RETURN THE FEATHERS.

Underneath their words stood a snowy egret, tall and regal on its black stilt legs. Crushed beneath its feet was the Floras' feathered hat. The girls stepped back and stared at their work. A bird-shaped shadow fluttered across the wall. Ofelia, Aster, and with some difficulty, Lane, joined Cat, casting their own shadow birds across the image. In the morning, when Sabal Palms awoke, only the most observant—the people who looked for stories and beauty in the world around them—would notice the egret with wonder.

THE OSTENTATION OF OTHERS AND OUTSIDERS

A HANDBOOK

Cat's Tips for Beginning Birders

Birdwatching is something you can do wherever you live, from big cities to suburbs to rural areas. Here are some tips for getting started.

* Study: get familiar with what you'll find so you know what to look for. Go to your local library to check out a field guide of local birds or take a look at websites like those of the Audubon Society or the Cornell Lab of Ornithology. You'll learn what local bird species look and sound like, where they live, what they eat, and more.

* Equipment: take a notebook to jot down what you see and hear and a field guide for reference. A pair of binoculars is helpful, but even the least expensive pairs can be an investment. Look into group outings and tours where you can borrow or rent binoculars before buying your own.

* Practice: visit your nearest park, nature center, or nature preserve to see what birds you can spot. Look for walks organized by nature groups specifically for beginners.

* Patience: be still and listen. Wait and watch. Appreciate birds. Repeat.

Lane's Crystals for Everyday Use

Crystals are minerals made in nature. Depending on their composition, they can come in different colors and shapes. Throughout history, crystals have been ascribed with different meanings, powers, and uses. Here are some of my favorites.

Tiger's Eye and Moss Agate: Got the jitters over an upcoming class presentation? Feeling unsure about how well you'll play at the next basketball game? Tiger's eye and moss agate have you covered! Keep one or both in your pocket and feel their confidence-building energy work.

Epidote: Complete that assignment! Write that story! Set a personal best on your next mile run! You can't go wrong with epidote in your possession to help you make progress and achieve your goals.

Lapis Lazuli: You don't have to be a superhero to be brave. With lapis lazuli, which helps foster courage and clear thinking, you can summon your own power.

Kunzite: You are great! Just ask Kunzite. This little crystal boosts self-esteem and banishes negative thoughts so that you can see how amazing you are.

Iolite: Do you find yourself stressed when reading a restaurant menu with a million items on it? Do you have a hard time picking out what to wear in the morning? Let iolite help guide your decision-making.

Aster's Chips + Chips Cookies
(AKA Grandpa's Weakness)

Makes 18 to 24 cookies

- 1/2 cup (one stick) unsalted butter, at room temperature
- 4 tablespoons granulated sugar
- 3/4 cup + 2 tablespoons light brown sugar
- 1 large egg
- 1 teaspoon vanilla extract
- 3/4 teaspoon baking soda
- 1/4 teaspoon coarse sea salt
- 1 3/4 cups all-purpose flour
- 1/2 pound (8 oz.) semisweet chocolate chips or chopped semisweet baking chocolate.
- 2–3 potato chips crushed to make crumbs (Crush more if desired.)

Preheat your oven to 360°F and line a baking sheet with parchment paper.

In the large bowl or mixer, combine the butter and sugars until they are light and fluffy. This can take about 5 minutes on low to medium speed.

Mix in the egg and vanilla. Add the salt and baking soda. On the lowest speed, mix in the flour. It's okay if the dough looks crumbly as long as the ingredients are combined well. Remove the bowl from the mixer. Add chocolate and mix with a spatula.

Scoop the dough into 1 to 1 1/2 tablespoon-size mounds, spacing them apart on your baking sheet. Sprinkle potato chips crumbs on top, and press down on them gently with a spoon to embed in the dough. Bake for 11 minutes. Let cookies rest on the baking sheet for a few minutes before eating.

These are best eaten soon after baking when still warm! If you aren't sharing or can't eat twenty cookies in one sitting (not recommended), bake half the dough and refrigerate the other half for another day!

OFELIA'S GUIDE TO WRITING WHAT YOU SEE

Always carry something to record notes like a notebook and pencil or a voice recorder.

Observe the world around you. Write down ten things you noticed during a specific part of your day. Did you notice something unusual? What was the funniest or most exciting thing you saw? What was the saddest?

Listen for sounds and conversations. Write down the things you heard today. Who or what did you hear—people, animals, objects? What's the most interesting thing you heard? What's the most surprising?

Seek ideas and information. Write down at least one new thing you learned today. Write down one idea you had. Write down five things you want to learn more about. How will you learn more about those things?

Follow leads. Take any of the sights, sounds, or ideas you wrote down and follow that lead. Where does it take you? How does the conversation end? What happens next? Who do you meet? What do you learn about them? What don't you know and need to find out?

Believe that, regardless of where you are, there are stories to be found.

DIY Badges

Supplies:

Craft felt (any color)

Large needle

Embroidery thread in different colors

Paper (preferably something like tracing paper that is light and easy to tear)

Pencil

1. Cut your desired badge shape out of felt.

2. Draw the badge image you want to embroider on a sheet of paper. Cut away the extra paper and place your drawing on one side of your felt badge. You can attach it with small safety pins or tape so that it won't move while you're sewing.

3. Pick a thread color for your embroidered image.

4. Thread your needle. Ask an adult for help, if needed. Tie the ends of the thread into a little knot.

5. Stitch along the outline of your piece of paper. The size of your stitches can depend on how big your image is, but try a quarter inch. Retrace your image with stitches until you are happy with how it looks.

6. If you are embroidering with more than one thread color, you will need to follow steps 3 and 4 as many times as the number of colors you are using. Whenever you cut the thread to start a new color (or when you're all done), make sure to tie a knot so that your stitches don't unravel. Tie the knots on the same side of the badge. That will be the back of your badge.

7. When your embroidery is completed to your satisfaction, carefully tear away the paper containing your sketch.

8. You can choose to stitch around the edge of the badge as well if you'd like for it to have a "frame."

9. Attach a safety pin to the back of your badge. Wear it proudly or give it to someone who has earned it!

AUTHOR'S NOTE,
or Sometimes a Feathered Hat Isn't Just a Feathered Hat

While many elements of this story are fictional, the killing of birds for fashion, sadly, is not one of them. The use of birds and feathers in hat decorations had become so popular by 1911, it was estimated that three hundred million birds were killed annually for use by the fashion industry in Paris. In the United States, feathers were imported from other countries, but much of the domestic feather supply came from states like Florida, Texas, and Louisiana.

Harriet Hemenway and Minna Hall were also real people. In 1896, after reading an article about a hunter's bird massacre, Harriet Hemenway, a wealthy woman from Boston, began a campaign against what was by then a multi-million-dollar business. Hemenway enlisted the help of her cousin, Minna Hall, and together they appealed to other women in their social circles to stop wearing hats that used feathers from hunted birds. Their efforts led to a boycott by about nine hundred women, and their continued activism resulted in the establishment of what is now the National Audubon Society, as well as the creation of local Audubon chapters, and the passage of the Migratory Bird Treaty Act of 1918.

While bird feathers in hats are no longer fashionable, many bird species are still under threat as the fossil fuel industry and companies that engage in potentially harmful activities seek to roll back environmental protections. The work to protect birds and their habitats continues today on local, national, and global levels through organizations such as the American Bird Conservancy, the National Audubon Society and its local chapters, and the Cornell Lab of Ornithology.

Another true element of the story is that activisim is for everyone, and it can take on different forms. Activists march in protests, organize fund-raisers, and lead boycotts to address issues that affect people around the world. But small revolutions that start in your community are important too.

Each one of us has the ability to speak up for what we believe in, challenge what we disagree with, and support what we care about. Start with yourself—changing personal habits and practices can have a big impact and set an example for others to follow. Are there issues you'd like to address in your town or school? What are the skills *you* possess and how can you put them to work for something you care about?

Sometimes it's overwhelming, not to mention difficult, to try to change things on your own. The beautiful thing about activism is that you're never alone. If you care about something, there are most likely others who care as well. Friends, classmates, teammates, family, teachers—there is community all around you from which you can recruit.

Change may not always come quickly, but making our communities and our world better is always worth the work.

SELECTED BIBLIOGRAPHY

One of my favorite parts of the writing process is doing research. Research is a lot like being a detective. Sometimes in the course of looking for one thing, you discover something else that is even more interesting. When I began writing *Strange Birds*, I had no idea the direction it would go, but research helped me create a map for the story.

Below I'm sharing a small selection of books, articles, and websites I worked with while writing *Strange Birds*. Some helped me fact-check and others served more as inspiration. I also included titles of the books that the girls encounter at different points in the story.

Remember that links to online articles can go the way of the dodo. (If you don't know what happened to the dodo, take a look at this https://www.audubon.org/news/why-dodo-deserves-new-reputation.) If the listed web address does not work, *this* librarian recommends seeing *your* librarian for help. We're pretty good with this type of thing.

Books Within the Book

Burn, Doris. *Andrew Henry's Meadow*. New York: Coward-McCann, Inc., 1965.

Child, Julia, Louisette Bertholle and Simone Beck. *Mastering the Art of French Cooking*. New York: Alfred A. Knopf, 1961.

Hoban, Russell. *Bread and Jam for Frances*. Illustrated by Lillian Hoban. New York: HarperCollins Publishers, 1964.

Konigsburg, E. L. *From the Mixed-Up Files of Mrs. Basil E. Frankweiler*. New York: Aladdin Paperbacks, 1972.

Birds and Bird Conservation

Baillie, Jonathan. "What Will Make Us Care Enough to Save Endangered Species?" Photographs by Tim Flach. *National Geographic*. https://www.nationalgeographic.com/magazine/2018/08/proof-endangered-birds-photography/.

Glassman, Sierra. "Passenger Martha." *Stone Soup*, 18 Dec. 2018, https://stonesoup.com/post/passenger-martha/.

Lasky, Kathryn. *She's Wearing a Dead Bird on Her Head!* Illustrated by David Catrow. New York: Hyperion Books for Children, 1995.

Plain, Nancy. *This Strange Wilderness: The Life and Art of John James Audubon.* Lincoln & London: University of Nebraska Press, 2015.

Sibley, David Allen. *The Sibley Guide to Birds,* 2nd Ed. New York: Knopf, 2014.

Souder, William. "How Two Women Ended the Deadly Feather Trade." *Smithsonian Magazine*, Mar. 2013, https://www.smithsonianmag.com/science-nature/how-two-women-ended-the-deadly-feather-trade-23187277/?page=2.

U.S. Fish & Wildlife Service. *Migratory Bird Treaty Act.* https://www.fws.gov/birds/policies-and-regulations/laws-legislations/migratory-bird-treaty-act.php.

Muckrakers and Activism

Bausum, Ann. *Muckrakers: How Ida Tarbell, Upton Sinclair, and Lincoln Steffens Helped Expose Scandal, Inspire Reform, and Invent Investigative Journalism.* Washington D.C.: National Geographic Children's Books, 2007.

Lindsay, Kitty. "Radical Monarchs: A Social-Justice Twist

on the Girl Scouts," *Ms. Magazine*, 29 May 2015, http://msmagazine.com/blog/2015/05/29/radical-monarchs-a-social-justice-twist-on-the-girl-scouts/.

Mahoney, Ellen. *Nellie Bly and Investigative Journalism for Kids*. Chicago: Chicago Review Press, 2015.

Myers, Walter Dean. *Ida B. Wells: Let the Truth Be Told*. New York: Amistad, 2008.

Paul, Caroline. *You Are Mighty: A Guide to Changing the World*. Illustrated by Lauren Tamaki. New York: Bloomsbury Children's Books, 2018.

ACKNOWLEDGMENTS

I have my thumbs locked, and I am flapping my shadow bird wings at *you*....

The Kokilas: Namrata Tripathi, Jasmin Rubero, Sydnee Monday, and especially Joanna Cárdenas who makes everything seem possible. Thank you for pushing me and helping me be a better writer. Stefanie Von Borstel and everyone at Full Circle Literary. Shannon Wright and Dana Li for the beautiful cover. Kaitlin Kneafsey, Carmela Iaria, Venessa Carson, Summer Ogata, Trevor Ingerson, marketing, publicity, sales, regional sales representatives, *everyone* at Penguin Young Readers who works so hard to turn a stack of printed pages into a book and to get that book out into the world. I appreciate you! Anne Heausler for copy editing, and Patricia Glinton-Meicholas for reading and lending her knowledge and expertise. The librarians, teachers, booksellers, parents, caregivers, guardians, and anyone who shares their love of books with children. Kelly McElroy, Caroline Joynson, and the University of Florida Libraries for assistance with the details. My sis, Virginia Perez, for letting me tag along when I needed to do research. The Radical Monarchs for being the original inspiration for this story. All the good people I have met in this publishing journey who have been so kind and encouraging and who are doing good work. La familia Perez, the Zeeb family, and friends, but especially Jenna. Readers! This isn't possible without you. Emiliano, Brett, and Mister Bagel. Thank you for holding down the fort, for letting me miss basketball games, for not biting me when you want to go out and I ignore you. You three are my favorite strange birds. I love you.

A DISCUSSION GUIDE TO
Celia C. Pérez

THE
FIRST
RULE OF
PUNK

ALWAYS REMEMBER TO
BE YOURSELF.

CELIA C. PÉREZ

Cover art © 2017 by Kat Fajardo

STRANGE
BIRDS

A FIELD GUIDE TO
RUFFLING FEATHERS

Celia C. Pérez
Author of *The First Rule of Punk*

Jacket art © 2019 by Shannon Wright

A 2018 Pura Belpré Author Honor Book

The First Rule of Punk is a wry and heartfelt exploration of friendship, finding your place, and learning to rock out like no one's watching.

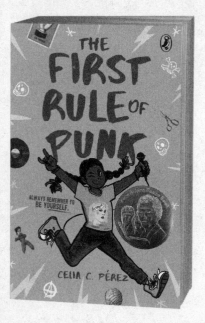

There are no shortcuts to surviving your first day at a new school—you can't fix it with duct tape like you would your Chuck Taylors. On Day One, twelve-year-old Malú (María Luisa, if you want to annoy her) inadvertently upsets Posada Middle School's queen bee, violates the school's dress code with her punk rock look, and disappoints her college-professor mom in the process. Her dad, who now lives a thousand miles away, says things will get better as long as she remembers the first rule of punk: Be yourself.

The real Malú loves rock music, skateboarding, zines, and Soyrizo (hold the cilantro, please). And when she assembles a group of like-minded misfits at school and starts a band, Malú finally begins to feel at home. She'll do anything to preserve this, which includes standing up to an anti-punk school administration to fight for her right to express herself!

Zines filled with black-and-white illustrations and collage art throughout make *The First Rule of Punk* a perfect pick for fans of books like *Roller Girl* and online magazines like *Rookie*.

"Armed with a microphone and a pair of scissors, this book is all about creating something new and awesome in the world. Malú rocks!"

—Victoria Jamieson, author and illustrator of the *New York Times* bestselling and Newbery Honor-winning *Roller Girl*

Discussion Questions

1. On page 33, Malú mentions Frida Kahlo is her favorite artist. What comparisons do you see between them?

2. On page 49, a girl in Malú's class asks the question, "What are you?" Have you ever experienced someone asking another person this question? It is what's considered a microaggression. What do you know about microaggression? What can kids do when they or their friends experience it? How does Malú react?

3. What are some words Malú uses to define the "modern girl" and how is she different from the "perfect señorita" she imagines her mother would like her to be?

4. On page 112, Malú and her mother talk about the difference between being "real Mexican" and "half-Mexican." Why does Malú feel she's not as Mexican as her "super-Mexican" mother? Why do you suppose her mother wants her to learn so much about what it means to be Mexican? How does this make Malú, who is biracial, feel?

5. On page 134, Malú learns that a "coconut" is brown on the out-side, white on the inside. This is another verbal microaggression Malú experiences. What does this mean? How does she react?

6. On page 143, Malú's dad says, "Turning an insult into something you embrace is a good way of empowering yourself." What are some other groups that have reclaimed words used as insults and began using them themselves? What does this mean both for groups that do this and those who have oppressed them by creating the name in the first place?

7. On page 180, Ellie suggests they start a petition. Why does she want them to do it? How do petitions accomplish social change?

8. Compare the mother-daughter relationship on page 190 between Señora Oralia and Mrs. Hidalgo to the relationship between Malú and her mother. What similarities and differences do you see?

9. On page 244, Malú sees an ofrenda and learns about Día de los Muertos, which Malú says is "NOT Mexican Halloween." What is Día de los Muertos? What is an ofrenda? What do you learn about the dead and their place in Mexican cultural practices from this scene and exchange?

10. What is "un pajarito quetzal"? Why does Malú look like one? Research what the bird represents according to Mexican history and tradition. How is this connected to who Malú is becoming? (283)

11. On page 296, Malú defines what it means to be punk. What does it mean to you to be punk? Why could this be considered a good thing?

From the award-winning author of *The First Rule of Punk* comes the story of four kids who form an alternative Scout troop that shakes up their sleepy Florida town.

When three *very* different girls find a mysterious invitation to a lavish mansion, the promise of adventure and mischief is too intriguing to pass up.

Ofelia Castillo (a budding journalist), Aster Douglas (a bookish foodie), and Cat Garcia (a rule-abiding bird-watcher) meet the kid behind the invite, Lane DiSanti, and it isn't love at first sight. But they soon bond over a shared mission to get the Floras, their local Scouts, to ditch an outdated tradition. In their quest for justice, independence, and an unforgettable summer, the girls form their own troop and find something they didn't know they needed: sisterhood.

"Thought-provoking, timely, and laugh-out-loud funny—*Strange Birds* explores friendship, community, and the role each of us plays in creating a better world"

—Aisha Saeed, *New York Times* bestselling author of *Amal Unbound*

"*Strange Birds* is an inspiring story about the power of truth, and of true friends."

—Rebecca Stead, *New York Times* bestselling author of the Newbery Medal winner *When You Reach Me*

Discussion Questions

1. What is a Flora? How do we know what they value? What other group oaths do you know about that communicate values? How does Lane feel like she might disagree with their laws and codes of behavior?

2. What is Cat's objection to the Flora hat? How does the hat's existence conflict with the values the Floras claim to stand for? (25)

3. On page 126, Lane says, "An oath [is] a promise. Maybe if her family had spit into their palms and made an oath, they would have stayed together. Maybe an oath was what made individuals a real group. Maybe an oath was what the girls needed." Have you ever agreed to an oath? If so, what were the agreements, spoken or unspoken, that you made? Do you agree that oaths have the power to hold groups together? If so, why? How?

4. Why did the Migratory Bird Treaty Act become a law? How does this connect to the Floras? What role does the MBTA of 1918 play in the story which takes place a hundred years later?

5. On page 198, Aster says, "White people don't usually come to this side of the Wall unless they're doing something touristy." What are the invisible walls that exist in your city? How do they separate or segregate the town's residents? What privileges or benefits exist on one side of the wall that do not exist on the other side?

6. On pages 200–201, Aster says, "But people see you for your skin color first regardless of what language you speak. Like, your pale cousins can go to places without thinking twice about how they'll be seen. I bet it's not the same for your Black cousins. Just ask them." What do you know about colorism? Read and discuss the difference between colorism and racism.

7. What does the group's peacock badge stand for? What other embroidered badges do you know that exist in the world? Where do people wear them? Why?

8. What does Aster discover about the connection between the Winter Sun orange trees and the DiSanti family? How does this confirm or conflict with the history she knows?

9. What does it mean when the girls use the slogan "RETURN THE FEATHERS"?

10. On page 265, Aster's grandpa says, "Being an activist isn't like moving from one job to another or changing shirts. It's something you always are." Explain what you think he means by this statement.

11. What do the girls mean when they refer to stealing the hat as "civil disobedience"? (271) What does that term mean? Do you think civil disobedience could work to create change?

The First Rule of Punk Activities

PRE-READING

1. Malú is Mexican-American, but her father is white. An important part of Malú's journey is understanding the role culture, race, and ethnicity play in her life. Use THIS glossary (www.racialequitytools.org/glossary) to choose seven or eight new vocabulary words to learn and use while reading the book. Post them near you and practice using them to write and talk about character and plot development in the novel. Consider using the instructions in the back of the book to make a zine with visual cues to help better define the words you have chosen.

DURING READING

2. On pages 104–105, we learn about some Mexican and Mexican-American punk bands. Research new bands by looking at their names, countries of origin, and band members. What are some quotes band members are known for saying? What are some connecting beliefs or ideas that unite them? Make a thematic playlist of songs that are all connected to the same idea, like "romance" or "rebellion." You may include some from page 197 to help you get started. Write a page or two explaining why you chose each song with specific lyrics and images to bring your explanation to life.

3. The Bracero program began in 1942 and brought many Mexican workers to the United States as guest laborers. It ended in 1964, but its legacy lives on. Use THIS site (www.labor.ucla.edu/what-we-do/research-tools/the-bracero-program/) to identify as much as you can about individual stories of farm laborers. Create a profile of one specific worker, capturing their story with a picture that symbolizes an important part of their narrative, a quote with their name, and their city or town of origin, as well as anything you can learn about what happened to them once they got to the US and after they left. Create a mini-poster with this information, then do a gallery walk with peers to learn about the workers they chose to profile.

4. Change.org is one of the leading sites used to start petitions for social action and change. What is something in your community or part of the world that you would like to change? Come up with a problem, identify the causes for that problem, and formulate a possible solution that has a deadline (so you have a better chance of seeing it happen). Make a petition on Change.org and use social media to send it to as many people as possible. Track your shares and responses as a class using a thermometer for each petition and color sections in as you get more and more responses. If your petition goes beyond your school walls to create change within your community, partner with a local organization that might benefit from your petition and see if they might help you spread the word!

POST-READING

5. The zines are a really important part of *The First Rule of Punk*. As such, there are instructions included in the back of the book for how to make a zine. You will notice that each of Malú's zines has a theme. Use words and symbols from online or offline resources to capture your thinking about a topic in a zine. You may consider some of the following: resistance, transformation, identity, race, culture, language, music, food.

Standards*: CCCSS.ELA-LITERACY.RL.8.2, CCSS.ELA-LITERACY.RL.8.3, CCSS.ELA-LITERACY.RL.8.4, CCSS. ELA-LITERACY. RI.8.7, CCSS.ELA-LITERACY.L.8.4.A, CCSS.ELA-LITERACY.L.8.4.C, CCSS.ELA-LITERACY.L.8.5, CCSS.ELA-LITERACY.L.8.5.A, CCSS.ELA-LITERACY.L.8.5.C

Additional Resources: The Forgotten Mexican Punk Rebellion of 1985 | https://www.change.org/ | Dress for Success: Public School Uniforms | Mexican X-plainer: Chiclets & Aztecs by David Bowles | Top 10 Things to Know about Day of the Dead | Bracero History Archive

Strange Birds Activities

PRE-READING

1. There are various times throughout history when kids and teens have formed clubs or associations for the purposes of creating social action or change. Conduct an internet search to find organizations run for and by women and/or an under-represented group and create a Padlet or other visual bulletin board that explains what the organization is, who runs it, and what the mission statement is. What social problem was it created to solve? Is there a local chapter in your area? How can you get involved?

DURING READING

2. On page 41, we learn about the Floras' codes of conduct, eight laws, and behavior expectations through their oath. "*A Flora is courteous. A Flora is cheerful. A Flora is helpful. A Flora is loyal.*" Complete the following chart for each character using a quote as evidence from the text to describe each girl in your first column. In the second column, explain what the quote reveals about the girl in your own words. In the third column, draw a symbol to represent the character. In the fourth column, choose one word to describe a value or trait for each character that either agrees with or is in opposition to one of the traits belonging to the Floras. Explain how your chosen word connects to the character.

Character	Quote	Quote Analysis	Symbol	One word value or trait
Ofelia/Aster				
Cat/Lane				

3. On page 166, the girls list several slogans, like "No taxation without representation" and "Give me liberty or give me death." Research historical and present-day slogans and the organizations that created them. Look for examples of banners or signs with people using them during demonstrations. What is the overall purpose of a slogan? Use your imagination to create a memorable slogan for a cause you care about. Connect the slogan to a social cause or reason for rebellion, rather than a commercial product. Make a visual representation of your slogan including the words and/or a picture to reinforce the idea. Hang the posters and signs with your slogans all around your classroom. What do they reveal about common concerns and/or beliefs? Try to eliminate all but one or two that capture agreements or beliefs held by the entire class. Can you limit it to one? If so, could that be your class slogan?

POST-READING

4. Many organizations mobilize youths using the model of transformational resistance and through referencing a critique of social oppression. Consider the critique of social oppression as a framework for looking at systems that work to oppress individuals in your community and the ways individuals can resist, as the girls did, to create positive change.

    At the end of the book, you'll find a handbook called *The Ostentation of Others and Outsiders*. It has several ideas for connecting with some of the girls' favorite hobbies and activities, as well as creating your own badges. In groups, research a social issue you care about and create a slogan, a badge, and a code of conduct, oath, and/or field guide to support the group's mission. How does the group's mission connect to social justice and move individuals or communities away from social oppression?

Standards*: CCSS.ELA-LITERACY.RL.7.3, CCSS.ELA-LITERACY.RL.7.3, CCSS.ELA-LITERACY.RL.7.4, CCSS.ELA-LITERACY. RL.7.9, CCSS.ELA-LITERACY.RI.7.1, CCSS.ELA-LITERACY.RI.7.3, CCSS.ELA-LITERACY.RI.7.4

Additional Resources: "What's 'Colorism'?" How Would Your Students Answer This Question?: Teaching Tolerance | CARE: Global organization for the elimination of poverty and spread of social justice among women | Malala Fund: Working for a world where all girls can learn and lead | Youth Participatory Action Research | https://www.girlscouts.org/ | United States Institute of Peace: Women in Nonviolent Movements | The Front: The Aesthetics of Female Resistance | World Wildlife Fund

ABOUT THE AUTHOR

Celia C. Pérez is the author of *Strange Birds: A Field Guide to Ruffling Feathers* and *The First Rule of Punk*, a 2018 Pura Belpré Author Honor Book, a 2018 Tomás Rivera Mexican American Children's Book Award Winner, and a 2018 *Boston Globe–Horn Book* Fiction and Poetry Honor Book. She lives in Chicago with her family, where, in addition to writing books about lovable weirdos and outsiders, she works as a librarian. She is originally from Miami, Florida, where roosters and peacocks really do wander the streets.

Visit her at celiacperez.com.

PenguinClassroom.com

This guide was written by Julia E. Torres. Julia is a veteran language arts teacher and librarian in Denver, Colorado. Julia serves teachers around the country by facilitating teacher development workshops rooted in the areas of social justice, anti-racist education, equity and access in librarianship, and education as a practice of liberation. Julia also works with students locally and around the country with the goal of empowering them to use literacy to fuel resistance and positive social transformation. Julia serves on several local and national boards and committees promoting educational equity and progressivism. She is the current NCTE Secondary Representative-at-Large, and she is also a Heinemann Publishing Heinemann Fellow and Book Ambassador for The Educator Collaborative. Connect with Julia on Twitter @juliaerin80.